PRAISE FOR *ALL THE QUIET PLACES*

"*All the Quiet Places* is a haun
power of Isaac's vision of young
Okanagan reserve in the 1950s is t
ticulous detailing and fierce attac
Every line is so carefully curatea
—Indigenous Voices Awards

T0044280

"Every single word advances the story. Each sentence presents the reader with vivid images that are so real, so familiar."
—Okanagan Indian Band Newsletter

"I feel that Brian Thomas Isaac has earned every single word,
every single sentence, every single line. There's so much hilarity
in here. There's so much wisdom... My goodness, what a journey
this book takes you on." —CBC *Unreserved*

"Isaac's unadorned prose is powerful and direct... *All the Quiet
Places* tells a moving tale of marginalization, loss and neglect."
—*The Fiddlehead*

"Beautifully crafted coming-of-age story..." —*Hamilton Review of Books*

"Isaac steps effortlessly into the shoes of young Eddie. Though *All
the Quiet Places* is Isaac's first novel, the writing is precise and
assured. Through Eddie's honest—and sometimes apathetic—ob-
servations of the world around him, Isaac deftly captures how the
angst and uncertainty that bubble within children can quickly
boil over when face to face with social inequity and oppression."
—*Quill & Quire*

ALL THE QUIET PLACES

All the Quiet Places

Brian Thomas Isaac

BRINDLE
AND GLASS

Brindle & Glass
An imprint of TouchWood Editions
touchwoodeditions.com

Edited by Susan Mayse
Cover design by Tree Abraham
Interior design by Sydney Barnes

CATALOGUING DATA AVAILABLE FROM LIBRARY AND ARCHIVES CANADA
ISBN 9781990071027 (softcover)
ISBN 9781990071034 (e-book)

TouchWood Editions acknowledges that the land on which we live and work is within the traditional territories of the Lkwungen (Esquimalt and Songhees), Malahat, Pacheedaht, Scia'new, T'Sou-ke and W̲SÁNEĆ (Pauquachin, Tsartlip, Tsawout, Tseycum) peoples.

We acknowledge the financial support of the Government of Canada through the Canada Book Fund and the Canada Council for the Arts, and of the Province of British Columbia through the British Columbia Arts Council and the Book Publishing Tax Credit.

Printed in Canada

This book was produced using FSC®-certified, acid-free papers, processed chlorine free, and printed with soya-based inks.

26 25 24 23 6 7 8 9 10

To my grandchildren, Sienna, Huxley, and Rebel

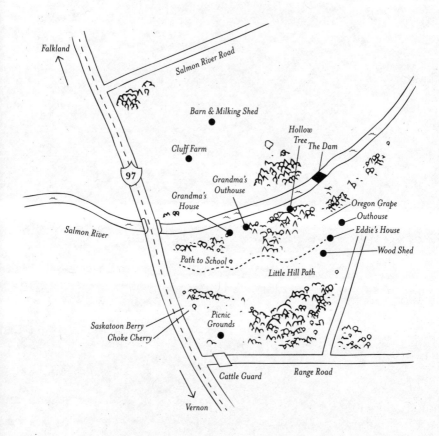

I

The sultry weather had been building for days until the air weighed on Eddie's bed like a damp blanket. His feet constantly searched for cool spots on the mattress but never found any. Even the burping frogs down at Heart Lake, a quarter of a mile away, stopped now and then to catch their breath. It was only when cooler air rattled the leaves on the poplars down by the outhouse and swept over the bed that Eddie fell asleep.

A screeching wind jerked him awake. The ceiling and walls cracked and thumped. He sat up. His little brother, Lewis, was fast asleep beside him, and no sound came from his mother's bedroom on the other side of the paper-board wall. The slop bucket slid across the porch, hit the ground, and rolled banging across the yard. Eddie stood on the bed and looked out the window but saw only pitch darkness. Then lightning flashed across the sky, showing trees that leaned at impossible angles to the ground. With a loud crack a bolt of lightning struck the top of a cottonwood down by the river, and pieces of wood scattered into the wind like dandelion fluff. Eddie saw spots in front of his eyes as if he had looked at the sun.

Lewis woke up crying and stumbled to join his mother, but five-year-old Eddie was drawn to the lightning like a moth to a coal oil lamp. His hand felt the shaking glass with each thunder clap. A nail holding a loose board in a wall squeaked like it was being pulled out by a claw hammer. His mother called to him, and the three of them huddled under her blankets, listening to fir cones and pieces of boughs that hit the roof.

The next morning Eddie let out a long yawn as he stretched and arched his back. He heard water dripping on the hot stove. *Psst, psst, psst.* He jumped to his feet, and with his nose touching the window, scanned the ground around the house. There were trees down everywhere. The ferocity of the storm had made him think the whole world had been flattened, but it wasn't as bad as he had imagined. Everything always looked better in the morning anyway. A squirrel ran along a trail of broken branches. Noisy birds chirped and swooped. Nuthatches flitting about on the roof of the outhouse were frightened away in a flutter when a robin landed among them.

Eddie jumped off the bed and was about to walk into the kitchen when he saw his mother at the table. Grace sat perfectly still, and a thin line of smoke from the cigarette in her fingers reached up to the ceiling like a string. The long ash on the end looked ready to fall, and the red glow was so close to her skin that Eddie wondered if she was getting burned.

Sometimes he found her sitting this way, red-eyed, quiet and still. He felt sad and wondered what he could do to make her feel better. She didn't move when he pulled out a chair and only looked at him when his knee bumped the table leg.

Grace sat up and looked around as if she had been caught day-dreaming. After snuffing out her cigarette, she filled a bowl with porridge from a pot on the stove. With a big spoon she scooped out a red glob of jam from the large can in the centre of the table and dropped it into the bowl. She slid it across the table to Eddie. Sitting back in her chair, she looked out at the downed trees.

"Looks like I'll have to sharpen the Swede saw," she said. "We're going to have to cut up all that wood and pack it up to the shed before it starts snowing. Seems like it might be enough for the whole winter. And you have to go on the roof and fix that new hole. Don't know how many shingles are missing."

The thought of all the work made Eddie push his bowl away with his elbow and rest his head on his arms. That was when he noticed a dark form moving among the trees down at the edge of the clearing close to the river. He sat up and looked through the cracked kitchen window. The slightest movement of his head made the image drift away and back again. He felt a chill as if someone had run a finger lightly up his back.

Whatever he had seen—bear, deer, or moose—was down close to the river at a piece of land where his mother, grandma, and uncle had cleared away the brush for a garden large enough for the two families. They'd stopped when they found that just under the top layer of soil was a thick layer of roots. It wasn't long after the work stopped that the ground became choked with Oregon grape.

When Eddie's mother stepped out of the house and strolled down the trail to Grandma's, he looked over to the wall where the .303 rifle rested on bent spikes. He stared at the gun for a long time. Grace always told him there were three things he'd better not do until he was older: make a fire in the bush without her, go down to the water by himself, or touch the gun.

But one day early this spring his uncle came home with a young deer slung over his shoulder. Uncle Alphonse hung the deer on a rail lodged in the branches of two trees. When the steaming guts fell to the ground, his blood-covered hands took out the liver and handed it to Grandma. She took it inside and sliced it into strips, coated the pieces with flour, and put them in a frying pan of hot lard. When she set the plate of meat on the table, Alphonse rubbed his hands together and smiled, something that didn't happen often.

Grandma laughed that nobody loved liver like Alphonse. "You don't want to try and take a chunk from his plate while he's eating. He'll bite your hand off."

The liver must be the best part of the deer, Eddie thought, but when he tried a small piece, it tasted terrible and had a funny smell.

The deer had made everyone happy that day. Getting a deer would make his mother feel better.

Eddie stood on a chair, lifted the rifle off the wall, and pocketed a shell. The gun was heavy and awkward. When he banged the end of the barrel against the table leg, he could almost hear his mother saying, Watch what you're doing! What's the matter with you? Someday he would have his own gun and do whatever he wanted with it. But this time, when he returned with his kill, he hoped she would be happy and call him a great hunter.

He stepped outside, wondering what he would find. A deer would mean plenty of meat for both families. A bear would be okay too. His mother said its sweet-tasting meat reminded her of pork chops.

Broken branches lay all around the yard. A potato sack was wrapped around the clothes-line tree, and under the porch steps was a ripped shirt Eddie didn't recognize.

As Eddie entered the clearing, the only sounds he heard were his breathing and his pants brushing against the spiky leaves of the Oregon grape. The slightest noise made him jump. A sharp thistle jabbed him above the knee, but he walked on without stopping or looking down. Keeping low, he crossed the clearing and crouched behind a shrub. After loading the gun the way he had seen his mother do many times, he held his breath, stepped out, and raised the gun to his cheek. But there was no game to be seen anywhere. Whatever it was that he had hoped to shoot and drag home had already moved on.

It was much brighter down in the Oregon grape now. Four trees had been blown over by the strong wind, and he discovered a ripe honeysuckle bush at the base of a tall cottonwood stump. At one time the cottonwood had been one of the largest trees around, but long ago another wind as strong as last night's had snapped off the huge trunk. Now it rested on the bush floor like the bones of a giant.

Eddie plucked a handful of honeysuckle and sucked out the nectar. A hole near the ground led into the cottonwood's hollow centre. He poked the barrel of the gun into the opening to scare out any animals that might be using the stump as a home. He squeezed his way inside, and his nose filled with the sweet smell of earth that had been disturbed for the very first time. He pushed rotting wood out through the opening with his foot until he had enough room so that when he lay down, his head and feet touched both sides of the stump.

The tree made the bush sounds louder: the screeching jays and magpies, the chatter of squirrels, and the woodpecker that hammered away from morning until night on an iron-hard fir. The sky through the stump opening looked different somehow. Closer, bluer, like water in a deep lake.

When Eddie closed his eyes and took long, deep breaths, he heard hummingbirds poking at the trumpets of honeysuckle above a mumble of bees. Then he made out the distant cooing of a mourning dove. The sound of the river washing over rocks and logs made him want to sleep, but a loud shout on the outside of the stump made him sit up. He looked through a small crack in the wood and saw his mother only feet away, swatting the brush with a large stick as she called his name. When she moved out of sight, he ran to the house and placed the gun back on the wall.

Grace slammed the door behind her, glaring at Eddie.

He spoke quickly. "I didn't hear you because I was playing on the other side of the house."

Grace didn't say a word. She took the gun down off the wall. Eddie watched helplessly as she drew back the bolt and the shell tumbled to the floor.

"What the hell are you doing taking the gun when I told you not to? You didn't even have the safety on. You could've shot somebody."

She hit Eddie with her switch until he fell to the floor.

Later that day Eddie made his way down to his new hideaway. He looked for a different way so he wouldn't leave a trail for anyone to follow. He still stung from his mother's switching and he mumbled his angry thoughts. "I hate you. And I'll never tell you or anybody else about my hiding place. I'll stay in there forever, and you'll never find me."

Once he crawled inside, his heart thumped in his ears, and it took a few minutes before the anger he felt toward his mother left him. After a few deep breaths, he felt safe and protected inside the space that was his and only his. The cool soft ground was his mattress, and the open top was his window.

"Maybe if I lie here forever, I can turn myself into a ghost. Uncle Alphonse says they're everywhere but nobody can see them. Invisible, he calls them. Yeah. Invisible. I can scare anybody I want and make them wet their pants because they're too scared to go to the toilet in the dark," he said aloud.

He fell asleep smiling. When he woke, he imagined he was the last person on earth. The small house above the Salmon River, on a corner of the Okanagan Indian Reserve, where his grandma and Uncle Alphonse lived, would be empty and deserted. His mother and little brother would be gone. And Eddie, who was two months away from his sixth birthday, would finally have what he often wished for, to be all alone in the world.

Eddie felt hungry and headed back to the house for something to eat. But when he got to the front steps, he saw through the open door his mother sitting in a chair sharpening the Swede saw with a file. He knew what would happen. She was going to start cutting wood and she would make him go with her to help. He looked down to the trail to Grandma's. Maybe if he visited her she would give him something nice to eat. Something out of a can or whatever she had. He ran down the trail. When he rounded the corner of Grandma's tiny house, he saw his uncle standing by a small fire. With a small axe he was scraping away the blackened part of a long pole. Then he returned it to the fire.

"Whatcha doing?" Eddie asked.

Alphonse lifted his head. "What's it look like I'm doing?"

Eddie shrugged his shoulders. "I dunno. Whatcha doing?"

"You already said that," his uncle said. "Gwan inside and bother your gramma."

Grandma stuck her head outside. "He's making a pole for his gaff hook. Maybe when he goes to the river for the salmon run, we'll get lucky and he'll fall in. Come in here, Eddie. You had dinner yet?"

Eddie shook his head.

"Well, you're just in time."

Eddie sat at the table as his grandma turned over the fried bread sizzling in a pan on the stove. She stabbed at one piece, laid it on a saucer and handed it to Eddie. Then she slid a jar across the table.

"Apple sauce. My favourite," she said.

Eddie spooned some on his bread. When he took a bite, he closed his eyes. The smell and taste of the apple sauce on the warm bread was so good it made him groan. "Mmm." Eddie wondered how so many nice things came from such a small cupboard.

As Eddie walked up the hill toward home, the trail was speckled with sunlight, but off to the right of the path, shade stretched out into the darkness of the trees. All around his house there were wasps and mosquitoes, and it would be so hot he would feel tired and want to sleep again. He couldn't decide if he should go to his secret place or down to the river. Then a chipmunk zoomed past his feet into the undergrowth. Eddie dashed into the bushes, but there were too many shadows to see the chipmunk. He stopped to listen for the sound of scurrying feet, but a light breeze swishing through the Saskatoon bushes and fir boughs made it hard to hear anything.

The hunt for the striped runner ended quickly. Eddie didn't care. For a long time he wandered around the bush until he heard his mother calling him. He went toward the direction of her voice, but when she called again, it sounded like she was coming from behind. Lost and confused, Eddie panicked and shouted to her for help. She was there in no time at all and shook her head as she approached.

"I don't have time to go chasing after you every time you get lost. If this happens again, I won't come looking for you, so you better start paying attention when you go into the bush. Go out the way you went in. Look for marks on trees, like broken branches, and anything that looks different. And don't stare at the ground. Look up once in a while."

It wasn't long before Eddie was back in the woods. He came across a rotten log in a beam of sunlight at a small clearing. He lifted a slab of bark, and underneath, white grubs twisted and rolled in the bright, warm light.

He kicked a large puffball that broke into pieces when it struck a tree. A noise above him made him look up. A dead tree leaned against a live one and squeaked when they rubbed together. When he found a tree scar covered in pitch, he smiled. He had found exactly what his Uncle Alphonse had told him to watch for.

"Keep an eye out for pitch because it'll be your lucky day when you find some. Bush candy, we call it. You chew on it and spit out the first taste. Then after a while, the longer you chew it, it turns into gum."

Eddie scraped his finger under the pitch until he had the same amount as a piece of bubble gum and put his finger in his mouth. He spit out the first mouthful and swallowed the next. His stomach rumbled, and he threw up. His sides were so sore that he doubled over holding his ribs.

His face and shirt were wet with tears and snot. When he was able to stand up straight, he looked for the way home but saw no such path. He was lost again. The small clearing had paths leading off in all directions. The fear inside him grew until he heard a squeaking noise off to his right. He moved slowly toward the sound and recognized the leaning dead tree he had seen earlier.

He found bits of broken puffball spread around the ground, then saw the slab of bark where he had left it leaning against the rotten log. He ran out into the open.

"I found my own way, Mom!" he yelled, bouncing up and down. "I know where there's worms, dry bark, and pitch for the fire. Want me to take you there and show you?"

"No. I got a job I need you to do."

Eddie's excitement left him. "We're not gonna cut up all the trees, are we?"

"No. It's too hot for that."

Grace used the back of a hatchet to flatten an empty syrup tin and handed it to Eddie. "You get up on the roof and find where the hole is. Look for a missing shingle. Shove this under a shingle as far as you can. And don't fool around up there and fall off. After you done that, go inside the attic and get the cat out of there. Damn thing was burying its shit in the shavings again last night. Kept scratching right down to the ceiling. I thought for sure it was gonna dig through and fall on me."

Eddie found the hole next to the chimney and made the repair. Then he swung down from the roof onto the ladder and crawled inside the attic. It was hot and smelled of cat poop and wood shaving insulation. The asphalt siding and roof shingles stank of hot tar, and the fir trusses sweating beads of amber added the sweet smell of pitch. Eddie heard whispering voices from the battery-powered radio in the kitchen below. His mother was about to make bread. It didn't matter how hot it was outside, she fired up the kitchen stove anyway. And because the old stove had so many holes and cracks, it burned armloads of wood until the temperature of the oven and the house felt the same.

Eddie carefully straddled the trusses and lay on his back. The wood shavings crunched softly under him. He closed his eyes, thankful to be alone if only for a little while, until he heard the squeak of the ladder. He sat up. Suddenly three-year-old Lewis appeared at the top of the ladder, smiling, with drool hanging from his chin. As he reached for Lewis, his little brother pulled away and almost fell backward off the ladder. It took a long time before Lewis allowed Eddie to squeeze past him and stand one rung below. They made their way slowly down to the ground.

"Lewis followed me up the ladder," Eddie said. "I can't go anywhere."

Grace went to the woodshed, grabbed the hatchet from the chopping block and knocked the first three rungs off the ladder. Then she took Lewis by the hand. "Both of you get in the house where I can keep an eye on you."

Dark clouds bunched overhead, and the air had a sharp, dusty smell—a sure sign of rain.

The moment Grace put Lewis on her bed, he fell asleep. In the kitchen Eddie kneeled on a chair to watch his mother punch down the dough. The table creaked, and a leg bumped the floor. She worked the dough hard, pushing and pulling, making it pop and snap. Then she cut off large chunks, shaped them and placed them into loaf pans. She covered the pans with a towel.

Eddie wanted to tell her about the flour on her cheek where she had scratched an itch or brushed back her hair, but the heat had made her grumpy. It was best to leave her alone. Squirming in his chair, he began tapping the table with his knuckles and swinging his legs back and forth harder and faster until the chair moved ahead with a squeak.

"Eddie, quit it," Grace said.

But his legs seemed to have a mind of their own and wouldn't stop swinging.

"Can't you sit still for a minute?"

He crossed his feet but they began pushing and pulling against each other.

"Eddie, sit still."

"I can't."

"It's like you got ants in your pants. Can't you do something else? Something quiet?"

"There's nothing to do, Mom."

"Boy, I can hardly wait until you start grade one. There's nothing to do, there's nothing to do. You need to be in school, not around here all day bothering me every ten minutes. Just sit there and be quiet."

She scraped the hardened bits of dough out of the chipped enamel bowl with a knife. The sound made Eddie shiver. He cradled his face in his hands to watch how long it would take for the bread to rise, but the weight of sleep began tugging at his eyelids. Just as his eyes were beginning to close, there was a brilliant flash of light followed by a booming explosion that rattled the windows. Eddie jerked awake.

"God almighty," Grace said, stepping away from the table. She looked up as though she expected the ceiling to come tumbling down at any moment.

Rain lashed down on the roof as if the bulging clouds had been stabbed by the lightning. Eddie's chair tipped over onto the floor, and he ran to the doorway to let the cool air wash over him. Mist rose from the roof of the woodshed as raindrops flew in all directions. The far end of the clothesline disappeared into the haze. Mud puddles scattered around the yard looked like they were boiling. Eddie stepped out onto the top stair to catch a mouthful of rain, but the stinging beads of water made it impossible to open his eyes.

"Get your new boots on if you're going out," his mother shouted.

The new boots had been in the box of used clothes she had brought home from a rummage sale in Vernon. Eddie had also found a pair of turquoise pants with an elastic waistband that he had been wearing for three days. They had no pockets and no fly but they had bright yellow flowers on the front.

He could hear the rain slowing as they hunted for the new rubbers in the jumble box that held the coats, belts, footwear that didn't have mates, and other bits and pieces that his mother didn't know what to do with. Finally she tipped the box onto the floor. Eddie fished out bubble-gum-pink rubbers from the pile, pulled them onto his feet, and ran out into the rain. But he was too late. The cloudburst was over. He had missed the best part. Robins were already swooping down from branches to snatch up worms sprouting from the wet ground, and the puddles were calming down.

Eddie was thrilled when his mother came down the steps. "Get your rubbers on, Mom."

"I don't need them. I'm only getting some wood. You can grab an armload and help."

She hurried toward the woodshed and skipped over a puddle on the path, but Eddie thought her shoes and dress didn't look quite right for playing. He jumped into the centre with both feet, splashing muddy water onto her legs.

"Oh shit, Eddie," she said.

She shook her dress, sighed, stacked her arm with wood, and walked back to the house. Eddie stomped his feet in the puddle again, this time splattering mud onto his new pants.

"Oh shit," he said.

Grace looked back over her shoulder. "Hey, don't say that." Her smile erased the worry lines from her face.

Eddie liked seeing her smile again. Then suddenly her expression changed as if she was about to sneeze. She was looking behind him up to the road. He swung around, but from where he stood, the wild roses, thistles, and weeds were too tall, so he ran into the woodshed and stood on the chopping block. That's when he saw a car driving slowly down the road.

"Get over here!" she shouted.

Grace dropped the wood in the box by the stove. Eddie ran to her. She pulled him close and looked into his eyes. "Now you listen to me. If I see who I think is in that car, I'll tap you on the back, and you run over to the Cluffs' as fast as you can. Ask them to call the police. Tell them Ellis Bell is back. That's all you have to say. They'll know."

The Cluffs were a white family that lived on a farm by the highway on the other side of the river, the reserve boundary. They had the only telephone for miles around. She didn't say why he had to do as she said. Her sharp voice, the look in her eyes, the tone of her voice, and the way she squeezed his shoulder until it hurt frightened Eddie like nothing before.

The car turned down the driveway. Grace put her hands on his shoulders, and they waited. The cold air hitting the warm soil had formed fog that floated fence-post high above the ground. The car rocked from side to side on the rut-filled road. Its wipers bumped back and forth to clear away the last drops of rain, and exhaust fluttered out of the tail pipe like a white silk scarf.

The front tires splashed through a deep puddle, spreading water onto the grass and rolling back down to form pools of brown, bubbling foam. Eddie felt his mother's nails digging into his skin.

2

A waving arm appeared out of the passenger window as two short honks sounded from the horn. Grace let out a deep breath. Eddie felt her body relax.

The car interior was too dark to see the faces of the people inside. All Eddie could make out were shadows against the rear window—a man at the wheel, a woman passenger, and a small head tucked between them in the middle. Red dingle-balls hanging above the rear-view mirror shook each time the wheels hit a pothole.

The car pulled up between the woodshed and house. When the engine was switched off, water that dripped on the hot mufflers sounded like sighing breaths. Steam rising from underneath smelled sweet, and as the motor cooled, it ticked like an alarm clock. The passenger door opened with a dry groan, and a woman emerged draping a sweater over her shoulders; her clothes looked brand new. She had on dark glasses and wore a red beaded necklace with matching earrings, belt, and purse. Eddie couldn't take his eyes off her jutting, wedge-shaped bosom.

The lady reached up and removed her dark glasses. "Hello, Grace."

Grace smiled and touched her arm. "Oh, Isabel. You look like a million bucks. I never get visitors, and who shows up? Elizabeth Taylor."

The lady laughed. "We haven't seen you for so long I figured it was time for a visit. How long has it been, three years?"

Eddie watched as the driver's door opened and a tall man eased out of the car as if he were unfolding himself. He had a flat-top crew cut, his sharp cheekbones looked like they were about to poke through his skin, and there were deep lines on both sides of his mouth. His face looked like it had been carved from a smooth block of golden cedar.

Eddie saw a small tattoo of a cross on the back of the man's right hand when he adjusted his pants. Running the palms of his hands along the sides of his head just above the cigarette tucked behind his ear, the man thrust out his jaw like he was pulling his neck skin out from a tight collar. His white shirt was unbuttoned below his chest, and the sleeves were rolled up. Eddie saw a larger tattoo on his left arm when he stepped around the front of the car. He wore black dress pants with sharp creases that ran from his belt down to polished cowboy boots.

"Grace Toma. Who the hell said she died?" the man said laughing.

"Hello, Ray. I thought you were a chauffeur for a movie star."

The man turned and looked at Eddie. His eyes were the colour of tea, and his frown made his smile look like a sneer. "Hello, Eddie."

Eddie wondered who the man was, how he knew his name, and why he was looking at him like he knew every bad thing he had ever done. The man motioned away from the car with a quick jerk of his head.

"Gregory. Get out here."

There was no movement inside.

"Eddie, you come over here."

Eddie had no desire to do what the man wanted. He was fine right where he was. Ray reached into his shirt pocket and pulled out two sticks of gum. Eddie immediately recognized the yellow wrapper with silver foil poking out each end. He could tell it was Juicy Fruit a mile away.

"Soon as you boys do something for me, you can have these."

Eddie stepped forward as the boy jumped out of the car. They looked the same age, but Eddie was a little taller. Gregory wore a brand-new shirt and a pair of pants, and the front went up to his chest with a strap that went around his neck. It looked like a baby's bib. Gregory looked at the flowers on Eddie's blue pants but didn't say anything. They stood side by side looking up at Ray. "If you find me an old bird nest, you can have the gum. Okay? But it can't be just any old nest. It's got to be a robin's nest. That's what I'm looking for."

They nodded.

"Well, don't just stand there. Get a move on."

Eddie looked at Gregory. "I know where one is. I seen it."

The boys turned and ran. They heard Ray's laughter until they were well into the trees.

They swung around thorn bushes, jumped over logs, and ducked under low-hanging boughs until they came to the place where Eddie had seen two turquoise eggs resting on the ground inches away from an overturned nest. Each time Eddie had come across robin's eggs, he'd thought they looked out of place. Their colour didn't look real. He'd even tried scratching the shell with his thumbnail to see if the colour came off.

Eddie had laid the nest over the eggs to protect them. But now the nest had been turned over, and one egg was in two pieces as if someone had cracked it open and placed the shells back down on the ground. He drew in his breath.

"What?" Gregory asked.

"Something broke my egg."

"How do you know?"

"Well, look. It was good before, and now something broke it and took out the baby robin. I covered it up and everything."

"Maybe it flew away?"

"Baby robins can't fly."

"Maybe it walked away?"

"Yeah. Maybe."

Eddie placed the shells inside the nest, and they rushed back to the house.

Ray was taking groceries out of brown paper bags when Eddie handed him the nest. He looked at the boys with a puzzled expression.

"What's this for?" he asked.

"You wanted it," Gregory said.

"I never said I wanted a bird's nest, did I?"

"Ray, give them the gum," Isabel said.

Ray held out the gum toward the boys. They each grabbed a stick, but Ray wouldn't release his grip. Eddie looked at his mother for help, but she looked away. Taking a larger hold of the gum, Eddie pulled hard just as Ray let go. He stumbled backward, embarrassed by the laughter, but held the gum tightly in his fist. He licked the inside of the foil wrapper before he folded the stick of gum into his mouth, and dashed outside with Gregory.

"Hey, hey, hey. Wait a minute," Grace shouted. "Don't you go near that river, Eddie. You hear?"

Eddie nodded. They jumped off the steps and were gone. Leaping over small puddles, Eddie led the way down to the hollow cottonwood. As Gregory looked at the tree stump that seemed out of place, Eddie tossed a rock into the undergrowth. When Gregory looked away, Eddie ducked inside the tree. Gregory turned around and Eddie was nowhere in sight. When Eddie reappeared, Gregory was amazed.

They walked deeper into the bush through a poplar grove. The trees seemed to wait for the boys to walk underneath before releasing the rain trapped on their leaves to sprinkle down their necks like cold fingers. The sounds of sticks breaking underfoot sent a squirrel speeding up to the high part of a cedar where it chattered down at them as if cursing.

Eddie pushed aside a salmonberry bush, and they stepped out onto the bank of the river. The sunlight was so bright that it hurt their eyes. A dragonfly speeding above the water's edge like an airplane looked like it was placing rings onto the surface with its tail. A haze rose from the damp grass on the riverbank like steam from a kettle. They tossed rocks and sticks into the water until Eddie heard his mother calling.

"Don't say where we went," he said to Gregory.

That night in the bedroom Lewis slept at their feet while Gregory and Eddie talked and laughed. Finally Gregory fell asleep. Eddie lay awake, thinking about what he and Gregory had done that day and wondering if there was anything better in the world than finding a friend.

The gas lamp in the kitchen spread light across the bed and threw shadows onto the bedroom wall. He listened to the grownups sitting at the kitchen table smoking cigarettes, their spoons ringing off mugs of tea, their conversation kept low.

Footsteps approached the bedroom. Eddie narrowed his eyes to slits. Someone stood beside the bed looking down at them. Then the door squeaked until the light shrank to a crack. The footsteps walked away.

"They're all asleep," Ray said. "I'm going outside."

The front door closed.

"So Eddie is going to grade one this fall. Are you sending him to the reserve school?" Isabel asked.

"No. He's going to Falkland," Grace answered.

"Falkland?" Isabel sounded surprised. "Oh, it's gonna be rough. He'll prob'ly be the only Indian there. I can already hear the name-calling."

"I thought about it a long time," Grace said. "Mom and me both. She's the one said we needed to move up here so he could go to the white school. Eddie needs to know how it's gonna be. It's not the same as when we were that age. Remember when we rode horses to the reserve school? Remember all the cousins and friends laughing and playing and thinking we had everything in the world?

"Well, where are they now? They're sitting in their shacks on the reserve, just like I'm doing. Sure, some of them have jobs, but I don't want Eddie sitting around waiting for his luck to change. He has to be ready to get out there when he's finished school. I want him to get a good job and have money so he doesn't have to live like this. He's a smart kid. He'll figure it out. He has to." Grace looked around the room. Then she sat up straight. "What are you guys doing up here, Isabel?"

"Ray wanted to see if anybody heard anything about his sister. It's over four years now she's been gone."

"It's been that long already? I thought the police said they knew what happened."

"They don't know. They're just guessing. All they said was they found her purse and shoes in the middle of a bridge in Vancouver. They think she jumped into the Fraser River and drowned. But Ray said, how do they know that it's her shoes anyway? Somebody could have stolen her purse too. If Ray could at least bury her, maybe he wouldn't think about her so much. I just think how lucky it was Gregory was staying with us by then."

"Poor Delphine," Grace said softly.

Eddie had just closed his eyes when he heard the front door open. Then he heard the creak of a chair as someone sat down. All talk had stopped, and it was quiet until Grace spoke in a clear voice.

"I can tell you got something to say, Ray. So you better get it off your chest. Spit it out."

Ray slid his chair close to the table. "Yeah, I'm gonna say something to you, Grace. You can go right ahead and get mad if you want, but I'm gonna say it anyways. Looks like things is really going to the dogs around here. It's not good. Not good a-tall. I don't know how you don't freeze to death in winter. I bet there's no insulation anywhere in the house, and that old heater stove looks ready to fall apart anytime. The walls inside are made of paper, and I can feel a breeze across my back just sittin' here. Christ, one morning you and your kids are gonna wake up dead."

"What business is that of yours?" Grace asked coldly.

When Eddie heard the warning tone in his mother's voice, he crawled out of bed and watched through the door crack.

"Eddie starts school this fall, right? It's one thing to let him run around here in girl clothes, but you send him to school dressed like that and he'll get his ass kicked every day. I seen them pants he was wearing and them pink boots. Good God, you don't know what you might be doing to a boy when you dress him up like that. You trying to turn him into a queer?"

Eddie looked down at his pants on the floor. His girl pants.

"Who do you think you're talking to?" Grace asked. "Just 'cause I'm not a man doesn't mean I can't cut wood. You come up here all shined up with money jingling in your pockets like a big shot and you think you can tell me what I'm doing wrong? When was the last time you put a gopher in a stew and told your kids it was rabbit? I bet you never had to do that. And since when does anybody give a damn about them except me and my mom, huh?"

Gopher stew and girl clothes. Eddie wondered what was to come next.

"I know it ain't been easy," Ray said. "All I'm saying is, if the Indian agent came out here today and seen how you lived, he'd grab your kids and send them off to residential school. They can do that, you know. They can just drive in with some cops and take away your family, and there's not a damn thing you can do about it. That's what almost happened to my sister Delphine after her old man left her. She laid around feeling sorry for herself the same as you're doing now. And don't say you're not. It's a good thing we got Gregory outta there when we did. Next thing you know, she took off for the big city, and nobody's heard from her since.

"She used to tell me to mind my own damn business. I did, and look what happened. If you tell me to, I'll walk out the door, and we'll leave you alone. But you never used to be like this, Grace. If you don't stop feelin' sorry for yourself and smarten up pretty quick, you're gonna end up the same way. You can't just sit around waiting for the Indian department to do something. You have to do it on your own. Your boys need a man to straighten them out, or Jesus H. Christ, the next thing you know, you'll have them both wearing dresses."

Grace replied angrily, but Ray wouldn't back down. From time to time, when their voices rose to near shouts, Isabel had to calm them down so they wouldn't wake the children. As the conversation went on and their voices lowered, Eddie crawled back into bed.

The next morning Gregory and Eddie were awakened by the laughter of people trying to talk at the same time. Eddie saw a pair of folded corduroy overalls on the floor where his girl pants had been. He pulled them on and hurried out before he missed anything. Eddie smiled when he saw his grandma and Uncle Alphonse sitting at the table, even though his uncle didn't have much use for kids. Grandma held Lewis on her lap while she blew on a steaming mug of tea. When she saw Eddie, the wrinkles on her face gathered in a smile.

The room smelled of fresh coffee. A crowded frying pan of bacon and eggs popped and spat fat onto the surface of the hot stove, sending up white puffs of smoke. Eddie sat beside his grandma, who filled his plate with fried potatoes, eggs, bacon, and toast made with town bread. The bread his mom had baked the day before was nowhere in sight, which pleased him, because if it wasn't fresh out of the oven, the crust would be so hard it cut his mouth. A small tin of peanut butter in the centre of the table caught Eddie's eye. He had tasted peanut butter only once before but remembered its creamy flavour.

"We've been workin' with this one guy for years. He's got clean cabins and he'll do anything to help because he wants good workers that'll stay until the picking is done," Ray said. "He gives you a little cash every Saturday and pays you when you're finished or when you ask for it. He's even got a list of other farmers that are looking for workers when his crop's done. We'll stay in one cabin so we can save money, and Grandma can do the cooking for us and look after the kids. If you tell the Indian agent in Vernon you got a job but no money to get there, he'll give you some to get you started. If you're leaving town, those buggers can't give it to you fast enough."

Isabel said, "We'll go into Seattle to this big army and navy store. You should see all the stuff they got, and it's cheap too, a lot cheaper than here. When summer's over you can come home with money and everything you always wanted. What do you think about that, Grace?"

"I'd like to get a truck so I can go out to get wood and go into town without having to always depend on other people for a ride. When are you going?"

"Day after tomorrow," Ray said. "You get all your stuff packed up, and we'll go to the Indian office first thing so you can see about money. We don't have any room in the car because we need to pick up a few things, so you'll have to take the train. I can drop you guys off at the station, and we'll be waitin' for you at the end of the line in Yakima. You never know, when you get back, Alphonse might have found himself a cook by then, eh Alphonse? You old mink."

"You go right ahead and pick them weeds in the hot sun. I'll stay right here," Alphonse said.

"After that we'll head on down to California for the macaroni harvest. They say you can make a lot of money picking that stuff. That macaroni comes off the plant by the handful, and you can fill over a hundred boxes in one day, I heard," Ray said grinning.

"Baloney harvest, more like it," Grace said. She turned to her mother. "What do you think about going back down to the States, Mom?"

Grandma nodded. "My mom looked after you and Alphonse while I went out and picked apples. Wonder if anybody I worked with in the orchards is still around there. Our fingers were always red and dry after picking all day, but we made each other laugh with a good story. Used to visit a lot more then." She shook her head. "I don't know what I'm talking about. They're prob'ly all dead now."

That afternoon Eddie and Gregory giggled when the car turned toward Vernon's town park. Saturday afternoon was the busiest time in Polson Park. Cars, trucks, motorcycles, and bicycles were parked off to the side of the tree-lined road. Some people pushed baby carriages while others lay on blankets on the grass. Children gathered around the slides and swings. The car had barely come to a stop before Eddie and Gregory bolted out onto the grass. With no weeds to slow them or thorny limbs to scratch and grab at their clothes, the boys raced to the fountain, circled around it twice, and ran back without stopping.

Hot dog buns, wieners—the uncooked kind, Eddie's favourite—potato chips, bottles of pop, a package of doughnuts covered in powdered sugar, and small jars of ketchup and mustard were laid out on a blanket spread on the ground.

Eddie was given a hot dog and a paper cup filled with pop. Ray held out a paper bag so everyone could see five Popsicles inside.

"Everybody can have one when you're finished eating all your food. But if you leave the table, that's it. Dinner's over."

Eddie watched a red kite with a long tail zigzag across the sky while a boy with a squirt gun chased a group of screaming girls. As he began to get up, Grace pushed down on his shoulder and told him to finish his hot dog. He wiped his hands on his pants and drank the pop down with a gulp.

Children by a pond were tossing chunks of bread to the ducks. A small piece of his hot dog bun had broken off and was the right size for throwing. Eddie couldn't sit still any longer; his legs were itching to run. He picked up the piece of bread and ran toward the ducks but stopped and came back.

"Come on, Gregory. Let's go," he called.

Gregory didn't move.

"Gregory," he called again.

But Gregory kept his head down and wouldn't look at Eddie. Grace grabbed his arm and pulled Eddie down to the ground. Ray brushed the crumbs off his pants, picked up the paper bag, and began handing out the treats. Eddie reached out his hand.

"Nope. I told you. If you leave the table before you finish eating, you don't get one."

Eddie's eyes filled with tears. He glanced over at his mother, but she looked away and took a bite from her hot dog. When Eddie saw Ray grinning, the tears ran down his cheeks.

The next morning everyone squeezed into Ray's car. Before Eddie knew what was happening, he was standing on the platform of the Vernon train station watching Gregory wave goodbye from the back seat as the car pulled away and turned a corner. Grace led him quickly inside the station with Grandma and Lewis following behind. It wasn't long until Eddie forgot Gregory and watched a new and exciting world hurtle past the train window.

3

Eddie and Gregory lay in bed snatching at dust motes that floated in a beam of sunshine. The cabin had no inside walls; everyone ate and slept together in one large room. Eddie shared a bed with Gregory and Lewis. Grace and Grandma slept in the bed next to theirs, while Ray and Isabel had a corner to themselves.

On a narrow stand beside the door sat a washbasin, two metal water pails, and a saucer that held a bar of soap. Hanging from a string draped across the open front to hide the slop bucket was a small grey towel. A cook stove stood on the other side of the door from the wash stand; its stovepipe disappeared up through the roof. There were no pantry cupboards, only shelves of unpainted lumber on both sides of a window. A small table was placed under the window so that a person washing dishes or peeling potatoes could see out to the fields.

Outside, next to each door, a small metal bathtub hung from a nail. Three outhouses sat in a row at the end of the cabins, and a water tap fastened to a nearby post dripped onto the ground.

Other workers soon filled most of the cabins. While the grownups worked in the fields, their children played outside. Gregory and Eddie tried to play with them, but the children walked away without saying a word.

"How come the other kids don't want to play with us, Grandma?" Eddie asked.

"Because they're Mexicans. They don't want no trouble. They eat their food, and we eat ours. That's all you have to know. Just keep away from them and mind your own business."

When the grownups went out the door to work in the fields, the three boys jumped up and down, laughed, and made faces at each other. Grandma smiled and put wood in the stove and began to make bread. She fried some of the dough for the boys. As soon as it came hot out of the frying pan, she gave them each one piece topped with a spoonful of jam.

"No more till supper," she said.

But whenever they were hungry, she gave them something to nibble on. Even if it was only a handful of uncooked macaroni, they were satisfied.

A fly buzzed past her ear while she washed the morning dishes. Without looking away from the window, she reached for the fly swatter hanging from a nail within close reach. Soapsuds hung down from her elbows like icicles dripping onto the floor. She glanced over and delivered a whack. Then she bent down, picked up the fly, and dropped it into the slop bucket.

The farm had four large fields, each surrounded by an irrigation ditch. Three of the fields grew fruit and vegetables, and one held a herd of cattle. Eddie didn't like the look of the large creatures, the way they whipped their tails or stared with their big eyes while chewing their cud. He became even more nervous when he saw that all that was keeping them away was a single wire that ran from post to post, looped around white spools. Eddie and Gregory stayed clear of the cows and always made sure to never look them in the eye.

At lunchtime Grandma loaded Gregory's small wagon with food and a large canning jar filled with sweet cold tea. The boys took turns pulling the wagon down to meet the grownups at the edge of a field, and Grandma walked behind holding Lewis's hand. The workers wandered over to what Ray called the chuck wagon and relaxed on the grass to eat every crumb of food.

Ray looked the same as always, but Isabel and Eddie's mom had dirt-streaked faces and mud stains on their knees. Grace had her hair neatly tucked under a tightly knotted kerchief, and Isabel wore an old cowboy hat, oversized clothes, and gloves with the tips of the fingers cut off. Eddie could barely see the red polish on her nails.

After the workers walked back out to the fields, Grandma let the boys rest for a while in the warm sun. They watched the cows by the fence.

"Don't worry about them. They won't bother us."

"How come?" Eddie asked.

"See that wire? It's electric. It gives them a shock if they touch it." Eddie didn't understand.

Just before suppertime Eddie, Gregory, and Lewis sat at the cabin table crunching on salted pieces of raw potatoes. Grace, Isabel, and Ray walked up the road toward home, heads down, too weary to carry on even the smallest conversation.

Isabel and Grace slumped down at the kitchen table. Ray grabbed a bar of soap and towel, took down the basin hanging on a nail by the front door, and walked out to the water tap. He let the water run until it was cold before filling the basin to the brim. When he noticed Eddie and Gregory watching, he told them to roll up their sleeves so they could wash up for supper. The soap burned their eyes until Ray held their heads under the tap. The two boys stood with their arms outstretched like wet scarecrows, waiting for a towel. Ray laughed at the sight.

After working the soap into lather, Ray spread it behind his ears and neck until his face was covered in a white mask. Then he doused his face with the cold water and scrubbed himself furiously and thoroughly. He tossed the dirty water into the yard, where it landed with a splash and rolled across the dusty ground in little mud balls. He dried his face and neck and dug a corner of the towel into his ears. Ray's mood improved after a good wash.

At supper time they pushed two beds back against the wall and moved the table to the middle of the room. The three boys sat on a wooden bench, and the grownups pulled up chairs. Grandma sat at one end of the table, and Ray sat at the other.

Ray smiled when he saw the food on the table. He picked up his knife and fork. "What's for supper, Grandma? I hope you made lots, because I'm so hungry I could eat a horse and chase the rider."

Grandma set a plate of food down in front of Ray, then poured tea into a mug and moved the sugar bowl closer. Ray scooped out three heaping spoonfuls. He stirred the tea quickly and finished with a tap on the rim. Grandma sat down and pushed the food along so the others could fill their plates.

After Ray wiped his plate clean with a piece of bread, he popped it into his mouth and reached over to the broom propped against the wall. He yanked out a straw, and working it back and forth in his mouth, he made loud kissing and sucking sounds until he laid the straw across his plate. He picked up his tea and drank it all without stopping. When he was finished, he set the mug on the plate with a bang and gave a loud "ahhh."

The others at the table were only half finished their food. Isabel and Grace looked over at Ray.

"He eats like he works," Isabel said.

"Always gotta be the one finishes first," Grace said.

"You betcha. Always," Ray said as he leaned his chair back on two legs.

"The kids are scared of the cows," Grandma said. "I told them the 'lectric wire kept them in. Maybe I didn't tell it good enough, I don't know," she said with a shrug.

Ray didn't answer. After the dishes were washed and the kitchen table was cleared, he stood and pushed back his chair. "Let's take a walk down to the cow pasture," he said. "Got somethin' I wanna show the kids."

Eddie saw Ray smile as he turned for the door. Grace and Isabel walked holding Lewis up by the hands while he swung his feet. Eddie and Gregory went on ahead with Ray, sometimes having to run to keep up.

Everyone gathered around Ray as he pointed to the fence. "Okay, you kids, look at the wire. Take a real good look. You see how it jumps like that every once in a while? That's the electricity turning off and on. See when it moves up a little, then falls down again? When it's up, the power is on. When it falls down, the power is off. See it? Can you see it?"

The movement reminded Eddie of a trout nibbling at a fishing line.

"Boy, this thing must be turned up full blast. I never seen one this strong before. Okay, now watch. Off . . . on . . . off . . . on . . . " Ray said as the wire jumped. Holding his hand over the wire he waited.

"Off." He grabbed the wire, but only for a second, before he pulled his hand away.

"On," he said and held up his palms.

"Why don't you leave your hand there so you can show the kids what happens?" Isabel asked with a smile.

"Yeah," said Grace.

Ray ignored them. He pulled out a handful of grass that grew just beyond the reach of the grabbing lips of the cattle and held it above the throbbing wire.

"Co-boss, co-boss," he called in a gentle voice.

Eddie watched a cow wander over. The grass disappeared into her great chomping mouth. Ray grabbed more grass, and another cow came up and lifted her head above the fence, but she couldn't reach Ray's hand. She stretched out her long tongue that was speckled with grey and black spots. Ray moved his hand away, and she tried again. He continued his game of keep away and finally held the grass just behind the wire. The cow clamped her mouth over the wire and the green treat he was keeping away from her. The animal let out an ear-rattling bellow as her eyes rolled inside her head. The ground sounded hollow under her heavy, stamping feet. The other cattle scattered as the creature stumbled backward, except for one slow cud-chewer that she knocked over like a bowling pin. Ray doubled over in laughter, slapping his thighs. When he saw the women and children hurrying toward the cabin, he laughed even harder.

Now Eddie was even more fascinated by the electric fence. For days he watched in case one of the cows touched the wire again. He'd lived his life without electricity and couldn't understand its workings. No one had explained why the wire jumped like it did, like it was breathing, like it had a heartbeat. The cattle were afraid of the wire. He needed to know why.

The next day Eddie and Gregory stood in the field, and Eddie's eyes were drawn back to the fence again. The mystery of the wire and why the cattle were so scared of it had grown in his mind so much that he needed to know exactly what made the cow act that way. The harder he tried to understand, the more confused he got. There was only one thing for him to do. If no one could help him, he would find out for himself.

Gregory followed him up to the fence. Cows grazing nearby lifted their heads to see what was going on as Eddie held his hands over the wire. Gregory stepped back. Eddie took a deep breath, and before he could change his mind, grabbed on to the wire with both hands. He felt as though he'd been kicked by a cow. His fingers locked onto the wire.

People on the far side of the field heard the scream. Ray dropped the flat of berries he was carrying.

"Oh God!" Grace yelled. "Hurry!"

Eddie's body arched backward as he tried to pull away from the wire, but his fingers wouldn't let go. His head shook from side to side, and his eyes shut tight as he strained and pulled. His voice buzzed in his ears, and he felt a strong thump to his hands.

Then through eyes blurred as if underwater, he saw his mother looking down at him. She patted his cheek with her hand.

"Hey, you."

Ray and Isabel appeared. Clouds floated behind their upside-down heads. Ray knelt on the ground for a closer look. His breath washing down on Eddie's face smelled of onions and cigarettes. Grace took Eddie's hands and turned them over, examining them. Eddie shivered as the effects of the electric shock began to fade away.

"Is he going to be all right?" asked Isabel.

"He's okay," said Ray. "He'll live. What the hell you doing, grabbin' onto the fence? I thought I told you all about it the other day. What's the hell's the matter with you anyway? Are you stupid or something?"

Even though it sounded like a question, Eddie knew it wasn't.

"Get up now. Let's go to the house. You can lay on my bed for a while," Grace said.

"You know, it's almost like this kid is tryin' to kill himself," Ray said.

"What would you say a thing like that for?" Isabel asked.

"Why the hell else would he grab on to the fence? To 'lectrocute himself, that's why. Now what else is he gonna do, huh? I don't know what it is about these dumb kids. You tell them one thing, and they go right ahead and do it anyway. Boy, if I'd done something like that, my old pop would've beat me with a harness strap," Ray muttered.

"It was a good thing Ray was there, because he knew what to do," Grace said to Eddie after he lay down. "When he saw you couldn't let go of the wire, he knew he couldn't touch you, so he kicked your hands away. If it was me, I probably would've grabbed on to you and got stuck too. Then Isabel and Grandma would have tried to pull me away, and they would be stuck, and all of us would've been hanging on to each other and dancing around like we were crazy."

Late Saturday afternoon the farm hands turned off the tractors and stacked the picking baskets, flats, and buckets in the sheds. Ray, Isabel, Grace, and all the pickers walked back to their cabins smiling and laughing. After working hard all week, Sunday would be a welcome day of rest.

"Not many farmers take Sunday off," Ray said. "That's why I picked this guy and the next one too."

Saturday supper was a bubbling pot of onions, fried hamburger, canned tomatoes, and pork and beans that Ray called slumgullion. They ate supper and cleaned the cabin. Then Isabel, Grace, and Grandma rushed to get ready to go into town.

Two women, fellow pickers that Isabel had known for years, joined them, and they squeezed into Ray's car. Eddie watched Isabel drive away. When the car bottomed out in a hole on the road, there was a shriek of laughter inside. A barking dog chased after the car, biting at the tires until the car turned onto the highway. A gear ground into place, the motor roared and they were gone.

The three boys sat on the steps trying to decide what they should do. They were tired from playing all day out in the hot sun. When the grownups caught them throwing rocks at cows, the boys played hide and seek behind the cabin until Lewis cried when he couldn't find Eddie or Gregory. It was hard playing with Lewis. He couldn't keep up in foot races and didn't understand Go Go Stop. It wasn't until he fell asleep after eating dinner that the older boys were able to climb the highest hill they could find and lie on their backs to watch the sky for jets. But what could they do for fun now?

Inside the cabin there was a loud clash of a pot lid falling to the floor, and Ray yelled, "Ow, goddamn it."

Eddie peeked around the doorway and saw the round metal tub in the middle of the floor, filled with steaming water. Ray blew on his hand. Eddie pulled back his head before he was spotted.

"You pot-lickers get in here," Ray said.

Eddie motioned Gregory and Lewis to go around the corner of the cabin while he pressed his back against the wall, hoping to blend in with the clapboards. Maybe Ray would decide that he had been mistaken in thinking the boys were near.

"Come on, I haven't got all damn day."

Eddie wanted to wait a little longer just to make sure.

"If you guys don't get in here right now, I'll drag this tub outside, and you can have your bath out there where everybody can see your bony little asses."

The three boys stood looking down into the tub of water that was clouded by a floating bar of soap.

"Why do we have to bath, Dad? We'll just get dirty again anyway," Gregory said.

"And Mom said as long as we use soap when we swim in the river, it's good enough."

"I don't care what any mom said. When I walk in the cabin sometimes, it smells like there's three wet dogs layin' on the floor. Now quit makin' excuses and drop them clothes on the floor. Make sure you guys wash everywhere, cuz I'm gonna check you over when you finish."

Ray drummed his fingers on the table while he cleaned his teeth with a straw, looking over to the open door every few minutes as if he were waiting for somebody. Eddie helped Lewis out of his pants and unbuttoned the straps of his overalls, letting them fall to the floor. Lewis grinned as he pulled and stretched his dink as if it were made of rubber. Eddie yanked his brother's hand away and lifted him over the edge of the tub. But the tub was slippery, and Lewis slid underwater, his eyes wide open in shock. Eddie lifted him off the bottom as he gagged and whimpered.

"Don't you start, or I'll give you somethin' to cry about," Ray said in a loud voice.

The boys complained about the open door until Ray set up two chairs, placed the broom on the seats, and draped a blanket over it. After mopping up the water splashed onto the floor by the bathers, Ray went around the cabin hunting down a buzzing fly and swept the floor a second time. When he couldn't find more jobs to do, he turned his chair toward the door and sat down. If there was a noise of any kind outside, he jumped up to have a look down the road dividing the cabins. Seeing no one, he wandered back inside. Ray added more hot water to the bath. Then Eddie heard bottles clinking.

A man appeared in the doorway looking out of breath, his face shiny with sweat. He held a twelve-pack of beer in each hand.

"Well finally, Abel. What the hell happened? I been waitin' so long my tongue is starting to swell up," Ray said.

"Generator, starter, something. I dunno," he said weakly.

"What?" Ray said.

"Car broke down."

"Where is your car?"

"Down the road. A car stopped. Some guys said they'd give me a ride for six beer. I told them to go to hell. I hadda walk two miles."

Slumping against the door frame, the man closed his eyes and took a deep breath just as the cardboard handles of the beer cases slipped down from his hands. But at the last moment, he crooked his middle finger of each hand and caught them before they fell to the floor. Ray rushed toward him.

"Abel!" he shouted.

The man smiled as Ray grabbed the cases out of his hand.

"Whatsa matter with you? Give it here before you break them all. Jesus."

Ray set the case on the table.

"There's nothing worse than warm beer. Maybe if I soaked them in cold water it won't be so bad . . . Dammit, Abel. Anyway, you better come on in and sit down. You look whiter than a sick *summa*."

Abel made his way to the table, his arms hanging useless at his sides. Ray pulled out a chair for him.

"Man oh man. I never seen you look this bad before. What happened to you yesterday anyway? After I gave you the beer money, I never seen you again. Why didn't you come to work? What the hell you been up to?"

"My old lady won't even talk to me today. She's mad because I went down to the tavern last night. I never made it home till daylight."

"What, you went and got drunk?"

"Oh jeez, Ray. I got drunker'n two Indians. And just now, when I was walkin' down the highway, I felt like layin' down on the road and hopin' a car would come along and finish me off."

Ray snatched the water pail off the stand. "Listen. You stay here while I go get some cold water to soak these beers. You just sit there . . . and . . . and don't die on me."

Eddie watched as Abel slumped in his chair, breathing hard out of his wide-open mouth. He wondered if Abel really might die. Sweat dripped off the end of his nose, and he had a bad smell like something was rotten.

Ray returned with a pail of cold water and placed the bottles of beer in the pail.

"Hey, what's going on here? There's three missing."

"When I come home, I went straight to bed, and I was sawing logs while you was out there all day humped over them rows of berries. Around two o'clock I got up and went back down to the tavern to get your beer, and while I was there I had me a couple eye-openers. Anyway, when I was on my way here, the car just up and quit. When I opened the hood, I could smell something was burnt. I don't know what it was, but it was burnt. And after a mile of walkin', I got thirsty and I had to drink somethin'. It's a good thing I had them beer with me, cuz boy if I didn't, I mighta died of thirst. Go ahead and crack me one, will you? Maybe it'll kill the pain in my legs."

Eddie rubbed at the dirt scab on his knee with the washcloth until he came to the shiny skin underneath, and then washed between his toes. He knew it was time to get out of the tub when his fingers were wrinkled like raisins and the water was too cold to make a good lather. If Abel's chair was facing the other way he could get dressed without being seen. He decided to wait until the man made a trip to the toilet. After ten minutes Abel still hadn't made a move toward the door, and Eddie began to shiver.

"I'm cold, Gregory. Are you?"

"Yeah, but I don't want to get out with that man watching us."

"Are you cold, Lewis?"

Lewis was strangely quiet and he stared at Eddie, unblinking.

"What's wrong with him?" Gregory asked.

Lewis's face turned red. Then Eddie and Gregory felt a warmth wash over their legs and heard an underwater squeak as if someone had rubbed against the bottom of the tub. When a bubble appeared on the top of the water, the two boys knew what was happening and jumped out of the tub as if a dangerous animal had somehow made its way among them.

Eddie helped Lewis get dressed and into bed. When Ray saw the boys sitting on the bed, he went to a shelf and brought down a paper bag. He tossed the bag of candy onto the bed and walked back to the table while the boys scrambled for their Saturday treat.

On Monday morning Ray was the first one out the door, and he picked as many flats of berries as Isabel and Grace combined. He didn't like to be second best at anything, so he worked hard, and the boys learned to stay away from him until the workday was over. Occasionally, after supper when the cabin was too warm or there was too much noise, Ray slipped out the door to go for a walk. No one wanted to go with him because they were too tired.

But one evening Eddie and Gregory saw Ray strolling up the hill behind the cabin and they crept along behind him in the tall grass. When he reached the top, Ray sat down on the ground, lit a cigarette, and took a long drag.

"Get up here, you little monkeys."

The two boys waited to see if he was angry at being followed, but he waved his arm for them to come over.

"You guys are the worst trackers in the world. Sounded like a herd of elephants was after me."

"Why did you come up here?" Gregory asked.

"We're movin' on to the next farm. About damn time too. I can't look another berry in the eye. We'll be leavin' Wednesday, and I just wanted to take one more look around. This farm's always been my favourite. There's not as many pickers as all the others, and it's quieter here than anywhere else. I been to a lot of places in the world. I seen funny things and I seen good things. But I sure like being here. This is the kind of place I'd like to own."

"What do you mean funny things? Like a dog doing tricks?" Eddie asked.

"If the dog had six legs and was dancin'. No, I mean funny like something that don't look right. When we were in Holland in the war, it was the first time I ever seen a windmill. They were lined up for miles and looked like big fans turnin' in the wind. They didn't look right. Like I was seein' things."

"What do windmills do?" Eddie asked.

"Damned if I know. One guy tried to tell me they sucked the water outta the ocean so they could use the land underneath. Imagine trying to tell a guy something like that."

A breeze swept across the field below and moved up the hill, blowing Eddie's hair back. The sun took a last peek over the distant hills. Its light clung to the heads of the dry, rattling grass until their hill turned into a sea of swaying candles. A small bird landed on the grass in front of them, so light the stalk barely bent. With eyes like black dewdrops, the bird launched itself from its spring-board with a chirp. Yellow salsify and dandelion fluff filled the air like snowflakes. A cotton-batting cloud that had drifted close to the sun blazed red as though on fire.

Eddie noticed tall white boxes in a treed corner of the farm. "What are those?" he asked, pointing.

"Beehives."

"They don't look like beehives," Eddie said.

"They're made so the bees put the honey near the ground, and the farmer can get the honey without fallin' from a tree. And it's where a lot of *summas* keep their money because nobody will go near it," Ray said.

Eddie looked over at Gregory.

"I took this out of a hive once and been keeping it for good luck ever since." Ray pulled a silver dollar from his pocket and held it up for the boys to see as he turned it around in his fingers. Then he flipped the coin into the air, and it landed in his palm.

"Okay," he said. "Time to get back to the cabin before your moms start hollerin.'"

Ray stood and stretched his back.

It wasn't until late afternoon the next day, when Grandma and Lewis had fallen asleep, that Eddie and Gregory made their way to the beehive boxes. They were out of breath when they poked their heads around the trunk of a tree and saw the hives sitting in bunches of twos and threes. The nearest one was thirty feet away. Eddie swatted something away from his face that he thought was a mosquito.

There was no plan. Eddie decided that all they had to do was get to the beehives, lift off the lid, grab as many silver dollars as they could, and run. Now, as they got closer, he wasn't sure if it was such a good idea. But it was too late. If he didn't do it now, Gregory would call him a chicken.

He ran to the first box and pushed at the top, but the lid was stuck. He pushed harder, but it still wouldn't budge, so he motioned

Gregory to help. Bracing their legs, they both gave a hard shove, and the box tipped over onto the ground with a heavy thump. A swarm of bees zoomed out of the hive.

Gregory screamed in pain. Eddie was stung on his neck and back. They raced blindly away until Eddie saw an opening in the trees at what looked like a road. He squeezed his eyes tight as he ran, waving his arms wildly, with Gregory close behind. The ground suddenly went out from under him, and he landed with a splash in a water-filled irrigation ditch. The cool water soothed Eddie's burning skin and blocked out the frightening humming noise. He swallowed a mouthful of dirty water before he felt the soft bottom of the ditch under his feet. The boys surfaced, wiping the mud from their eyes. The water was chest high.

When they climbed out of the ditch, the bees forced them back underwater. Just when they thought it was safe to leave, the bees returned and drove them back. Finally, they grabbed onto weeds and pulled themselves out of the ditch. They lay on the ground, moaning and crying from the pain of their stings.

Grandma was shocked to see them when they walked into the cabin. She cleaned them and changed their clothes. Gregory couldn't stop crying.

"Shut up," Grandma said as she washed the mud from their faces.

At the supper table, Eddie and Gregory sat puffy-eyed and sore.

"Why did you guys do something so stupid? Why?" Isabel asked.

"We wanted to take some money from the beehives so you wouldn't have to work," Gregory said.

"Where did you hear a bonehead thing like that?"

The boys looked over at Ray.

"Is that right, Ray? You told the kids there was money in the beehives?"

"No. I said honey, not money. Dumb bastards. They must've heard me wrong," he said with a smile.

Just as Ray had said, two days later the berry crop was finished, and it was time to move to a new farm. They drove until the sound of the car slowing down made Eddie sit up. The hum of the motor had made everyone tired, but now they forced themselves awake. Eddie and Gregory pressed their faces close to the windows, and Lewis wedged his way between them. Ray opened his window, and cool air filled the car. He pointed to the fields.

"Well, here we are. And just have a look at them fields. Criminy, they're just thick with crop. This is gonna be a lot easier too. We don't need to be foolin' around with them little berries anymore. No more fartin' around. Yep. Now we're gonna be makin' some real money."

As the car turned in to a long line of cabins, Gregory grabbed Eddie's arm and pointed toward a building with white clapboards and large black lettering high on the front of the building. The boys couldn't read the words, but they recognized the Coca-Cola sign.

"Here we are. Tolliver Farms. This is where we make our fortune," Ray said as he grabbed Isabel on the leg.

Eddie saw twice as many cabins as at the last farm, but they looked the same. Toilets and a clothesline were at the back, and on a raised platform in front of the cabins was a single water tap. A metal tub for bathing and hand-washing clothes hung by its handle from a nail beside each doorway. Each cabin had a car or pickup truck parked out front. They were old vehicles, much older than Ray's. Some had different-coloured fenders and doors, but they all had one thing in common: rust the colour of dried blood was spreading through the metal.

Ray drove to the end of the cabins and parked around the side of the last one. While he went to tell the farm owner they had arrived, Grandma opened the door of the cabin. Gregory and Eddie ran in ahead, and Lewis followed behind Grandma, clutching at her dress. The air smelled of coal oil and smoke. Curtains were bed sheets cut into squares, a honey-coloured flycatcher strip hung from the ceiling, and a small stool was tucked under the washbasin stand. Above the window by the pantry cupboard hung a store-bought fly swatter.

Grandma pulled back the curtain and pushed up the smudged window to shove a prop stick underneath. She sent Gregory out to the car for the extra broom, and Grandma and Grace swept the dirt out through the door. The floor had been swept so many times before that the wood grain stood up in ridges. After the dust settled, Isabel mopped the floor until it looked new again. Ray returned, lifted the thin mattresses off the beds, and carried them outside. One by one he laid them on their sides and pounded them with a large stick to get rid of any bedbugs and dirt. He put the mattresses back on the bed springs, and the women spread blankets over each one. Soon they were eating supper around the table in their new home.

4

Eddie and Gregory followed Ray through the centre of a large pasture. The late afternoon sun was setting, and the air felt cool and smelled clean. They looked around nervously for signs of cattle. Ray stopped at a patch of ground that was circled by weeds and bushes. Eddie caught the swamp smell that often drifted in through the cabin window.

Ray pointed toward the tall circle of greenery twenty feet away from where they stood. "What do you boys see?"

"Thorns," Gregory answered.

"Stinging nettles," Eddie said.

"Oh, there's a lot more than that going on in there. The farmer told me this slough was a pain in the ass. He tried to drain it, but the water came back a week later. When he comes to do the summer fallow, he has to slow right down and crawl past this damn thing. There's soft ground about ten feet out around it, and once his hired hand sunk the tractor down over its big rims. It took a bulldozer to finally get it out. He tried hauling in gravel, but it just sinks down like it's on quicksand. They even used it for a garbage dump and threw in empty oilcans, tires, lumber, boulders, broken windows and bottles and everything he didn't need. But it just keeps disappearing. So, I'm tellin' you kids, stay the hell away from there. I mean it. If you don't listen to me and I see you anywhere close to it, I'll give you a whippin' you won't forget. Because whatever goes in that swamp never comes out."

Despite Ray's warning, the next day Eddie and Gregory stepped carefully through the stinging nettles and thorns. Their bare feet had become thick and hard as boot leather. Pebbles that had once stuck like tacks rolled away from their feet harmlessly, unable to break the tough skin. They held the nettles back with sticks until they came to the edge of the slough. Just then the thick scum let out a belch like a simmering pot of porridge. At the centre, where the water was clear, spidery-looking creatures called water skippers that they had seen in the pond at home raced everywhere like ice skaters. Sitting on their heels, Eddie and Gregory watched the skippers darting about, fascinated that the unsinkable little creatures left only tiny dents on top of the water.

Eddie heard a flying locust somewhere behind them, coming closer and closer. Cracking and snapping, the locust landed in the slough in front of them. It pushed forward across the clean water, its legs churning like a frightened duck's until it climbed on top of the scum. The locust hurried toward the edge, and with only inches to go to safety, it stopped. One eye looked above while the other looked below. Then, with a sound like a raindrop on water, the locust was pulled below the surface.

An old door that was lodged in the muck looked safe enough to hold their weight. Eddie jumped up and down on it just to make sure. Then he and Gregory held onto the tall grasses and shuffled out to the end of the door. They watched clusters of water bugs running in circles as if in a game of tag, their feet sending small ripples across the reflection of the sky. When they were within easy reach, Eddie was tempted to snatch one up, but a horn honked back at the cabin, and someone called his name.

The skippers suddenly scampered off in different directions, and the boys saw movement down in the deep water. They cupped their hands around their eyes and leaned over for a better look. It took a few seconds before Eddie could see down to where the swamp was deepest. The bottom had been stirred up, and a cloud of mud, grass, sticks, small ferns, and some thin and shiny things the size of a penny tumbled inside the underwater storm. They looked like fish scales, but they were bigger than anything he had ever seen before.

"See anything?" Gregory asked.

"No, there's too much—"

Just then something large floated up and came to a stop close to the surface. The way it swayed ever so slightly back and forth reminded Eddie of a salmon resting in a slow current. Lowering his hand into the water, he reached down until his finger touched the peculiar shape. The boys saw a streak of silver like the underside of a fish or snake just before the water rose like a wave and broke over them with a loud splash. They ran out from the slough talking excitedly, unsure of what they had seen.

Grandma, Grace, Isabel, and Lewis were gathered around a red pickup truck. Ray had the hood up and was looking at the motor. "I never thought I'd see the day when I could save enough money to buy my own truck. Do you remember, Mom, when you told me a long time ago you always wanted to see the ocean? Well, now we can. We can go wherever we want and we don't have to ask nobody to take us."

Eddie slid his hand over the rounded fenders. The bumps coming through the paint felt like scabs. The mirror on the passenger's door and a tailgate chain were both missing. The single dented chrome hubcap made the vehicle look off balance, and a strip of roof fabric hung down over the driver's seat like an untucked shirt.

Gregory stood on the running board, and Eddie sat behind the steering wheel. He pressed on the horn, and it gave a piercing beep. Ray jumped back from under the hood and glared through the windshield.

"Dammit, leave things alone," he warned.

He closed the hood and wiped his hands on a rag. "Like I said in town, Grace, this truck don't look like much, but the motor and transmission is good. Should last for a bit, as long as you change the oil once in a while. That's what's wrong with people. If they just kept the oil clean, they wouldn't have so much trouble. Anyway, it's a good old truck. Might be a little hard to get started in the winters, but she's got a good rear end. Kinda like Işabel."

Isabel turned away, uninterested.

"Why is your hair wet, Eddie?" Grace asked.

"I dunked my head under the tap. Can you take us for a ride?"

"Yeah. Let's go for a drive," Gregory said.

"I guess we can go for a short one to the gas station and back," Grace said smiling.

The boys ran around to the back, climbed over the tailgate, and began jumping up and down, rocking the truck and laughing at the rattling noise. Eddie and Gregory sat down facing the back. Inside the cab, Lewis crawled up onto the front seat. Grace slammed the door twice before it stayed shut. As they turned left onto the highway, Eddie felt important. Grace went through the gears, picking up speed. Isabel waved, and Ray watched with his hands in his pockets.

When the truck rounded a sharp corner, Eddie was thrown against the side. Gregory held out his hand to help, but just when their fingers touched, the truck hit the train tracks and bounced them both into the air. They landed hard on the metal deck. Eddie raised himself up to his knees to rub his sore tailbone. Gregory was trying not to show how much it really hurt, but couldn't force a smile.

What was to have been a short trip turned into a long afternoon drive. Grace stopped at a gas station to refuel and bought an ice cream cone for herself and each of her passengers. As the truck picked up speed on the road again, Eddie and Gregory had to pull their shirts over their heads to keep the dust off the ice cream.

So they banged on the back window until the truck pulled over and they climbed in front. By the time Grace came to a stop in front of the cabin, all three boys were fast asleep beside her on the seat.

Eddie was surprised by the attention his mother gave the truck. After work and during any spare time she had, she worked on the truck. She hauled out the rubber mat, swept the floorboards, and washed the mats until their colour changed from grey to black. Ray found three hubcaps at a junk dealer's, and Grace sewed the ripped roof cloth back into place. Isabel and Ray polished the dull paint with floor wax until the truck shone bright and clean. Eddie couldn't remember seeing his mother smile so much.

On Saturday morning, the boys awoke to see everyone seated at the table drinking coffee. They should have been out in the fields already, but they sat leaning on the backs of their chairs as if they had all the time in the world. Eddie stood by his mother and gave her a puzzled look.

"Day off today. The farmer said the crop needs two days before it's ready. We're just talking about what we should do. We're thinking maybe Isabel and me and you kids could drive over to Yakima to the theatre and see a movie. We can have buttered popcorn and cokes. What do you think of that? Think it's a good idea?"

"When are we going?" Eddie asked to laughter.

Two hours later, Eddie, Gregory, and Lewis sat in the truck, their faces scrubbed clean, wearing their town clothes, anxious to get going. Eddie couldn't understand what was taking so long. Just then the door opened, and Isabel and Grace came out of the cabin.

Eddie stared. He had seen Isabel all dressed up before, but he had never seen his mother look like she did now. She had on a new dress and wore red lipstick and earrings. Her straight hair was curled and seemed darker, her eyes looked sharp, and she had a red glow on her cheekbones. But the biggest difference was when she laughed at something Isabel said. Eddie didn't know she had so many teeth.

The first thing Eddie noticed as he walked up the red carpet inside the theatre was the smell of popcorn. He had never smelled anything so mouth-watering. Even when his mother made bread pudding, and the smell of cinnamon, raisins, and sugar filled the house, nothing made him swallow as much as the popcorn spilling out of a large gleaming pot in the glass case.

Eddie couldn't believe all the candies and chocolate bars. And inside a long glass counter were ice cream bars laid out in neat rows. The line moved quickly, and before he knew it, Isabel was speaking to the girl behind the counter. The girl opened the door of the giant popcorn maker, scooped popcorn into two large containers, and ladled melted butter in a circle over the top.

"Salt?" she asked.

Grace nodded, and the girl shook salt from a large jar onto the popcorn.

When Isabel and Grace settled everyone in their seats, Lewis shoved both hands into the popcorn and almost knocked the container out of his mother's lap onto the floor. "Hey, watch what you're doing, Lewis. You can only eat one handful at a time, you know."

Isabel laughed.

Eddie's mouth was stuffed with butter, salt, and popcorn. When he could chew no more, he sipped the Coke through the straw and swallowed it all in one gulp. He could feel the pop fizzing as it went down his throat. It was such a new and delicious experience that if he was allowed, even if he had to sit in a pasture of cows all by himself, he would do nothing else. Every day.

Above the loud chatter Eddie heard soft music. A man wearing a white shirt and tie told parents to stop their children from climbing over the seats. When he saw teenagers throwing empty popcorn boxes, he hurried over and pointed his finger at them.

The lights dimmed, and the curtains in front of a large screen began to open. A cheer went up.

Afterward, as people filed out onto the street, Eddie wiped the tears away before anybody noticed. Poor Bambi's mother, killed by hunters. He couldn't imagine how someone could shoot a talking deer. He saw Lewis and Gregory rubbing the sleep from their eyes as they made their way through the crowd. Isabel stopped. "Oh, dammit. I left my purse in there. You guys go ahead, and I'll catch up."

Grace asked, "Is that why you're holding that empty popcorn box? Gimme that, and you hurry up and get in there before somebody finds it."

"Holy cow. Old age starting already," Isabel said.

She laughed and turned back toward the theatre. Grace stuffed the box into a garbage can. Ten minutes went past, and the crowd thinned out until the sidewalk was almost empty. Grace looked back to the theatre. There was no sign of Isabel. "Jeez. What's taking so long?"

Down the street, Eddie noticed a car drive out of a large parking lot and turn toward them. It was shiny black with chrome hubcaps and trim that reflected the sunlight like mirrors. Even though the car was a half block away, Eddie could hear the radio was turned up loud. Grace heard the noise and looked down the street. She stood perfectly still as the car came closer. Just as it drove past, Eddie clearly made out the words of a song. "Your cheatin' heart . . . " And then he heard his mother curse under her breath. Without taking her eyes off the car, she pushed her purse against Eddie's chest.

"Hold this," she said.

She reached down, pulled off her shoes, and ran out into the road.

"What the hell . . . " Isabel appeared at Eddie's side as she watched Grace chase after the black car. Lewis jumped off the sidewalk to go after his mother, but Isabel grabbed his arm and stopped him.

A few other people stopped and watched.

Just as the car looked as if it was about to leave Grace behind, the traffic light turned red. Eddie heard laughter coming from inside the car as Grace appeared beside the driver's rolled-down window. She swung her fist as hard as she could and struck the driver on the side of the head. She hit him so hard that he fell over onto the lap of his passenger seated next to him. Grace stuck her head inside as she reached down with both hands. She had the man by the hair and looked like she was trying to drag him out of the window. The woman passenger screamed. Grace let the man go and ran around to the other side of the car. She managed to get the door open, but the car lurched forward with squealing tires and just missed a vehicle that had entered the intersection. Grace swore at the car as it took off down the street.

Isabel picked up Lewis and hurried over to where Grace stood with her hands on her hips.

"Come on! Let's get outta here before the cops show up," Isabel shouted.

Grace stared at the car until it turned a corner and was gone.

"Grace!" Isabel yelled. "Let's go. Now!"

Eddie stared up at his mother as if he didn't recognize her.

A siren wailed a few blocks away. Isabel handed Lewis to Grace. "You look after him. I'll drive."

Eddie and Gregory climbed into the front of the truck as Isabel started the engine. Grace slammed the door and set Lewis on her lap.

Isabel turned up an alley, and the truck wove around cardboard boxes and garbage cans. As they turned onto the highway, Isabel gunned the motor.

"Are you gonna tell me, Grace, what's going on?" Isabel asked as she checked the rear-view mirror. Lewis was curled in a ball on his mother's lap.

"It was Jimmy," Grace said.

"What? Oh jeez, Grace."

"It was him. That's for damn sure. My cousin Mabel told me he was down here. She said he's got a nice car now and a new woman. It was fluky they showed up like that. I just couldn't stand to see him and that slut driving down the street, sitting so close like they were showing off how much in love they were. It was almost like he was rubbing my face in it, Isabel. I could hear Hank Williams on his radio. I wonder what I woulda done if they didn't have the radio on and I never heard old Hank. Jimmy and me always used to sing along with Hank Williams every time we heard him on the jukebox or radio. Didn't matter where it was, neither. Sometimes he'd grab me and swing me right off my feet. That's what I liked about him—he wasn't scared to do things like that. I hated it that he was doing it with her. It made me so damn mad.

"I guess them *summas* never seen a Indian doing the hundred-yard dash before. She had one of them cigarette holders in her hand. The phony bitch. All Jimmy had to do was look in the mirror, and he woulda seen me. So when he stopped at the light, that's when I punched him in the face as hard as I could. I used to have dreams about what I would do. And there I was, doing it where everybody could see. That felt good.

"I scratched him right across his neck and over his ear, good and deep too, like a bear marking her pissing tree. He was scared. Like a little girl having a nightmare. He yelled at me and asked me what I was doing. Then I heard her scream and say, 'Let's get out of here.'

"At first I just wanted to take a good look at her to see what was so special about her. And when I seen how ugly she is, I figured there must be another reason why he's staying with her. Maybe she's rich, or maybe she has big tits. I dunno. There has to be something, because it sure isn't for her looks. But what I really wanted was to remember her face in case some day I get lucky and come across her walking somewhere all by herself. But Jimmy peeled out before I could get my hands on her. You know, even with all that burning rubber around me, I could smell her cheap hairspray. The hell with him and his ugly woman."

Isabel laughed.

Eddie studied his mother's angry face. Did he dare ask her who the man in the car was? Why did his mother want to hurt him? And who was the lady? He'd heard those swear words before only when Grace was mad at Alphonse, so this wasn't the time to ask.

"I know one thing for sure. No matter where it is they're at, if they're in a beer parlour or at a dance, or just riding around in the car, the next time they hear Hank Williams, those bastards will think of me."

It was the middle of August, just days away from Eddie's sixth birthday. The temperature had risen to over a hundred degrees, and it was so hot the workers had to be out in the fields first thing in the morning while it was dark. They soaked rags under the tap which they wore on their head or wrapped around their neck. Dust collected everywhere in the cabin. Grandma washed the floor every day trying to keep it clean, but the soaked wood made the cabin humid. Eddie and Gregory felt tired most of the time and needed to take naps in the afternoon. They even joined Lewis to play under the tap with a little boy from four cabins away until a water fight sent the little boy home crying.

At 9:00 AM Grandma filled a cardboard box with lunch and cold tea and covered it with a small blanket. She placed the box in the wagon and turned to Eddie.

"Here, you and the brats take the food down to them pickers. And don't run with it either. You get the lunch dirty or spill something, they'll knock you on the head."

Eddie pulled the wagon as Gregory walked behind with Lewis. The cool of the morning had been replaced by a dusty heat that made Eddie itch all over. He felt a trickle of sweat run down his leg and when he scratched his head, his hair felt like it was on fire. The boys sat in the shade and watched the grownups eat.

"Can we go down to the river for a swim?" Gregory asked Isabel. Before she could answer, Ray spoke in a loud voice. "No. You kids stay away from that river. And if I ever catch any one of you there, I'll whip you good. Go back to the cabin. Maybe after work, and if you guys listen to Grandma, we can take a walk down there and find a little swimming hole."

It felt such a long time before Eddie and Gregory saw the grown-ups walking up from the fields. Eddie hoped Ray kept his promise about finding a swimming hole. And when Ray walked up to the cabin and smiled at the three boys sitting on the door ledge, waiting, Eddie knew he would keep his word. Everybody, even Grandma, followed Ray down to a shallow spot close to shore. She took off her shoes and stepped into the river. After splashing water over her face and arms, she sat under a bush to watch while Gregory and Eddie had swimming races upriver. Gregory was a strong swimmer who could paddle upstream easily with his swinging arms and kicking legs, but Eddie couldn't gain an inch on the strong current. Grandma laughed as if she were swimming with them.

Grace and Isabel held Lewis by the hand and walked into the water until it came over their knees. They dabbed water onto their shoulders and necks before turning back to the shore. At a deep spot upstream, Ray used a bar of soap and covered himself with lather until his entire body looked coated in ice cream. He dove under and disappeared inside a milky cloud. When he surfaced, Eddie couldn't see a speck of soap on him, but when he turned around, there was a patch of suds on the back of his head.

Later in the cabin, waking from a nap, Eddie wiped the drool from the side of his face and gave a long yawn. Looking around, he saw that no one was home except for Grandma.

"Where is everybody?" he asked.

"How the hell am I supposed to know? Nobody tells me anything. Go look for them."

Eddie walked outside and sat on the steps. It bothered him to hear her talk that way because she was the most fun of all the grown-ups. Now she had become short-tempered. Even Ray was careful what he said to her.

"The heat is making everybody grumpy," Grace had told him. "The best thing we can do is leave her alone and hope for rain. It's not easy for us either, getting out of bed so early and working till we feel like we're going to fall over. And it's hard to get a good night's sleep in this old cabin. She'll be her old self pretty soon. Just stay out of her way."

Gregory came around the corner of the house. "Wait till you see what my dad found in the field," he said.

Ray held his hands against his chest and sat on the steps. He pushed up on the bottom of his shirt pocket, and out popped two furry ears. Ray eased out a baby rabbit.

"You can pet her if you want. Not too hard, though."

Eddie touched the bunny's soft ears and lightly stroked its trembling body.

"Why is it shaking?"

"She's just a baby. She's scared."

"Can I hold it?" Gregory asked.

"No," Ray said.

He held the bunny up to the boys' faces so they could feel the soft fur and pet the bunny. Gregory and Eddie began pushing each other's hand out of the way.

"Okay, that's enough," he said.

Ray went inside the cabin and put the bunny in a cardboard box. He set it down in the corner by his bed.

"I don't want anybody to touch the bunny when I'm not around," he said. "Or else."

That was all he needed to say. Except for work, Ray took the rabbit with him everywhere. And he told everybody that since he'd found the rabbit, his fortune was about to change. "Some people pack around a rabbit's foot for good luck. Me, I got the whole damn rabbit."

He named it Honey, and when he went for a walk after supper, he took Honey from the box and carried it inside his shirt pocket. If he came home in a miserable mood, he always felt better when he saw Honey and began talking baby talk.

"How's my little Honey, huh? How's my little girl today?"

But Ray's behaviour bothered Isabel.

"Why can't you be nice to everybody else like you are to that stupid thing?" she asked. "When I came home the other day and I seen you cutting up vegetables, I thought you were making supper. You were making supper. But you were making it for your damn rabbit."

"She's just jealous, isn't she, my little Honey girl? Yeah. She just wishes she could have ears like yours," Ray said and kissed the rabbit on the nose.

On Saturday night Ray and Abel walked into the cabin. Ray carried a twelve-pack of beer and a small paper bag that he tossed onto the bed. "Here you go, you pot-lickers. Bet you thought I forgot, didn't you?" he said.

His voice sounded different to Eddie.

Isabel jumped off the chair where she had been reading a movie star magazine. "About time you got here. Don't need to guess where you both been. Boy, if Grace leaves without me I'll skin both of you yahoos." She hurried out the door. Just as Grace started the truck, Isabel waved and called, "Wait for me, wait for me." Isabel climbed into the truck, and they drove away.

"Hello, boys. How are my boys today, huh?" Ray asked. Eddie had seen how Ray could change after a few bottles of beer, but this time he thought Ray's voice sounded even fuzzier than usual.

Eddie and Gregory sat on the bed going through the bag of candy while Ray pulled over a chair. He took a drink of his beer.

"Is that like pop?" Eddie asked.

"It's grown-up pop. Too strong for kids. Too sweet."

"Can I have a taste?"

"Yeah, sure. Come here and I'll give you a taste."

Eddie stood in front of Ray. "Here you go. Make sure you swallow fast now, okay?"

Ray tipped the bottle up. When Eddie's mouth was filled with liquid, he swallowed and choked. Beer shot out his nose. Ray and Abel laughed until Abel began coughing. The fumes burned inside Eddie's nose. Ray drank from the bottle, and his neck throbbed as the liquid bubbled down his throat. He drank all the beer without stopping. Eddie was impressed. The next time he had a pop, he would try to drink it just like Ray.

Abel and Ray sat at the table and opened another beer.

"Did I ever tell you I spent time in London, England, in the war?" Without waiting for Abel to answer, Ray continued. "There's this place called Trafalgar Square, and they say if you sit there for two hours, somebody you know will show up. We used to go down there to see the sights and have a couple of pints. We didn't have any beer for so long it tasted damn good, even if it was piss-warm English beer. The first time I ever laid eyes on the place, I couldn't believe it. There was people walking everywhere, thousands of 'em, and big double-decker buses, kinda like a bus riding on top of another bus, all red and shiny. Fountains spraying water up in the air, and people feeding pigeons. The pigeons. Jeez, I never seen so many of the little bastards in my life. This guy, he's standing there holding his arms out and he's covered with pigeons. My pardner Bill, he was from some reserve close to Calgary. Foothill Bill we called him. He said they were probably shitting all over the guy.

"The inside of the square was the size of a couple berry fields, and all around the outside there was these old rock buildings, churches, art galleries, cafés, and fish shops. You could see where some of them were hit by a bomb. Christ, you couldn't go anywhere in London without seeing where a bomb landed. You know, with all the horns honking and people all dressed up, laughing and eating fish and chips outta newspapers, it was like there wasn't even a war going on.

"They had places that looked like big beer parlours where soldiers could go to down a few drinks and meet up with other soldiers. The Americans went to their own place and we stuck to ours. Canada House, they called it. It was bigger and friendlier, but mostly because the Americans wasn't there. But a few Yanks come in anyway, and sure enough, a fight would start. After everybody started getting a little drunk, Canadians even started fighting Canadians. It didn't really mean nothing, though. We were just like a bunch of horses that finally got let outta the corral so we could kick up our heels. And that Bill, oh, he was a good-looking Indian, and boy, he could round up the women. Him and me, we started sniffing around like two stud pigs after we heard them English women had the biggest tits in the world. So, we went out hunting. It was gonna be open season on tits. Christ, I was so horny I'd a humped a pile a rocks hopin' a snake was in there. And good old Bill, he found us two real nice girls, and man oh man, they were right. You wouldn't believe it, Abel. You had to see 'em with your own two eyes."

Abel swallowed and sat up straight. "Zat right?"

"I'm telling you, some of them looked like they had their knees tucked under their sweaters. Anyway, we ended up back at their place. Bill and his girl went in one room, and me and mine went in the other. Her name was Pamela. Good old Pamela. She was after me the minute the door was shut.

"'You're a Indian, right? A red Indian?' she asked me. 'Sure am,' I said. You know, somebody said them English people really liked Indians. I didn't believe it at first. What the hell they like us for anyway? But you know what? They really do.

"'You sure you're an Indian, you better be sure,' she said.

"'Sure as cold shit in a dead dog,' I told her.

"I never had a woman like that before, breathing like she run a mile and pulling off my clothes so hard my shirt buttons was bouncing off the wall. I tried to tell her to slow down, but it didn't do no good. I couldn't believe it. There I was on the other side of the world with a woman that was just as squirrelly as I was, and we was both gonna do what we always dreamed about. Any minute I was gonna bury my face between the biggest pair of tits a man could ever hope to see in his whole life, and she was gonna get screwed by a real, genuine Indian.

"We was going at it like dogs for a few minutes and then I hear that old London clock, Big Ben, gonging outside somewhere. And just when I get to the vinegar stroke, that's when she started squealin'. You shoulda heard it, Abel. Me, Pamela, and Big Ben, all going off at the same time."

Ray closed his eyes and looked up at the ceiling. Eddie looked over and saw the corner of his mouth was curled up and he had a funny grin. "Jeez, Abel," Ray said. "I can still see her tits bouncin'."

Ray finished his beer and stood. He pulled a bottle out of the case and walked over to the box where he kept his precious Honey and looked inside. "What the hell. Where is she?" he asked and turned slowly toward Eddie and Gregory.

"I said—where's Honey?" he repeated.

"What's the matter?" Abel asked.

"Honey's gone. The kids did something to her."

"You said not to touch her, and we didn't," Gregory said.

Ray walked toward the boys. His glare was frightening, and his shadow on the ceiling and walls bent forward as if he were coming at them from all directions. His hands clenched and unclenched.

"I told you both what I'd do if you ever did anything like this. So you better tell me right now. For the last time, where is Honey?"

Abel's loud shout made Ray jump. Abel had one hand over his mouth and pointed with the other.

"What's that in your pocket?" he asked.

Ray pinched his shirt and pulled out his wallet. "What's the matter with you Abel? What are you talking about? There's nothing in my pocket except my wallet."

"Did you forget you had your rabbit in the tavern? What the hell did you do? Your back pocket. Look in your back pocket."

Ray put a hand on his back pocket. He squeezed and quickly drew his hand back as if he had touched a hot stove. "Oh no."

He pulled out a furry shape and held it up in the air.

"Oh no . . . my Honey?" he whimpered. Honey was lifeless. Ray sank down in a chair holding Honey close to his chest. Sobbing, he rocked back and forth.

"Not my Honey. Not my little Honey. My poor little Honey."

At the breakfast table the next morning, Ray didn't take part in any conversation and ate with his head down.

"Boy oh boy," Isabel said. "You didn't even remember taking your stupid rabbit out of the box, did you? And how did Honey end up in your pants pocket and your wallet in your shirt pocket?"

Ray gave an uninterested shrug.

"I bet I know. You and that dumb Abel got cut off by the bartender because you both had too much to drink. Didn't you?"

Ray looked up at Isabel with a frown. "Whyn't you just drop it?" he said.

"I bet the bartender told you to put your money in your pocket and go on home. You thought he said Honey, not money. You must've heard him wrong, Ray. Dumb bastard. I'm surprised he even let you bring that stinking thing in there."

Grandma, Isabel, and Grace began laughing. Ray stood to go outside. When the door thumped behind him, Grandma was the first to speak.

"It's too bad about his little bunny, though," she said.

"Yeah, too bad she wasn't fatter. Way too skinny for the stew pot," Isabel said.

Eddie couldn't understand how they could all laugh at what happened to little Honey.

5

It took a few days for everyone to stop talking about what happened to Honey. Sometimes, when Ray asked what was for supper, Eddie saw Isabel, Grandma, and his mother smile.

One night after everyone had gone to sleep and the house was dark, Gregory and Eddie whispered to each other as they watched the bats fly in front of the window, thankful Ray had nailed up bug screens. They had gotten used to the smell of the outhouse that sat twenty feet from the back door. But tonight the wind changed direction, and the warm air held the stench over their bed like a stinking cloud. It drove them under the blankets until they came out gasping for air.

Night in the small cabin felt like a place of safety to Eddie, and he usually fell asleep looking through the window at the stars in the sky. But this evening the ceiling ticked and thumped with new sounds. Suddenly the cabin seemed filled with ghosts. The coats hanging on nails by the door with their arms hanging down and elbows bent, their bodies leaning forward, seemed to be waiting for a signal to come to life and step down to the floor. Just when the noises had gone quiet and it seemed danger had passed, he heard light steps of clawed feet scratching on the ceiling.

"What's that?" Gregory whispered.

Eddie stared through a gap in the boards into the moonlit attic and saw a shadow sweep by. An animal of some kind was right above them. The sound of crunching bones coming from a corner of the attic meant sleep was out of the question. Only the breathing of the sleeping grown-ups interrupted their miserable silence.

After breakfast on Sunday morning, Ray and Isabel announced they were going for a long walk. When Grace said she was going into town, Grandma said it would be nice to have the house all to herself for an hour.

Gregory and Eddie watched Ray and Isabel walk quickly out of sight. Grace opened the driver's door of the pickup, and Lewis crawled inside. She slid behind the wheel. "Don't you guys go anywhere. You stay right here at the house."

"Why can't we go, Mom? We didn't do anything wrong," Eddie pleaded.

"I know. But it's not going to hurt you to stay home for once," she said.

She dug into her purse for change. "Here's enough for some bubble gum or something. You can go to the store, then get right back home. You hear?"

"Yeah," Eddie said.

She started the truck and pulled away. The rear wheels kicked up dirt that left Eddie and Gregory in a swirling cloud of dust.

The two boys stood in front of the store window eyeing up the treats inside. There was so much to choose from, but with only a nickel to spend between them, it wasn't going to be easy to agree on what to buy. They ran inside and lifted the lid of the water-filled cooler. They'd learned all the names of the pop inside it. The bright green Lemon-Lime, the yellow Grapefruit, the purple Grape, the Orange Crush, and the red Cream Soda shone in their eyes like neon lights.

When they couldn't decide what they wanted, the storekeeper offered a few suggestions. "You can buy bubble gum or share a pop if you return the bottle right away. Or you could have one of these." He held up a large green sucker.

"How much is it?" Gregory asked.

"The all-day sucker is five cents." Eddie's stomach was set on pop even though "all-day" had a nice sound. Agreeing that licking the same sucker was worse than drinking the same pop, they chose a bottle of Orange Crush from the cooler and sat on the store steps. They passed the bottle back and forth until one thought the other was taking too much, and the bottle emptied quickly. When Eddie let out a loud burp, it brought back the aftertaste, burned his nose, and brought tears to his eyes. Gregory sucked the empty bottle until his tongue was drawn inside. Then he held both hands in the air, and the bottle hung suspended as if by magic.

Eddie waited while Gregory went inside to return the bottle. The store had become busy, and Gregory seemed to take a long time. When he finally came out, he raced around the corner of the store and called Eddie to hurry. The pop sloshed in Eddie's belly as he ran past Gregory at full speed before stopping at their cabin door, a full three strides ahead of him. As they sat on the door sill to catch their breath, Grandma turned from a chair where she had been fanning herself with a magazine.

"Why don't you guys go somewhere else? I can't even sit and think sometimes with everybody hanging around. Go on, get outta here until your moms get home."

She waved the back of her hand at them as if shooing away a cat.

They walked behind the cabin to think of where to go, and Eddie saw a plank propped against the house leading up to the attic. The boys quietly inched up the plank and sat side by side on the ledge. They searched the clouds for shapes of animals or people until Gregory pointed out a cloud he thought looked like Ray. Eddie thought there was much more to see and hear from a place high above the ground.

Sunlight glinted off the river a half mile away, and the swallows warbled as they ducked inside nests under the overhanging roof. A dog chased a gopher to a hole in the ground and began digging and barking. Clouds of dust floated through the dry weeds, and flies buzzed in the attic.

Gregory dug into his shirt pocket and pulled out the all-day sucker. "Look what I got."

"I thought we didn't have enough money to pay for it?" Eddie asked.

"I took it when he wasn't looking."

Gregory peeled off the cellophane wrapper. The sucker shone like green glass in the sunlight when he held it up to his mouth to take a lick.

"Wait, let's break it in half," Eddie said.

Holding the horseshoe-shaped candy in the palm of his hand, Gregory gave a hard bang on the ledge. Pieces of the sucker slid across the ceiling boards into the attic. They gathered up as much as they could find, except for a large chunk that had slid farther back into the dark. On hands and knees, they searched for the missing piece. Eddie saw something at the edge of the light, but it didn't look solid enough to be a sucker.

"Gregory, come here," he said, pointing to the bones and feathers of a bird. "It's a robin."

Even in the dim light they could make out the red clump of its breast. The skin of the bird had been stripped and tossed aside like a banana peel. Eddie couldn't connect the grey-brown feathers spread around the attic floor to the funny sight of a robin hopping across grass to pull a stretchy worm from the ground or the way it rested on the bottom bough of a tree, chirruping to the world. Nearby lay the feet that had once plucked sticks and grasses off the ground for a nest. Gregory pointed to a dot-sized drop of blood on the wood.

"Are you kids up there? Get outta there right now," Grandma yelled.

They backed out of the attic space and climbed down the plank to the ground.

Eddie noticed Ray watching him and Gregory all during supper and wondered if they had done something wrong. It was as if Ray wanted to say something but didn't know how. After supper Ray stepped out the front door and turned back to the boys. "Let's go for a walk to the store. Bring Lewis. I'm thirsty for an ice-cold pop, and my lucky dollar is burning a hole in my pocket," he said smiling.

It was cooler outside, but the grass and weeds beside the path, dried out by the hot summer sun, gave off a powder that made their eyes burn. Other people were also outside, trying to get away from the trapped heat of their cabins. A man and a little girl with an ice cream cone walked up the trail from the store that narrowed to single file. The little girl turned the cone each time she took a lick so she didn't lose a single drop. Ray walked toward the approaching man without making any effort to move out of the way. The man pulled the little girl with him, and the grass crunched under their feet as they stepped off the path. The man smiled and nodded, but Ray ignored him.

Ray picked out a mixture of flavours from the pop cooler. He wiped each one with the towel hanging beside the bottle opener and put them into an empty cardboard case. He held an extra one in his hand. Setting the bottles on the counter, he reached for his wallet.

"Okay, let's see here," the storeowner said as he counted the bottles. "Seven bottles plus deposit makes forty-two. And I'll be needing a nickel for the sucker the boys made off with today."

Ray's eyes narrowed. "What?" he asked.

"These two took an all-day sucker without paying for it. I don't want any trouble, so just pay me the nickel, and I'll forget all about it. No point getting the sheriff involved over a nickel, is there?"

The storekeeper drummed the counter with his fingers. Ray reached inside his pocket and pulled out a nickel. He dropped it on the counter and it bounced off the glass with a loud crack, and then he turned and walked out the door. Lewis cried because they were leaving the store empty-handed.

Gregory and Eddie were quiet. They knew they were in a lot of trouble. How quickly things had changed. A moment earlier, Ray would have bought them anything they wanted, but now they were being led home like prisoners. Eddie and Gregory stopped at the cabin door.

"Get in here," Ray ordered.

The boys walked carefully as if the steps were made of thin glass and stepped inside. Grandma and Isabel looked up from where they sat at the table. Grace took Lewis by the hand to the basin to wash his face. Eddie's heart thrashed inside his chest. Ray stood in the middle of the room with his hands on his hips. A moth fluttered against the ceiling as it circled the electric light bulb, unable to pull away from the draw of the light. The flycatcher hanging down next to the bulb was speckled with dead bluebottles. The moth landed on the flycatcher, and its wings beat madly.

"Did you two steal a sucker from the store today?" Ray asked.

"Yeah," Gregory said.

"No," Eddie said.

"Did you or not?"

"Gregory did. I was outside waiting."

"So you knew he took it, but you thought you wouldn't get blamed if you got caught? Is that right?"

Eddie didn't answer.

"Did you?"

"No. I dunno," Eddie answered.

Ray reached over to the washstand and picked up a red willow stick. He bent the switch into a bow and swung it back and forth in front of him. The white tip beneath the bark flashed as it filled the room with a whooping sound. Tears welled in Eddie's eyes as he backed away.

"I got this down at the river. I was gonna make a fishing pole and take you guys fishing so we could catch us some trout. Here I was feeling bad about leaving you behind today and I find out you're nothing but little thieves."

He pulled out a small paper bag from his shirt pocket and tossed it into the woodbox. "I don't go fishing with thieves."

Gregory ran to Isabel. "Mom?" he pleaded.

She pushed him away, and Gregory fell to the floor crying. Ray reached down and pulled him to his feet.

"No, no, no," Gregory begged.

Eddie looked away, but the shadow on the wall showed Ray reaching back and swinging the stick hard. It landed with a horrible sound. When Gregory tried to pull away, Ray jerked on his arm pulling him back. Gregory's feet kicked madly. With one more solid whack, Ray let go of Gregory's arm. He crossed the room in two strides and grabbed Eddie by the elbow. Eddie put his hand behind his back to stop the blow, but it fell on his thumb. He shrieked with each stroke. Finally Ray let go of his arm.

"Get to bed. The both of you. And stop your damn crying."

6

Eddie was awakened in the morning by rain tapping on the roof
of the cabin. The heat had finally lifted, and the odour of the toilet
and dust on the grass had been washed away. The air smelled sweet
and clean. The grown-ups had already left for the fields.

Gregory said something to Eddie during breakfast, but Eddie
spooned the porridge into his mouth. His hand still hurt from the
night before, and he still felt angry. Gregory pushed back his chair
to leave the table, but Eddie kept his head down.

Gregory fumbled around in the wood pile. "Coming, Eddie?"

Eddie looked over at Gregory standing in the doorway holding
the switch that Ray had used on them. He wanted to run over and
break it in two. Gregory had on the new runners Isabel had been
saving for his first day of school. They didn't look right with his
ragged corduroy overalls. A single suspender held up his pants
while the other was unbuttoned. Eddie wanted to laugh and point
to the tail hanging down between Gregory's legs, but his thumb
throbbed and he looked back down at the floor. Gregory paused
a moment before he walked away. Stones rolled under his feet as
he broke into a run. For a moment, Eddie had an urge to jump
off his chair and go after Gregory, but he listened to the footsteps
growing fainter until it was quiet.

Grandma walked in the door carrying a handful of vegetables.
She looked around the room for Gregory. "Where did he take off to
already? You guys are not supposed to go anywhere. Where is he?"

"He went out."

"Where?"

"I don't know."

"You pick your lip off the floor and quit acting like a baby." She placed the vegetables on the counter and sat at the table across from Eddie. "Did you hear me?"

"Why did he lie that I stole the sucker with him? I was waiting outside on the steps for him to take the pop bottle back. I never helped him steal it. I didn't even know."

"It doesn't matter if you did or not. You helped him eat it. And you didn't tell him to take it back. Now you get out there and look for him."

Eddie half expected to see Gregory waiting on the trail, but he was nowhere to be seen. Maybe he was hiding somewhere, waiting to jump out to scare him. Eddie ran to the field. It was hard to make out Ray, Isabel, and Grace among the arched backs of the other pickers in the field. They all looked the same, and it took a while before he spotted Ray walking down the row. Eddie stopped in front of him, breathless and excited.

"Is Gregory here?" Eddie asked.

Beads of sweat dripped off the end of Ray's nose as he looked impatiently down at Eddie. He shook his head and turned to walk back to his row.

"Do you see him here? Doesn't Grandma know where he is?"

"No. He left without telling her."

Ray turned back toward Eddie. "Damn kids. If it's not one thing, it's something else. You go find him, and if you can't, come back here and tell me."

Eddie took off as fast as he could. With so many open fields, there were few places to hide. He ran around to the back of the cabin and scurried up the plank, but no one was in the attic. His eyes squinted in the bright sunshine as he scanned the area. Sunlight reflected off the windshields of cars on the highway, and Eddie thought he saw a vehicle parked on the side of the road, but it was too far away to tell. Every dot in the distance could have been Gregory. He slid down the plank and went into the cabin.

"Where is he?" Grandma asked.

"I'm trying to find him. Ray told me."

Grandma reached down for Lewis's hand. "Let's go," she said. When Lewis couldn't keep up, she carried him on her hip. "Where did you look?"

"I looked over there and there and there." Eddie pointed.

She started down the path to the river. "You run ahead and see if he's down there." Her voice sounded shaky, something Eddie hadn't heard before.

"Ray said we weren't supposed to go down there."

"Just get down there."

Eddie raced down the path. Stopping at the water's edge, he called out in his loudest voice. He listened for an answer but heard only the sound of water. Grandma came up beside him. Lewis struggled out of her grip down to the ground. She yanked him around by the arm.

"Keep still, damn you."

Lewis looked fearfully up at his grandma.

"Grey-gree," she called.

Her voice broke. She cleared her throat and called again, but her answer was the peep of a curlew on the far bank. She turned to Eddie. "Now, you run as fast as you can and get Ray. Tell him I said to get down here right away. Hurry."

Eddie ran as if all the ghosts in the world were after him. His feet thumped like a drum as he crossed the footbridge over the irrigation ditch. When Ray saw Eddie on the hill at the end of the field, he stood to wipe the sweat from his forehead with a hand-kerchief. Shading his eyes from the sun, he was about to turn away when he saw the urgency in how Eddie's arms swung, the puffs of dust swirling in the air behind him and how he caught himself just before he fell. He met Eddie in the middle of the row.

"Grandma says come quick," Eddie blurted.

"Did you find him?" Ray asked firmly.

Eddie could only shake his head.

Ray called to Isabel. "Gregory's gone off somewhere. I'm going back and see if I can find him."

Pickers within earshot looked over. Ray set off down the row. Without breaking his stride, he turned back to Eddie. "Where's Grandma?"

"Down at the river," Eddie said.

With his long, loping gait, Ray quickly disappeared out of sight. Grace and Isabel walked with hurried steps, even breaking into a short run at times. "Why would Gregory run off like that, and why aren't you with him?" Isabel asked.

"He just took off before I finished eating," Eddie said.

Isabel and Grace spoke to each other in excited voices, but Eddie barely heard them. Why had he lied when they asked him a simple question? But he would be blamed again for another bad thing Gregory had done. He just didn't want to talk to Gregory. That was all.

After a quick search of the area, Ray returned to the cabin. "Okay, Eddie. You have to think now. What happened this morning?"

"He asked me to go with him somewhere, but I didn't want to. I wasn't finished eating yet. But he left anyway. He was wearing his new runners and he took the willow switch with him too. That's all."

Ray went to the woodbox and set the wood on the floor. He dug around in the dust for a minute then stood. "He took the fish hooks and line too."

Ray went outside and spoke to the farm owner and foreman. Within twenty minutes the foreman and three men walked the wide banks of the river, prodding under the overhanging shore with long poles, digging and poking in the mud and reeds, until dark. Still there was no sign of Gregory.

At Eddie's bedtime they still hadn't found Gregory. Ray was down at the river with the other men. Grandma, Isabel, and Grace sat at the kitchen table drinking tea. Their low talk was interrupted by their hushed crying that didn't sound like crying, but more like halting whispers. Even though his brother slept beside Eddie, the bed felt empty. If Lewis touched him with his foot, Eddie kicked him away. He didn't want to sleep in case Gregory came back. Staring at a small crack at the bottom corner of the window, Eddie wondered if Gregory would get another switching. Beyond the window screen a dog barked, and a flashlight waved across the night sky. Someone far away called Gregory's name.

The next morning Eddie was awakened by the sound of breaking china. He sat up in bed and saw the sheriff standing in the doorway with a bulging holster on his hip and his Stetson in his hand. Grace steered Isabel by the shoulders to a chair and picked the broken pieces of a cup off the floor. Placing her hand on Ray's arm, Grandma led him over to the table where he sat down. His strong shoulders sagged. Grandma stroked his back.

The sheriff turned to Ray and cleared his throat. "Ray."

When Ray lifted up his head, Eddie saw that for the first time since he had met him, Ray's frown was gone. The sheriff motioned him to come outside. Ray stood and walked hunched over out the door.

"I'm going out there too," Isabel said.

Grace put her arm around Isabel's shoulder and they went out into the bright sunlight. Grandma tried to stop Eddie, but he ran past her.

Two men turned the corner of the cabin carrying a stretcher. Other pickers stood with the farm owner behind the ambulance, shifting their weight from one foot to the other. The stretcher bearers walked past, their shoulders bouncing as their heads bobbed. The red light on the ambulance clicked with each turn.

Ray, Grace, and Isabel stood near the ambulance door, and Eddie ran around to the other side. Peeking through arms and bodies, he saw the men slide the stretcher inside the ambulance. A small arm dropped out of the blanket and swung back and forth. One of the men quickly shoved it back out of sight.

"You know we usually don't do this out here, out in the open. You sure you want the mother to see this?" the sheriff asked.

"I can't stop her," Ray said.

The sheriff nodded to the men at the ambulance.

The starched sheet rustled as it was drawn back. Eddie recognized the mop of Gregory's hair. His once brown, smooth face was colourless and covered in scratches. Specks of dirt dotted his mouth like whiskers and his long lashes looked like a doll's. Black silt leaked from his ears and nose.

The next day all of Eddie's family's belongings were packed in the truck under an old wooden canopy the farm owner had given them. Ray and Isabel had arranged to have Gregory's body shipped back for burial to the reserve in Lillooet where he was born.

"I don't want you to go there for the funeral. It's too far, and the kid's seen enough," Isabel told Grace.

Isabel kissed Lewis on the forehead and bent down to Eddie. She handed him a paper bag and held his face in her hands. "Well, my little man. I want you to take this colouring book and the crayons I got for Gregory. I want you to have fun with them. Just look after yourself, Eddie. You're gonna be all right, you know. But I want you to do me one little favour, will you? Don't go grabbing them 'lectric fences no more. Okay?"

Eddie nodded.

"Bye, sweetheart," she said. She hugged him one last time and crossed the yard to the car. The door closed, and they drove away.

In the truck Lewis sat by the window on Grandma's lap, and Eddie sat in the middle. As they drove past the store, Eddie saw the signs and displays in the window and the steps where he and

Gregory had sat so many times. They had both loved spending time at the store. What had once been a place of fun to them both now seemed to blame him for what happened.

Grace turned onto the highway. "It's going to be a long drive to where we're going, so we only stop for pee breaks. If you or Lewis get hungry, there's a bag with sandwiches and drinks on the floor."

As the miles passed by, Eddie was nagged by a puzzling feeling. "Did we forget something, Mom?"

She looked down at him. "No."

"You sure?"

"Yeah, the cabin was empty. The only thing we left behind was the bedbugs."

Eddie kept his eyes on the highway. He thought he heard a swish of sound as the white lines disappeared underneath the truck. Grace clicked on the radio to a country music station. While a singer sang a sad song, Eddie noticed a crack in the bottom corner of the windshield and his mind wandered back to the farm, to the rows of vegetables and the irrigation ditches and the kitchen table where Ray sat like royalty. And when he remembered the small crack in the window above his bed, he started to cry. Even when he began to fall asleep to the whine of the transmission and his head nodded forward, Eddie couldn't stop crying. He awoke once or twice feeling that he had never stopped crying though there were no more tears.

Someone was shaking him, calling his name. He pushed away the hands, but they persisted.

"Don't," he said.

"Eddie, come look," Grandma said in a hurried voice.

"I'm tired."

"Look at this. Holy cow," she said.

Eddie sat up. Through the open door of the truck he saw water washing up on land and for a second wondered if they had driven into a lake. Waves slammed onto a broad shore with a deafening noise.

"Come on. Get outta the truck and run around."

"Where are we?"

"At the ocean. I always wanted to see the ocean. All my life I heard people talk about it. Now I finally get to see it. Look how big it is. Come on, hurry up. You don't need your shoes. Let's go," she said.

Eddie pulled off his shoes and socks. "Where's Mom and Lewis?"

"They went up ahead. That's why we have to hurry."

Their feet left perfect footprints in the sand until a sheet of water rushed onto the shore and took them away. The water around their ankles bubbled and fizzed like pop. Eddie looked down the beach stretching out in front of them and saw his mother and Lewis. Grace strolled slowly down the sandy beach while Lewis ran ahead of her picking up shells and sticks. After a bigger wave surrounded them, Eddie felt something slimy touch his foot and saw what looked like a large green snake wrapping around his legs. He jumped back and fell.

"Look out. It's gonna get you!" Grandma said.

Eddie scrambled backward.

"It's just weeds," she said laughing. "What did you think it was?"

Eddie stood up, embarrassed, and saw Lewis bent over looking at something that had washed up on shore. He ran over to see.

"It's a starfish," Grace said.

Eddie ran his fingers up and down each of the five points. It felt like a corncob with the kernels removed. Lewis placed it gently on the sand as another wave came over their knees. Scooping a fistful of water to his mouth, Lewis made a face at the salty taste.

They sat around a driftwood fire eating sandwiches and drinking warm pop. Eddie and Lewis crawled under the truck canopy to sleep. Grace and Grandma kept the fire going and talked until after dark.

The next morning, before they set off for home, Grandma wanted one last walk along the water. Eddie thought the wind felt even stronger than the day before, but without any trees nearby to tell, he couldn't be sure. The screeching gulls hung in the air like kites. Eddie hadn't seen such empty space before, and the endless stretch of water reaching out of sight left him with a nervous feeling in his stomach that didn't go away until the pickup truck crossed the Canadian border.

7

Early one morning, three days before he was to begin school in Falkland, Eddie was awakened by the sound of tires on gravel. Crouching at his window, he saw a white car coming slowly down the road. He hurried into the kitchen. Through the sheers and streaky glass, he watched the car come to a stop only feet from the door.

A man stepped out, took off his suit jacket, and tossed it into the back seat. After closing the door, he rolled up his cuffs and nervously watched the windows of the house. His skin was the whitest Eddie had ever seen, and he was funny-looking. His thick glasses rested on his long nose, and a narrow band of hair peeked around the back of his bald head. He walked hunched over, and his long skinny neck reached out in front of him with each step. A noise somewhere in the bushes made him stand up straight, and his head swung toward the sound. He looked like a buzzard.

Eddie hurried into his mother's bedroom and shook her shoulder. She rolled over and looked at him, sleepy-eyed. "What's the matter?"

"Somebody's here in a white car," Eddie whispered.

"An Indian?" Grace asked.

"No. And it's got letters on the side."

Grace threw off her blankets and grabbed her dress from the bedpost. She checked to make sure she was buttoned up before swinging the door open.

"Good morning, Grace," the man said as he approached. "I know it's early, but I'm in a hurry. I need to know what your plans are on sending your boy to school."

"Why?"

"I just want to be sure. Will he be going to school in Falkland?"

"Yeah. Where else would he be going? Or are you gonna come pick him up and drive him into Vernon every day? What do you mean, wanted to be sure? What are you talkin' about? You don't think I want my boy to go to school?"

"You know he will be the only Indian student in that school, don't you? You sure you want to do that? Wouldn't it be better for him to be with his own kind?"

"His own kind? Why do you not want him to go to school in Falkland? Got a better idea?"

"I just want to present another option for you. For you and all the Indian families that have school-age children. It can be a burden for some having to deal with it all. Have you considered sending him up to St. Mary's school in Kamloops? He'll be—"

"Don't you say another word, Mr. Cooke. So that's why you're here. I know you're a bit new to your Indian agent job, but if you think I'm gonna let you take Eddie away, you got another think coming."

"I'm not going to take anybody away. I just wanted to present you with what I think is a viable option."

"You must think I'm stupid or something after what the priests and nuns did to Alphonse. Whipping him like a dog if he didn't do everything they wanted, and him pissing the bed till he was sixteen. And if the reserve didn't open the school at Six Mile, I would have been dragged away too."

"Hey. What are you tellin' him that for?"

Eddie hadn't noticed Uncle Alphonse standing by the wood-shed, gaff pole in his hand, on his way to the river to catch salmon.

"If you really give a damn about my boy, why don't you come inside? We can talk about why we don't have power out here yet. We can talk about a lot of things," Grace said.

"I don't have time for that, Grace. Boy, seems like you're always cranky, or do you save it all up just for me? Like I said, I have a lot of families to see. I'm just wasting my breath here."

"You are wastin' your breath if you think me or anybody else on the reserve would ever think of sending their kids to St. Mary's. Somebody should go up there and burn that place to the ground."

Eddie watched the buzzard shake his head before he turned and walked to his car. He climbed inside, started the engine, and drove away.

8

After his face was scrubbed and a wet comb was pulled through his hair, Eddie stood in the middle of the kitchen in his new clothes.

Grace told him to turn around and studied him a moment. She had one hand on her hip, the other under her chin. "Wait," she said. "Go around again—hold it."

She pulled the price tag off the back pocket of his brown corduroy pants. Then she unsnapped his pants and pulled out the shirt tail caught in the fly. After zipping him up and closing the snap, she held his face in her hands and looked him in the eye. "Now listen to me. And listen real good. When you get to the bridge, make sure there's no cars coming before you go across. When the coast is clear, you run as fast as you can. You hear?"

"You already told me, Mom."

"Well, I'm telling you again. Just don't fool around. That bridge is too long for anybody to get across without damn near gettin' killed. Don't go daydreamin'."

She handed Eddie a brown shopping bag. "I didn't know if you're supposed to be taking anything with you or not so I put your colouring book and crayons in there. Isabel wanted you to have them, so you look after them, all right?"

Eddie nodded. She held up a sandwich loosely wrapped in wax paper and shook it at him. A piece of crust fell on the floor.

"Here's your lunch. You make sure you eat it all and don't go wasting it." She placed the sandwich inside a yellow lard pail. "Look at that, eh. Perfect lunch kit for your first day of school.

Funny how it ended up in the garbage pit. Know how it got there?" Eddie shook his head.

After adding a piece of white cake, she snapped the lid shut. Eddie tried not to show his disappointment that the pail had made its way back into the house again. He should have taken it way out in the bush.

"I know you wanted the new one with cowboys shooting at a stagecoach. But we're not rich. We're not millionaires. You think money grows on trees? Huh? Do ya?"

Eddie shrugged his shoulders.

"You better get going. You don't want to miss the school bus on the first day."

Lewis gawked at Eddie. His finger was shoved in his nose up to the first knuckle.

"Aren't you coming with me, Mom?"

"What? You want me to take you to the bus and have the other kids laugh at you? No. You get a move on, and if you don't know what to do, just watch what everybody else is doing. The Cluff kids will be there anyway. Ask one of them. And don't you be scared neither. You get right in there and don't let anybody push you around. Stick up for yourself. If anybody gets funny with you, just punch him on the nose."

Grace opened the door. Placing her hand on Eddie's back, she nudged him outside to begin his first day of school. When the door closed, he heard muffled voices on the other side and wanted to be let back in. Now he knew how the cat felt after it was put outside for the night.

As he walked past his grandma's house she tapped on the glass and waved.

"Goodbye, schoolboy. Learn lots," she said. "Boy oh boy, you look pretty darn smart already. What you gonna look like when you get home?" She laughed and put her hand over her mouth to keep her false teeth in.

Grandma had never set foot inside a school. She couldn't read or write, so she had to make a mark with an X, and Grace had to print her name and sign underneath as a witness.

Eddie started up the road. When he saw the path ahead that he had taken many times before, it looked strangely longer, and he had a funny feeling in his stomach. But the sound of his rubbing corduroys, the smell of the new jacket and shirt, and the new socks inside his runners that felt as snug and warm as his mother's hands when she rubbed his feet on cold mornings made him feel better and a little braver. He walked faster and made his way toward the highway with the shopping bag in one hand and his lard pail lunch bucket in the other.

He turned onto the path to the bridge. It crossed a grassy area partly hidden from the highway by a line of trees. Eddie called it the picnic grounds. It was a place where he often imagined himself, Lewis, his mother, and grandmother sitting on a blanket, eating hot dogs in front of a fire. But after trying to convince them to have a picnic, he gave up.

"Why do you think it would be fun sitting close to the road so the *summas* in the cars going by could stare at us? It's a stupid idea. Just stupid," Grace and Grandma told him.

Now Eddie was glad they stayed away. He had always felt comforted by the rushing tires and car sounds. Whenever he didn't feel like talking to anyone but didn't want to be completely alone, he went to the picnic grounds and watched the passing cars for hours. He wondered what the people inside them were like, what they were thinking, and where they were going.

In the centre of the grounds was a Saskatoon bush that in the summer would be so full of plump berries that the branches bent down to the ground. A gooseberry shrub once loaded with ripe fruit the size of marbles was now picked clean. Even though his arms would be covered in scratches, he always dug around a little deeper because he knew where the sweeter berries hid, down inside the thorny branches.

The trail skirted around a steep horseshoe-shaped hill that sloped down to the river. It was where he had taken Alphonse's snow shovel and skimmed down the hill over dead mulleins and thistles poking out of the snow. A wall of brush stopped him from sliding out onto the frozen river.

A snowberry bush at the edge of the trail was covered in white berries that looked so tasty that he had tasted one once, but it was sour and bitter. His grandma told him later that if he had eaten enough of them, he would have gotten very sick.

Stripping off a handful, Eddie kicked them high into the air and they landed on the ground around him like hail. He stopped at the fence where a chokecherry bush grew from the side of the steep riverbank at the end of the trail. He had always thought it was funny that a bush with a name like snowberry was bad for him, and one called chokecherry wasn't.

He crawled through the page-wire fence and slid down the bank to the pavement. Stopping at the bridge, he looked across the hundred-foot distance to the other side. He looked in both directions, and when he saw the coast was clear, began to run.

Halfway across, he glanced down to the river and saw the tail of an animal slip into the water. He stopped and stuck his head through the railing and watched an otter swimming close to shore. It looked up at Eddie before ducking under the logs jammed against the bank. The noise of the river was loud, but the sound of a loud motor made him stop and look up the highway. A tanker truck towing a long trailer had rounded the bend. Eddie knew that if he tried to run he wouldn't have enough time to make it across, so he held the shopping bag and lunch pail in his left hand and grabbed the bridge railing with the other to brace himself. He spotted a car coming from the opposite direction. Both would meet right where he was standing.

The truck driver blasted his air horn. Eddie stepped up onto the bottom beam and squeezed his eyes shut as a wall of wind pushed him up against the railing. The shopping bag was ripped out of his hands, and the colouring book flipped end over end in the air and landed in the river below. Eddie watched helplessly as it floated away. There was a flash of white paper just before the book sank into the darkness. After the truck had gone by, he saw crayons rolling in circles on the pavement. Eddie wanted to pick up as many crayons as he could, but another car came along and finished off the rest. Most of them had been squashed, and they bled purple, green, and yellow. The colours were in even layers, but the red crayon seemed to cover the rest. It looked like blood. Eddie couldn't look away. A loud car horn brought him back to attention. He switched the wire handle of his lunch pail to his other hand, and ran toward the bus stop.

Just across the bridge to the right of the highway was the Cluff house. The house was at the edge of a circle of buildings bordering the barnyard. A white arch-rafter barn with red sliding doors surrounded by white plank corrals faced the road. A shelter for a milk cow had been added onto the barn, and just outside the door was a growing pile of manure. Gas tanks sat in front of the milking shed, and a pair of bicycles leaned against the wall of the house.

Whenever Eddie went to the mailbox with his mother, he always tried to see inside beyond the open curtains. A green armchair sat next to a record player, and chesterfields stood on opposite sides of the room. The couch facing the window had a view of the school bus stop. A tapestry of elk grazing below snow-capped mountains hung on the wall. On the other side of the living room he had once seen a girl sitting straight-backed at a piano, her head moving from side to side while she played.

Eddie saw a girl and a boy walking side by side up the driveway toward the road. The boy was tall, and his hair looked almost white in the morning sun. The girl's hair was a shade of brown and bounced with each step. They met at the bus stop. The girl wore black cat's eye spectacles, a white dress with red polka dots, and a red sweater that she had on backward. Her smile made Eddie feel shy.

"Hi. What's your name?" she asked.

"Eddie."

"Eddie, my name is Eva, and this is my little brother, Albert. It's his first day of school too. Me, I'm in grade three."

Albert stared ahead as if half asleep. His hair was covered with bare spots. Eddie had seen himself in the mirror look the same way after a quick trim from Alphonse's sharp clippers. Eva repeated his name, and Albert looked up. He wore brand new cardboard-stiff Cowboy King jeans with a belt cinched tightly; its buckle was in the shape of a horseshoe. His white snap-button shirt had black fringes on the pockets and cuffs, and he wore scuffed western boots with pointy toes. To Eddie the only things missing were a cowboy hat and a horse.

Albert looked down at Eddie's lunch pail. "You having lard for lunch?" he asked with a sneer.

"Albert Cluff, you stop that right now," Eva said. "Don't listen to him, Eddie. He's a little scared about going to school today."

"I'm not scared," Albert shouted, his face turning red.

"He really is. A little anyway. Oh Eddie, you have the most beautiful brown eyes. And your lashes are so long. They're like girls' lashes. Anybody ever tell you that before?"

Eddie shrugged his shoulders.

Eva began to sing. "Beautiful, beautiful brown eyes, beautiful, beautiful brown eyes, oh beautiful, beautiful brown eyes, I'll never love blue eyes again."

Eddie didn't know what to say.

"Not bad, huh?" Eva asked.

"Uh-huh," Eddie said.

"I sing in the choir at Sunday school. We go to church every Sunday, twice actually. You're welcome to come with us anytime you want."

When Eddie saw a yellow school bus coming down the highway, he felt weak.

"You really should come. Sunday school is a lot of fun. We get to do all sorts of things and hear stories about the baby Jesus Christ," she added.

Eddie heard only half of what she said. He was thinking of all the quiet places down by the river and wishing he was at any one of them right now. He wondered what Lewis was doing. His mother had been talking about his first day of school since they returned from the States. She promised he would have fun going to school, making friends and learning how to read and write. Suddenly the new running shoes and clothes didn't feel like a good enough reason to go to school.

Brakes squealed as the bus pulled up in front of them and the door swung open. The driver wore a toque and had long fuzzy sideburns that drooped down and looked like dog's ears. He kept his hand on the door lever and stared at Eddie and the Cluffs with an impatient expression as they filed up the steps.

Just when the bus seemed to pick up speed, it slowed down to pick up other kids his age. Some looked out the back window at a waving parent as the bus pulled away. One little girl sat by herself and rubbed her eyes.

When the bus was almost full, the driver pulled over. Two older boys slid onto the seat beside him and squeezed him tight against the window. "Move over, you little Comanche," one said to him. When they saw his lunch pail, they whispered to each other and laughed.

In Falkland the bus stopped in front of the school, and the driver swung the door open. The older students talked loudly as they left the bus and went off in different directions in twos and threes. Eddie and the other first-graders looked around for someone to tell them what to do and where to go.

"Hey, Eddie. Come here."

Eva Cluff waved for him to join her. Eddie looked back and saw other kids hurrying to catch up to them. They walked through the big doors, and Eddie jumped when a man at the top of a long set of stairs yelled for quiet. Eva left them at a door where a small woman stood. She had red cheeks and perfume so strong that Eddie coughed. Smiling, she pointed to the door. "Just go on in and sit down. I'll be there in a minute."

As Eddie turned to walk down the rows of desks, he felt as if a million eyes were watching him. He found a place by a window. A girl stared unblinking at him. Boys in front stole glances over their shoulders and spoke to each other in whispers. Finally the woman entered the room and closed the door behind her.

"Good morning, students." She turned and began printing letters on the blackboard. "My name is Miss Ferguson. Can we sound out my name together?" She pointed to the letters. "Miss Fer-gus-on."

She brushed her hands and faced her class. "First things first. Does anybody need to use the washroom? It's okay. Don't be shy. All you need to do is raise your hand and ask politely. We don't want any little accidents, do we?"

A girl with red hair seated two rows over lifted her arm. "May I go to the bathroom, Miss Ferguson?" she asked in a loud, clear voice for everyone to hear.

Miss Ferguson nodded her head, and the red-haired girl walked to the door. As she went out, she turned and smiled smugly at the class.

While his fellow students cut out shapes with scissors or coloured with crayons, Eddie looked around the room. Long bookcases full of storybooks lined the back wall, and in the corner stood an open box of musical instruments that Eddie had never seen before. The blackboard behind the teacher was almost as wide as the room. Above it colourful pictures, each labelled with a letter of the alphabet, circled the room. Eddie saw a picture of a dark-faced man wearing a row of feathers that fell to the sides of his head and down past his shoulders. His piercing eyes glared at Eddie. When Miss Ferguson noticed Eddie staring so intently, she walked over and asked in a quiet voice, "Eddie, what on earth are you looking at?"

Eddie sat up and pointed to the picture.

"Which one is it? Can you tell me what letter it is?"

Eddie felt embarrassed. He shook his head. "The man with the feathers."

Miss Ferguson looked up at the wall of pictures. "That is the letter I, and that man is an Indian chief. You've never seen an Indian chief before?"

"No. And why is he so dark? And if I rubbed his face, would it get on my fingers?"

She held her answer for a moment. "Some people have darker skin than others. That's all."

She patted Eddie on his shoulder and returned to her desk. As she gathered up loose papers, Eddie saw she was smiling.

At noon Eddie popped the lid off his lunch pail and pulled out his sandwich. It slipped out of the wax paper and landed on his desk with a clunk. He looked around him and saw his classmates take neatly wrapped sandwiches out of shiny new lunch kits. They unwrapped the packages as if they were Christmas presents. He saw peanut butter and jam sandwiches, cheese and pickle sandwiches, and meat sandwiches in white town bread that was sliced perfectly. He took a bite of his baloney and butter sandwich, set it down on the wax paper, and pulled it under his arm so no one would see it.

After they ate, Eddie and another boy kicked a ball back and forth. They were having so much fun that he was surprised when the bell rang for everyone to go back inside. As he ran up the steps among the running and shouting children, he noticed Eva Cluff standing by the swings, watching him. She turned and disappeared into the crowd.

Eddie needed to use the bathroom. He should have gone at lunchtime, but he'd forgotten. Now he would have to ask, and the whole class would know what he had to do. He began to raise his hand and felt a hard kick on his desk. He turned around and a boy with snot crawling down his top lip shook his head at him.

"I'm going first," he said as he put his hand in the air. "Can I go to the bathroom, Miss Ferguson?"

She looked over, and the smile dropped from her face. "Rodney Bell. You go ahead, but don't take all day. You can go up next, Eddie."

Rodney was taller than anyone else in class, even Albert. Five minutes had gone by when Miss Ferguson spoke up. "Eddie, you go ahead and tell Rodney to get back here. The first bathroom is the boys'. Go."

Eddie hurried up the stairs. When he turned into the boys' bathroom and saw no sign of Rodney, he felt relieved. Something about Rodney scared him. Just as Eddie zipped himself up and was headed for the door, he heard the sound of breaking glass and loud ringing out in the hallway. The noise was frightening. He didn't know what to do.

A man stuck his head into the washroom, and when he saw Eddie, he asked in an angry voice, "Did you do that? Set off the fire alarm?"

Eddie couldn't speak and could only stare at the tall man blocking his way. The man put his hands on his hips and watched Eddie closely. Eddie heard doors open and the sound of people coming out of classrooms into the hallway. The man looked up and down the hallway, walked up to Eddie, and placed a hand on his back. Eddie could feel himself shaking. "Okay. Go back and join your classmates."

Eddie and his class stood out on the sidewalk. What was happening? Miss Ferguson raised her hands. "Quiet now, please. This is what is called a fire drill. We usually practise a few times before the principal rings the fire bell, but I am going to call out your names. All you say is, 'here' or 'present.'"

Rodney Bell did not answer when his name was called. Miss Ferguson looked back to the list of names and wrote something on the page.

Eddie walked up the steps of the bus carrying rolls of paper tucked under his arm that Miss Ferguson said he should show his mother. Halfway down the aisle he saw Eva sitting alone. She patted the space beside her.

"I saved you a place. Come on, sit down."

Eddie slid onto the seat.

"Look at his lunch kit," a boy behind them said. "Wonder where he got it? The Hudson's Bay in Vernon?"

They laughed, and Eva spun around. "Oh, Kenny, you're so funny."

She turned back and patted Eddie's arm. "The only way you're going to stop people teasing you about your lunch kit is to get rid of it. Look at the grade sevens. They bring their lunch in a plastic bread bag and tie it onto their belt loop over their front pocket and let it swing around. They think they're the real cat's meow. Just hide the pail in the bushes and take it home with you at night. Parents. They just don't have a clue, do they?"

Eddie shrugged his shoulders.

"My cousin goes to high school in Vernon, and I can't wait to go. They have a cafeteria there, so you don't even need to take a lunch. You just walk up and tell them what you want, and they hand it over to you. I'll get to see what kinds of clothes they're wearing and hear the new slang words. Oh, I can hardly wait to get out of this school. There isn't anything at all to do here. Falkland is such a hick town."

The bus doors swung open, and Eddie hurried down the steps. He had to stop at the bridge to let one car go by before racing across. Up the bank he went, through a large stretched square in the page-wire fence. When he ran by Grandma's house, he saw her sitting at the table where he had seen her that morning. She waved as Eddie flew past.

At his house, Eddie showed the picture of the Indian chief to Grace. "Look what I did today. And look what the teacher gave me."

"Boy. That's a mean-looking Indian," she said.

"Do we have a chief, Mom?"

"We sure do."

"What does he do?"

"Nothing. If he was any kind of chief, he'd be helping us. He doesn't do a damn thing."

"What does he look like?"

"Like anybody else."

"Like him?"

"No. This is something a *summa* made."

"*Summa*?"

"You know what that means, don't you? Sure you do. You heard me and your grandma and Alphonse say it lots of times."

"What does it mean?"

"It means white people. Boy, Eddie, I thought you knew."

Eddie shook his head.

"Well, what did you think we were talking about?"

"I didn't know it was a Indian word. I thought it was a real word."

"What did you think it meant?"

"The other people. The people that got money. I don't know. Sometimes when you say something, it sounds like a swear word, and when somebody else says it, it doesn't."

"Like what?"

"Eva said at the bus stop this morning they go to Sunday school and I could go with them so I could learn all about the baby Jesus Chrissakes."

His eyes were open wide as he waited for his mother to say something.

"Eddie, I don't know what you're talking about. Just never mind about learnin' Indian. This was only your first day. You can't figure everything out in one day. Look how old I am, and I don't know. You'll learn all about things like that at school. That's why you have teachers. And after you got everything figured out, then you come and tell me."

9

Even in the dead of winter, when everything was frozen solid, the odour in the outhouse persisted. Eddie did his best to not breathe through his nose but imagined floating bits of stink somehow making their way into his mouth. Lewis had been getting on his nerves lately, even more than usual with the cold weather keeping them locked inside the house. Eddie needed to get away from him before he gave him a good hard punch. The outhouse was the only place he could be alone.

When they were younger, if Lewis saw Eddie on his way to the toilet, he always followed. Eddie tried to hurry because he felt strange doing his business while being watched. When threats didn't work, he picked up the catalogue they used for toilet paper and flipped through the pages. It took fifteen minutes before Lewis gave up and walked away. After two or three times, Eddie was able to go by himself.

Sitting in the outhouse, Eddie could see past the snow-covered trash pit all the way down to the thick brush and trees along the river. A pink light in the clouds to the east made him think of cotton candy. Red willow branches against the white looked painted. Tracks of small animals, weasels probably, dotted the ground.

A large spider in the centre of a web above the corner of the doorway was so still that Eddie couldn't tell if it was frozen or just resting. When a gust of wind blew through the cracks of the toilet walls and shook the web, the spider gathered itself into a ball. The harder the wind blew, the smaller the spider got. As snow sifted across the outhouse floor, the air was fresh for a moment.

Suddenly something wet and cold touched Eddie on his bare behind, like the nose of an animal. Jumping off the seat, he looked down into the hole for the dirty beast he had always thought lived at the bottom of the pit. But there was no animal. The outhouse cavity was filling up and was only inches away from the wooden seat.

He went back to the house. "Mom, the toilet is almost full. It's up to the seat."

Grace was seated at the kitchen window. "What are you telling me for? Get a stick and knock the top over."

"Knock the top over," Lewis said mockingly.

"Why doesn't Lewis do it? He doesn't do anything around here."

"Because you were the one that filled it up," Lewis said.

Eddie had been fed up for some time with how Lewis got out of doing any work, so the moment Grace turned back to the window, Eddie stepped forward and grabbed him by the shirt.

"Mom," Lewis shouted.

Grace looked back. "Leave him alone."

But Eddie was determined Lewis was going to get it this time.

Grace hurried to separate them. "Jesus, Eddie. Don't you do that again. And you, Lewis, keep your smarty mouth shut. You always got something to say. The both a you are starting to get on my nerves. Any more from either one a you guys and I'll whip you—" Grace stopped when she heard the thump of a car door outside.

Eddie walked to the window and moved back the sheers with his finger just enough to look out with one eye. He saw a woman in a dress that was as white as snow.

Grace looked over his shoulder. "Looks like the public health nurse. Well, it's about time."

"For what?" Eddie asked.

"Shots. Everybody else got their kids done, and nobody said a thing to me. I just wrote a letter last week, and here she is. I don't believe it."

"I got mine at school. I'm not going to get more, am I?" Eddie asked.

Grace lowered her voice. "No."

Lewis jerked open the curtain to have a look. Grace and Eddie ducked and stepped back. "Who is that?" he asked.

"The nurse," Eddie said.

"What do you mean shots, Mom?"

Eddie smiled. "She's gonna give you a needle."

"A what?"

"She's going to poke you with a long needle," Eddie said.

"Does it hurt?"

"It really hurts when she sticks it in right there," Eddie said, poking Lewis's buttock.

"Quit that, Eddie," Grace said.

"It hurt so bad even some of the fifth-graders cried. You can't sit down for a long time. You can't even walk without it hurting. Mine hurt for a whole day."

Three loud bangs on the door made Lewis back away.

"Smarten up, Lewis. You stand right there and don't move," Grace said.

"Let her in, Eddie," Grace said as she grabbed Lewis by the arm. "Now, you keep still or I'll give you a licking that'll hurt worse than ten needles, and you won't be able to walk right for two days."

Eddie opened the door to a stern-faced woman.

"Toma?"

"Yeah, come in," Grace said.

The nurse locked her eyes on Lewis. "I see you've been expecting me. Is that Lewis you've got hog-tied?"

"Yes."

"Well, Lewis, let's try to do this without any fuss. You don't want me to bring out the handcuffs, do you? It's been a long Saturday, and this is my last call. I just want to go home so I can put my feet up and have a cup of tea. It'll be over before you know it."

As she walked past Eddie, her stiff white skirt brushed his hip and felt like cardboard. The nurse set a black leather bag on a chair and brought out a white cloth that she placed on the table, smoothing out the wrinkles. She pulled out a needle and a small glass bottle, held the bottle upside down, and eased the tip through the rubber stopper. She pulled on the end, and the glass filled with clear liquid.

Lewis tried to pull away, but Grace had him in her strong grip. The nurse held up the needle and pushed on the bottom until a line of liquid squirted into the air. She flicked it with her finger before setting it down on the cloth. Then she brought out a bottle which she opened and poured liquid onto a piece of cotton batting. Eddie thought that if pain had a smell, it would be the odour coming from the cotton.

"Now, let's drop those pants, son."

Lewis broke free, but Eddie stepped in front of him. He turned to go out the back door, but Grace stood in his way. His only escape was into the bedroom, so he ran past the nurse and slammed the door. Eddie put his shoulder against the door and pushed. Lewis was trying his hardest, but Eddie rammed his shoulder against the door and Lewis fell to the floor. As Eddie swung the door open Lewis began to crawl under the bed. If he had been just a little quicker, he might have made it, but Grace caught him by the ankle. The nurse handed Eddie the syringe and cotton. She yanked down Lewis's pants and placed her knee on his back. She took the cotton and smeared it across Lewis's bare buttock, then tossed it aside. She took the needle from Eddie and jabbed Lewis.

While the nurse gathered up the bottles and needle and placed them in her bag, she took a good look around. Even as she walked to the door, her head swept from side to side. When she grabbed the doorknob, she looked back for one last peek. Without saying a word, she opened the door and walked away.

"Ow, ow, ow," Lewis cried as he rubbed where he had been jabbed. He brought his hand to his nose. "What is that stuff?"

"Poison," Grace said. "Now quit yer cryin' and get down to that toilet. If you're gonna act like a baby, well then, you got yourself a full-time job. Go get a good long stick and push the top of that stuff over."

10

Headlights lit up the faces of Eddie, Grace, and Lewis at the cattle guard. They stood shivering in the cold air that was thick with tumbling snowflakes.

"It's not coming, Eddie. They wouldn't send the school bus out on a night like this. This is crazy. We're all going to freeze to death," Grace said. "If it's not here in five minutes, we're going home. I'm gonna look like a fly in a sugar bowl anyway around all them *summas*."

A snowflake landed on Grace's eyelash and she swatted at it as if it were a bug. She shook her head. "This is what happens when you're poor. Always waiting for somebody else to do something for you, like they are doing you a favour, and you better be thankful. And if you bugger it up, they're going to have something to say.

"One time my mom made me a nice white dress. First time she ever done that. She made me wash off my horse's back and even gave me an old shirt to sit on because I rode bareback to the day school, and she didn't want the dress to get dirty. So I hopped on and loped down the road. Well, the horse spooked, and I fell onto the wet ground, and the dress was covered in mud. Got a good lickin' that day. But it just shows that sometimes, no matter what you do, people think you will prob'ly just land on your dirty ass anyway."

Eddie looked up at her. "You had a horse?"

"What? Oh Jesus, never mind about the damn horse. Just saying that if we coulda taken the truck we coulda driven in style to the concert. Just needed winter tires, new battery, windshield wipers, gas, and oil. That's all. Damn truck put us on our asses, just like that horse did."

Eddie hoped the bus would hurry. His mother rocked from side to side on her feet and groaned with each passing vehicle, ready to give up any minute.

"You said you'd go to the Christmas concert and watch me sing, Mom," he said.

Grace didn't answer. Rubbing her hands together, she looked back to the trail where snow was quickly covering their tracks.

"That's it," she said. "I waited long enough."

Just as she reached for Lewis's hand, Eddie heard the light bump of tires hitting the bridge decking, and the lights of a large vehicle waved up and down. The amber lights on top of the bus came into view, and the driver changed gears, swung off the highway, and did a wide U-turn in front of the cattle guard before coming to a stop. The doors flapped open.

The unsmiling driver nodded at them. As if it were just another day at work, he was wearing the same clothes as earlier that day, the lined denim jacket, the toque, and the green pants Eddie had seen gas station attendants wear. Grace took a seat behind the driver by the window.

"Can I sit in the back?" Eddie asked.

"No. You stay with me," she answered.

The bus pulled back onto the highway. As they drove over the bridge, Eddie crossed the aisle and rubbed the frost from the window. In the Cluffs' driveway under the barnyard light, Eva and her family were getting into a station wagon. When Eva looked up, Eddie waved to her. She looked away and opened the door to the backseat. Eddie was disappointed. Maybe when he saw her at the concert, he would ask her to ride home on the bus with him. But any courage he had to even imagine asking her left him, and he settled down in his seat.

The wipers could barely keep up with the snow gathering on the windshield. If it weren't for the tracks left behind by other vehicles, it would have been hard to see the road. At the outskirts of Falkland, Grace grabbed Eddie by the arm.

"Look, out there," she said.

Electric Christmas lights were strung around windows and doors of some of the houses. Eddie and Lewis rubbed the frost off the bus windows with their palms to see. On one house the lights blinked off and on in red, then yellow, then blue, then white, and then green. In the living room of another house stood a Christmas tree lit up by smaller lights.

"How can people afford to buy stuff like that?" Grace asked.

"Can we get lights like that, Mom?" Eddie asked.

"Sure. But we'll need a really long cord to plug into one of these houses."

The bus pulled to a stop in front of the Falkland community hall. When the driver opened the door, the noise coming from inside the hall sounded as if people were yelling at each other. Parents with children dressed in costumes streamed in through the wide doors. Just as Eddie was about to go into the hall, he was hit on the back by a snowball. He turned around to see Rodney Bell grinning at him. He turned and followed Grace and Lewis inside.

A ten-foot tree covered in decorations stood to the right of the stage. The large star on top of the tree rose above the cigarette smoke that stretched from wall to wall in a thin cloud. Men leaned against the walls on each side of the hall in a line that ran up the stairs to the balcony. Some people bunched together in small groups talking with one another while others stood by themselves looking uncomfortable. Eddie noticed two men looking at his mom. One leaned his head back as if to ask the other man a question. The man looked away, shrugging his shoulders. A spotlight swept back and forth across the folds of the blue curtains.

An older student approached Grace. "What grade?"

"What?"

"What grade is your kid in?"

"Grade one."

"The grade one class is at the front. I'll show you," he said.

As Grace followed down the centre aisle of the hall, Eddie saw people turning in their seats to watch. Their eyes went from head to toe, but his mother looked straight ahead.

A woman was motioning Eddie over to where she stood at the side of the stage.

Grace asked, "Who's that waving?"

"Miss Ferguson, my teacher," Eddie said. He felt important when Grace patted him on the back as he walked by.

Eddie and his classmates were guided onto the stage behind the curtain. They giggled as they waited. Then the curtains slowly drew back, and the house lights went down. The spotlight shone in Eddie's eyes as he looked for his family in the crowd. Miss Ferguson walked to the microphone to introduce her class before she sat at the piano.

The choir sang three songs, the audience applauded politely, and Eddie and his classmates took a bow. The curtains came together as Miss Ferguson led her group offstage. Just before Eddie walked down the steps, he saw his mother smiling at him and couldn't wait to hear what she had to say. When he stepped onto the floor, he lost sight of her because of all the people crowded around the bottom of the little stairs. As he made his way toward his seat, he saw Eva through the backs and legs of the grown-ups. She was holding a sheet of paper in her hand as she followed her teacher toward the stage. When she saw Eddie, she smiled and reached out. Suddenly Eddie felt someone push him hard from behind, and he tripped and fell to the floor. He looked up at Eva, who stood with a surprised expression. A man grabbed him by the arm and helped him to his feet.

Eva's teacher, Mrs. Stanley, rushed over. "Are you okay?"

Eva pointed behind Eddie. "Rodney Bell pushed him. I saw it," she said.

Eddie looked around but couldn't see Rodney.

"Mrs. Stanley, I saw what happened. I saw the whole thing."

Mrs. Stanley held her finger to her mouth. "Hush now, Eva. We don't have time for this now. It will be dealt with at school. You join the others and get ready to do your presentation."

The dirty melted snow on the floor left two dark patches on his knees. Eddie tried brushing his pants clean but gave up and made his way through all the legs back to his seat.

The bus stopped in front of the cattle guard, and after its door closed, spun its wheels in two feet of new snow. Rocking back and forth, the driver changed gears from forward to reverse until he made it over the slippery spot. The bus drove back onto the road, backfired, and sped away into the night.

"Let's take the long way around. It'll be easier than going up the hill by Grandma's." Grace walked ahead to break trail with Lewis on her back. Holding two bulging paper bags, Eddie found it hard to step in the holes she left in the snow.

It had stopped snowing, and the light of a half-moon lit up the snow-blanketed road ahead. As they walked, Eddie began losing the feeling in his unprotected fingers, and his back tightened when a light wind blew from behind. Snow slid off a drooping tree branch that sprang up, relieved of its weight, and the spilling snow freed more snow from the lower branches until the air filled with a swishing, sparkling mist.

Grace opened the door and swung Lewis down to the floor. He let out a cry as he slumped against the cupboard pantry. Eddie shut the door with his foot while Grace felt along the wall until she found the match holder. Then she struck a match and lit the coal oil lamp. After putting Lewis to bed, she opened the fresh-air grill on the stove, opened the damper, and filled the stove with wood.

The fire crackled to life, and an orange glow appeared on the side of the stove.

She sat down at the table and noticed Eddie's fingers were bright red. She blew on his hands and rubbed them until Eddie felt his fingers tingle.

"That better?" she asked.

"They hurt."

"You'll be okay after you get warmed up. Next time I go to town, I need to get you guys a good pair of mitts with wool lining and maybe even lined pants. I seen how the *summas* dress their kids, and I'm gonna make sure you have what they have."

"And a new lunch kit too?"

"Darn rights. You know you can tell me what you need, and if I got money, we'll get it. I don't want anybody saying how poor we are." She smiled at Eddie. "Let's have a look inside one a them bags."

She laid the bag on its side, spilling the contents onto the table. There were candy canes, hazelnuts, almonds, walnuts, hard candy, chocolates, and a ball wrapped in green tissue paper. She pulled off the tissue paper.

"Look at this. That's the best-looking orange I ever saw. We didn't have these when I was a kid. Boy, if I was rich, I'd have one of these every day."

She peeled the orange, broke it into pieces, and handed one to Eddie.

"You know when the principal called your name and you took Lewis up to Santa Claus, you grabbed the bags from him like you didn't have a care in the world. You weren't scared at all. You're a lot braver than me, Eddie. I guess old Santa does know everything. He even had a bag for Lewis."

"My teacher asked me if I had a brother or sister at home."

"Anyway, it was good seeing you up there on the stage singing. Like I said, you're a lot braver than me. And I'll tell you something else: this year we're going to have a good Christmas. We'll get a better tree than Alphonse got last time, and we'll all have presents under it too. You wait and see."

Grace used pliers to break open the nuts and put them in a bowl. Eddie picked out the hazelnuts and chewed as he watched the smoke from the chimney swirl around the window. He looked back at Grace and caught her smiling at him. Neither spoke. Earlier that evening up at the road, waiting for the school bus, she didn't want to go to the concert. Now it looked like she'd even had fun. But there was an ache in Eddie's stomach he couldn't explain. Christmas or presents or even decorated trees weren't on his mind. All he could think of was Rodney. And he didn't feel very brave.

11

It was ten below zero. The temperature had dropped twenty degrees in one night. Outside, Grace had almost finished shovelling the path to the toilet. Before she went out, she had told Eddie to help clear the trail down to Grandma's. First he was to dump the slop bucket over the bank.

Lewis ran out of the bedroom. "I gotta pee."

"Go outside, then."

"No, it's too cold."

"Not if you hurry. Just go out and pee off the steps."

"It's too cold. I really have to pee, Eddie."

"Well, hurry up and go in the pail before Mom comes in."

Lewis stood on his toes and let loose a loud stream into the pail, stirring up the contents. The smell bothered their eyes. Eddie heard the doorknob turn and wondered what would happen to Lewis when he was caught. The door swung open, and a well-dressed man stepped into the room. Eddie recognized him right away: the buzzard.

Lewis couldn't stop peeing. Eddie was surprised that he didn't hear a knock until he realized that the buzzard had just opened the door and walked in. He peered at Lewis and glanced around the room.

"You boys here all alone?"

Eddie shook his head.

"Where's your mother?"

"Toilet," Eddie said.

"Oh. Well, I'll just come in and wait for her."

He unhooked the clasps on his overshoes and pulled them off, using the toe of his boot against the other heel. Snow landed on the floor. His brown, shiny oxfords inside were bone dry. He unwound the scarf around his neck and was removing his gloves when Grace opened the door.

She was caught off guard seeing the man standing in her kitchen, and when she saw Lewis giving a last few squirts into the slop pail, her body jerked as if an electric shock went through her. Without saying a word she took quick steps to grab the handle of the pail away from Eddie and regarded Lewis from under her eyebrows. Lewis was slow to move, and Eddie knew that if the man wasn't there, that Lewis wouldn't be standing still at that moment. And the big knuckle on their mother's right hand would have left a lump on his head.

Lewis ran into the bedroom as Grace set the pail out on the step.

"You might as well sit down," she said to the man.

She scowled at Eddie and set the kettle over the heat. She brought the teapot down from the top of the stove and took two mugs from the cupboard pantry. Eddie felt warm in his layers of clothing. He leaned against the wall by the door to wait.

"What are you doing out here on a Saturday anyway, Mr. Cooke?"

"I'm on my way down to the coast to spend Christmas with the old folks, and I thought I'd kill two birds with one stone. I was going to wait until after the holidays to talk to you, but it seems the high school in town has sent your family a Christmas hamper."

"A what?"

"Some food and Christmas presents for the children. I think you're pretty fortunate they had one for you. If I were you, I'd send them a nice letter of thanks. You're good at writing letters."

"What do you want to talk about? You finally gonna put in the electricity?"

"No. I wish I could tell you that I was, but we're still working on it."

"Working on it, hah. You should put one of them signs in front of the Indian Office that says, 'Slow men working.'"

"Grace, I didn't come all the way out here to get into an argument."

"I thought you said you were driving through to the coast?"

"You know what I mean."

"You always got an answer for everything, don't you? Well, if you're so smart, then tell me why me and my mom still haven't got electricity."

"I don't have that kind of authority. It's out of my hands. If I could, I would phone the hydro company and give them the go-ahead, but I can't. I just can't do whatever I want."

"Like I said, you got an answer for everything."

"I just walked through two feet of snow from the highway to tell you something, and you jump on me. So, you know what, if you want to know why you don't have power yet, I'll tell you. But if this comes back to me, I'll just deny I ever said it. I'm not supposed to put power out here until I know for sure you won't just up and leave for the States or move to another far-flung corner of the reserve. God knows why you want to live out here in the boondocks so far away from your people anyway. The only way you will get power out here is if another family decides to build out here so the cost won't be as great. It can't be done unless there are at least three homes to service. That's why, Grace. You're a migratory people—you move around a lot. The department wants to be sure before they hand out that kind of money."

"Hah. We'll probably be dead by then. Froze to death or died of old age."

"You're exaggerating."

Grace poured water from the kettle into the teapot and set the sugar bowl and canned milk on the table. She dropped a heaping teaspoonful of sugar into her cup, poured in the sweet milk and filled the mugs with tea. After stirring her cup, she slid the spoon across the table. Eddie could see that she was tiring of the man already.

"No sugar or milk for me," he said.

"Umm," Grace mumbled.

He slurped the hot tea. Eddie took off his coat.

"Besides playing Santa Claus, why are you here? Why did you walk through them snow drifts from the highway?"

The man put down his cup. "Do you remember a while back when the public health nurse came out here? Well, she didn't file a report on you or anything, but she thought I should have a look in on you."

Grace had her cup to her mouth to take a drink. She set her cup down hard, sloshing the tea. "For what?"

"She was concerned about your living conditions, so I thought I'd look into it myself."

"What did she say?"

"She was concerned about your living conditions."

"You already said that."

The man sat up in his chair. "It isn't that bad. She mentioned a few things like the slop pail, the smell of the house, and how you have coats on the bed for blankets. I think what concerned her most was that she didn't see a lot of food in your pantry."

"How does she know that? She didn't have time to look around. She was only here for a minute and then she left."

"You know what? I'm not going to argue about every little point with you." He stood and pulled on his overcoat.

"Are you leaving because of the smell of my house?"

"No. Everything seems okay to me, under the circumstances. And I'm going because I want to be through the Fraser Canyon before dark. I should never have stopped here and wasted good driving time. I should have let somebody else deliver the hamper.

All I'm going to tell you is that any other Indian agent might have simply made a few calls, and your kids would be living at a residential school right now. See, that's what happens when I get a report. If I think the children are at risk, I have them removed. It's that simple."

Mr. Cooke wrapped his scarf around his neck and pulled on his gloves. "Like I said, I'm not going to argue. I noticed that you don't have enough firewood to see you through the winter. I'll order a dump truck load of wood from the sawmill in town. It's seasoned slab wood that's been cut to stove lengths. And if you can get your driveway cleared in the meantime, say two weeks from today, I'll send the truck out. And I'll pay for it myself. I wouldn't want anybody to hear that I don't help out. Get your brother Alphonse to bring the hamper down here from the highway. I'll put it off to the side of the trail away from the road. I just hope dogs don't get to it first."

He pulled on his overshoes and opened the door. "And if you really want to get your power out here, maybe you can stop sending letters to Ottawa. It makes me look bad."

He walked out. Grace couldn't take her eyes away from the door. Lewis came to the edge of the bedroom doorway just out of Grace's sight.

"Is he gone, Eddie?" he asked.

Lewis stepped through the doorway and saw his mother. When he turned to run back into the bedroom, Grace reached around and gave him a hard slap on his behind.

12

1962

Eddie, Grandma, Lewis, and Grace stood under the hazelnut tree and looked up at the sagging branches that were heavy with nuts. After picking from the low branches, they moved the ladder. Eddie climbed up and picked enough to fill two water buckets while Lewis gathered the nuts that had fallen to the ground. They put the nuts into gunnysacks and laid them on the roof and trunk of one of Alphonse's wrecked cars. The four cars were parked right where they had broken down, wheel-less, their axles resting on blocks of wood. Grandma hated the cars, but Alphonse said when he found all the parts he needed, he could have them all up and running in no time.

"I guess these damn cars is good for somethin' after all," Grandma said. "We'll let the sun dry them out before we put them away for winter. Should only be a few days. I wanted to do this before, but the squirrels always got there first. This time we beat them to it."

Alphonse walked over and shook his head. "Wouldn't leave them there if I was you."

"Why?" she said.

"They don't give up that easy," he said, walking away.

A week passed, and Eddie gave up thinking about the nuts. Alphonse had taken off again, so Eddie now had to look after two houses. He brought in firewood, hauled water from the river, and did whatever his mother or Grandma needed until at night he fell into his bed exhausted. After Eddie did his morning's work, he was sitting at the table eating bread and jam when Grace walked in.

"Alphonse just showed up. Right after you did all his work for him. Anyway, your grandma wants to see you," Grace said.

"Why?" he asked. "What for?"

"Don't know. She just told me to send you down there. Get your coat on. It's a little chilly."

Eddie slipped on his jacket and walked down the steps. He wondered what his grandma wanted and if he were in trouble. He couldn't remember breaking anything in her house, spilling water, tracking in dirt, or leaving a mess. Maybe she wanted something else done, as if it weren't enough to fill her pails with water and pack in wood for her that morning.

Most of the time Grandma was fun to be around, especially with Alphonse gone for days or even weeks at a time. Eddie liked having supper with her and staying the night, and she made him feel important when she poured him a cup of tea and placed it on a saucer. He always drank carefully from the cup, unlike an old woman who stopped to visit once; she poured her tea into the saucer and sipped at it like a cat. As he drank, his grandma would reach up to a special place in her old cupboard and bring down a cake wrapped in a tea towel.

Grandma loved cake but couldn't read the recipe, so Grace showed her how to use different sized spoons and teacups instead of the exact measurements called for. It took time, but she learned how to do it on her own. Her cakes were all the same. Only the icing was different: white, pink, green, or sometimes a colour he couldn't recognize. When she learned how to make matrimonial cake, it became Eddie's favourite. It had a sweet date filling and toasted oatmeal that crumbled in his hand, and he always bent over his plate so not a single crumb would land on the floor. But sometimes she sat at the table with a mean look on her face and stared out her window as if he weren't there, which reminded him of his mother. He hoped she was in a good mood this time.

Eddie zipped up his jacket, shoved his hands into his pockets, and walked hunched over. When he came to the little hill above her house, he saw her in the small garden at the back, turning over dirt with a shovel. He ran down the hill and cut across the wild grass that his feet crunched under a layer of white frost.

"What are you doing?" he asked.

Grandma stopped digging and looked at Eddie. She was out of breath but smiled as she leaned on the shovel.

"I know school starts again pretty soon and I want you and me to go fishing. I'm all out of meat too. I had baloney, but it turned green yesterday and now it smells like one of Alphonse's socks. Damn him anyway. He's like a tomcat, wandering off to the bushes or I don't know where. And he never thinks about going to the store for me, that bugger. Seems like he's getting worser and worser. So let's gather up some worms and get down to the river and find us some fish."

She turned over a large chunk of dirt, and Eddie fell to his knees to snatch the worms before they could shrink back into their tunnels. Using the shovel handle for support, Grandma lowered herself down; her knee clicked twice.

"Grab that fat one before he gets away. We don't want to lose him. That's the one that's gonna catch us the biggest fish."

After Eddie topped off the worm can with a handful of the soil, Grandma placed it into a large purse that Alphonse had found on the side of the highway. Looping the shoulder straps she'd made from binder twine around her neck, she swung the purse around so it rested against her back. She picked up her fishing pole that doubled as a walking stick, and they set off.

They hiked along a seldom-used path close to the river. Eddie had always avoided going that way because of the thorns and stinging nettles.

"There's a better trail from our house down to the river," he said. "We'd miss a stretch of deep water that might have fish."

Eddie knew there were no fish between her house and his trail. He had walked up and down the far bank before and hadn't got a single bite. The river was too fast and shallow.

Patches of early frost dotted the trail, and the still autumn air in the bush made Eddie shiver. Finches huddled together on a tree branch with their heads drawn inside fluffed feathers. One of the little birds let out a peep, and its breath made a circle like a tiny smoke ring.

They turned into another trail that led down to the spot where Eddie came to watch minnows swimming under a large cottonwood log that stuck out halfway across the river. He called it the dam. The cottonwood couldn't be budged even in high water. He wanted to show her where he had seen fish swimming close to the bank, but she sat down on the log, swung her legs over, and slid down to the other side. Eddie sighed. He couldn't understand why she would walk right past a perfectly good fishing hole. She was so stubborn sometimes.

Pushing through tall grass, he came to an open shore littered with smooth rocks left behind by high water. The stream made a wide sweep around the dam and carved a new path into the far bank. Thirty yards ahead, the river swung back to the right. He expected to see his grandma waiting for him, annoyed that he'd taken so long, but she wasn't there. Eddie jumped across a small stream that had broken off from the main flow and looked downstream, but saw no sign of her anywhere. He listened for a sound, for her voice calling to him, but heard only splashing water. Then he saw her pole and purse lying on the rocks just two feet away from the deepest, darkest hole he had ever seen. A prickly feeling spread over his scalp as he leaned over and looked into the gloom, frightened at what he might find. He was about to call out her name when she shouted from the trees.

"Did you bring any paper?"

"No."

"Dammit."

She came out from behind a bush tucking her shirt into her pants and saw Eddie looking inside the purse. "We're not stopping here. Maybe on the way back. We don't want to pack all our fish down the river and all the way back again."

They tramped through thick brush. Eddie stayed close behind her with his eyes glued to her boot heels until a branch hit him in the face. He was tired and wanted to stop for a rest and had no idea where they were headed. When they stepped out into the bright sunlight at the edge of a narrow field, Eddie saw the river a hundred feet away.

Grandma stopped at the riverbank and sat down on the stony ground.

"I should've listened to you, Eddie. We shoulda stopped at that first fishing hole. If I knew it was gonna be this hard, I woulda stayed home."

Her words made Eddie feel better, especially coming from her. There seemed to be very little that his grandma couldn't do, and he thought she was the most fearless person in the world. Once long ago, when he and Lewis hid under her bed after a loud thunderstorm sent streaks of lightning whipping across the sky, she said that she would fix it so they would be safe. They didn't believe her, and it took a lot of convincing before they crawled out and stood in the doorway to watch. She took a knife from her pantry and stuck it in the ground with the sharp end pointing up. She said it was a magic trick shown to her when she was little. Nothing would happen to them as long as the knife was there. When they saw her standing unafraid in the wind and lashing rain with her face turned up to the sky as if teasing the storm, the boys ran outside with their arms held away from their sides, running and swaying through the rain like airplanes.

Grandma didn't fish for fun; she was all business. She had a knack for knowing where the fish were hiding in shady spots and how to coax them out. Today she pulled trout after trout from the water, rebaited the hook, and tossed it back into the river. She didn't use weights because the hook would sink and tangle in tree roots or sticks. Her method was to toss the line above a deep hole and let it float downstream on the top of the water. When she felt a strike, she pulled the line with a hard jerk, yanked the trout out of the water, and slammed it onto the rocks behind her. The fish would die instantly, saving Eddie the trouble of knocking it on the head with a stick. Once a fish came off the hook in mid-air and flew deep into the bushes. He found it by listening to it flipping around in the undergrowth.

Eventually Eddie put down his fishing pole because he was too busy removing fish from Grandma's line. After he hooked twenty pan-sized trout through the gills with sticks, she said they had caught enough. It wasn't soon enough for Eddie, who had lost the thrill of fishing hours earlier. She had turned his favourite pastime into work. Now he was so hungry he didn't think he had the strength to pack home all the fish.

"Go find birch bark and some dry wood," Grandma said. "I gotta have something to eat before I fall over. And bring back clean moss if you see any."

Ten feet from the river two logs, one higher than the other, looked as if they had been placed there so that a person could sit down above the stony ground on one and lean back against the other. Grandma gave the log a thankful pat as she sat down. She squeezed her eyes together and let out a weary breath. Eddie watched her to make sure she was all right, but when she opened her eyes, she was irritated to see him watching her.

"What are you standing around staring for? If you hadda gone when you were sposed to, you coulda been back by now."

Eddie walked into the trees until he came across an old birch log with its white bark split open and curled up like rolls of paper. He peeled off long strips and gathered up dry branches and green moss from the side of a large stump. When he returned, he saw she had fallen asleep, so he worked as quietly as he could to make a pile with the smallest pieces of tinder on the bottom. Now all he needed was a match, but he hadn't been allowed to carry any since the day he set fire to the Oregon grape below his house. He'd been fascinated by the noise of the blaze that sounded like popping firecrackers and the way the fire devoured everything in its path. He had been so spellbound by the strange beauty of the flames that he hadn't realized he was surrounded until his mother pushed him out of the way and began beating at the fire with a shovel. She gave him a terrible whipping that day, and for a long time afterward, Eddie caught her watching whenever he went near the match holder on the wall.

Grandma's bag lay on the ground near her feet. Inside it he found a salt shaker, hooks, fishing line, a knife, and a baby food jar filled with wooden matches. He unscrewed the lid, removed two matches, and placed one in his shirt pocket. Then he scratched a match on a rock and held it under the pile of tinder. When the crackling of the fire awakened Grandma, her eyes were on Eddie instantly. He was so unnerved by her stare that he took the match out of his pocket and put it back in the jar.

"You got a fire going already. Good boy."

She brought out the knife from her bag and rubbed it across a flat stone. "We might as well clean them right now. House is stinky enough. Jeez, that Alphonse can really smell a place up. His feet are so bad it's like they died and he don't know it."

His grandma ran the knife along the white belly and pulled out the guts. Eddie's job was to rinse the fish in the river and scrape out the black stuff next to the backbone with his thumb. He felt proud to see so many cleaned trout on sticks in the river. She skewered four nice-sized ones onto green willow branches which she stuck in the ground close to the fire. White beads of fat dropped into the fire and filled the air with a mouth-watering smell.

"Looks cooked to me, but I'll show you how to tell."

Eddie leaned forward.

"Give it a good squeeze. Be quick or you'll burn your finger."

With his thumb and forefinger on each side of the fish, Eddie gave a quick press.

"Does it feel hard or soft?"

"Hard."

"That means it's cooked. You see how the skin is split down the back? That's another way to tell, but it's almost cooked too much by then. Anyway, cooking lessons is over. Gimme that salt shaker."

Grandma was so hungry she couldn't wait for the fish to cool. She picked off a piece of steaming meat that she tossed back and forth in her palms before popping it into her mouth. She was almost finished her first fish before Eddie could even touch his. He waved the stick back and forth in the air for the fish to cool. Then, leaning back on the log, he sprinkled salt on the trout, picked off big chunks, and gulped the pieces down whole.

"Hey, you make sure you don't swallow any bones. I don't want to have to stick my finger down your throat. Do like I do and feel around with your tongue."

Eddie was ravenous but he took his time. Feeling a bone in his mouth, he picked it out and tossed it into the fire.

Grandma pointed a bent finger at him. "See."

Clouds floated in front of the sun. The cool early autumn brought down leaves tinted in brilliant shades of yellow and red like the colour of fire. Some were so bright that when they landed in the water, Eddie almost expected to hear a hiss. The sun pierced a hole through the clouds, and a shaft of light appeared on the mountains across the valley. While the fishermen ate, they watched the beam move slowly over the dull forest. Where it touched the trees, the colours became brighter. As the beam moved on, the colours darkened.

Eddie peeled off the crispy skin, and it crackled in his mouth as he chewed. It had been a long time since he'd eaten anything so good. After picking the fish clean, he sucked on the bones for the last salty bits.

Grandma licked her fingers and wiped her mouth with the back of her hand. "All we need now is a cuppa hot tea with three spoons of sugar in it and a chocolate cake this high," she said, holding her palm two feet off the ground. "Find any moss?"

Eddie reached into his pants pocket and handed it to her.

"Oh, it's nice and warm too."

She limped off toward the trees and was gone ten minutes before she returned smiling. "That stuff's better'n toilet paper any day."

Eddie had put the fire out and was leaning against the log when she sat down beside him.

"Let's have a little snooze before we go. We had us a good day, and we can come back to that other spot whenever we want and pull every one a them fish outta there. That's far enough for me. We'll go through the field this time so we don't hafta go trampin' through the bush.

"You know, Eddie, school starts pretty soon, and you'll be too busy to go fishin'. Tomorrow, after you help me and your mom get them hazelnuts done, I won't hardly see you no more. You'll be gone all day. You're the only pardner I got left," she said, patting his hand.

The next morning Eddie and Lewis walked down with Grace to collect the nuts, and Grandma came out her door. They walked up to the first car. When they lifted the gunnysack, they were shocked.

"It's empty!" Eddie blurted angrily. "All that waiting just to have them stolen."

A quick check of the other sack revealed the same. Every single nut was gone.

Alphonse walked over to them and looked over Grandma's shoulder. "I told you the squirrels would find them." He walked back to the house laughing while the others stood in silence.

"Them little devils," Grandma said. "They better start runnin.'"

Eddie grabbed his slingshot and filled his pockets with the roundest, smoothest rocks he could find. Grandma loaded the .22. They searched for hours but didn't see a single squirrel. Grandma was sure they chattered warnings to each other when they heard her coming.

13

Eddie sat by himself staring sleepily out the school bus window. When they pulled to a stop in front of a mother and son standing at the side of the road, he looked in curiosity. Though he had seen them in movies, Eddie had never met a Negro.

A red kerchief tied in a knot at the back covered the mother's head. Her skin was as dark as burnt wood. She was a big woman; everything about her was oversized. Her folded arms rested on top of big breasts. Her hips were wide, and her behind stuck out as if she were hiding something under her blue skirt. The son was tall and slim with long hands, arms, and legs. His nervous eyes reminded Eddie of a panicked horse as he looked at the kids inside the bus. Some kids stood on seats and craned their necks over others who'd gathered at the windows.

The boy took a deep breath before he climbed up the steps and walked down the row of seats as his mother spoke to the driver. He stopped at Eddie's seat.

"Can I sit here?" he asked in a soft voice.

Eddie nodded and sat up straight. The boy slid onto the seat as the driver closed the bus door and pulled away from the woman.

"My name is Joshua," the boy said to Eddie. "What grade are you in?"

A younger boy and girl kneeled on the seat ahead, bewildered and curious, staring at Joshua.

"Turn around," Eddie said sharply. The boy and girl spun around and sat down.

"Grade five. My name's Eddie."

"I'm in grade five," Joshua answered.

They didn't speak the rest of the way.

When Joshua walked into the school, kids watched open-mouthed. The smallest children stood rock-still and stared, almost frightened. Eddie had experienced almost the same reaction in his first days of school.

In class Molly Watt, who sat in the desk behind Joshua, leaned forward to sniff at his back and reached up to touch his hair. Joshua ducked his head and turned to glare at her. Rodney Bell sat strangely quiet, but Eddie saw even the teacher watching Joshua when he wasn't looking.

At noon hour Joshua sat on a bench by the playground watching the boys and girls play games and take turns on the swings, looking as if he wanted to join them. Then Rodney and the Mullen brothers, Sam and Sid, walked up to Joshua and spoke to him. Eddie couldn't hear what they said, but Joshua jumped to his feet. Sam stepped forward and took a swing, but Joshua ducked and punched him on the jaw. Poor Sam fell backward, landing on the ground hard.

Rodney had more than likely convinced Sam to find out how tough Joshua was.

From the boardwalk Eddie saw Joshua and Sam standing side by side in the principal's office awaiting their fate. The curtain was snapped closed. Later he learned they both received four straps on each hand.

Joshua made a few friends—Eddie often saw them talking and laughing—until some big boys in grade eight began to make his life miserable. Then his friends disappeared. A month later, when he saw Joshua sitting by himself near the gymnasium eating lunch, Eddie felt bad about the way he was being treated. But he was also thankful that the spotlight was off him and shining brightly on Joshua instead.

One morning Eddie needed to use the bathroom before the bell sounded. When he walked in, two boys from his class who always regarded him with contempt were writing on the walls.

"Get outta here," one said.

"No." Eddie walked up to the urinal. He knew they wouldn't bother him because they were always big talk but no action.

When he finished, one of the boys handed him a red crayon. "Here. Take it."

It felt strange being asked to join in, even though he didn't understand what he was supposed to do.

"Just write something."

Eddie watched for a minute, reading what they wrote, and scrawled the same bad word on the mirror.

An hour later the door to Eddie's class opened and the principal walked into the classroom. "Eddie Toma, Freddy Beauchamp, and Herbert Tobin. Follow me to the office."

The three boys lined up side by side in the office. When the principal took the strap off its peg on the wall beside his desk, Eddie felt sweat run down his back. He had been strapped before, once on each hand. It stung a lot, but the trick was not to stick your hands in cold water right away. They needed to cool off naturally. And you never cried. You could make a face or say ouch, but no tears. Only sissies cried.

The principal slammed the strap on the desk so hard Eddie's ears rang. Mr. Latimer spoke in a calm voice. "Are you the ones responsible for the vandalism in the bathroom?"

"No," they answered.

"I'll ask one more time, and if you answer truthfully, I'll let you off with washing the walls in the boys' and girls' bathrooms and a week of noon hours sitting in my office. If you don't, well, I'll give you three guesses what will happen. And the last two don't count."

Freddy and Herb confessed immediately.

Mr. Latimer gave Eddie a hard look. "Looks like you're all alone, Toma. Are you sure you didn't have anything to do with this?"

"Yes."

"You two, wait out in the hall."

Sitting on the edge of his desk, the principal handed a note pad and pen to Eddie. "Do me a favour, will you? I want you to write something down for me. Think of the worst word you can come up with that would describe a coloured person and write it down for me."

Eddie hesitated. He looked up at the principal. Something didn't feel right. He was being tricked somehow.

"Don't look at me. Just write it down. Now," the principal said loudly.

Eddie scribbled quickly and handed back the pad.

"Are you sticking to your story that it wasn't you that wrote on the bathroom mirror? Last chance."

Eddie wanted to tell the truth but couldn't bring himself to admit to doing such a thing. He felt like the worst person in the world, and he was embarrassed that people would think he was like the ones that called Joshua by that same name.

"You know, Eddie, you're not only a liar, and a bad one at that, you're a lousy speller. There are two Gs in that word. For the life of me, I can't understand how you can write a word like that. You of all people. What were you trying to prove? How did you think he was going to feel? Was it your intention to scare him to death after everything that boy has been through? Please tell me. I'd like to know."

"I don't know," Eddie said softly.

"Speak up."

"I don't know," Eddie repeated louder.

"Well, I do. I know you think it's only a word, but when people use words that are so hateful, it shows the level of that person's intelligence. Or lack thereof. How do you react when people call you names? And I don't mean names like 'stupid' or 'sissy.' I mean names like 'redskin' or 'Comanche' or 'Cochise.' Do you like being called those names?"

Eddie looked away.

"Answer me."

"No. I mean, I don't like it."

"I don't suppose you do. You know, Eddie, I know just about everything that goes on around here. I hear the names kids call other kids, and when I do, I try to deal with it as swiftly as possible because I have no time for bullies and name callers. But of all the people in this school, Eddie, I thought you would be the last person in the world to call someone a name just because of the colour of their skin."

The principal turned to reach for the curtains. Eddie wanted to say that he had only done what the boys were doing so they would think he was one of them. But he knew there was nothing he could say now. It was too late. Just before the curtains closed, Eddie saw Eva on the sidewalk looking up at him.

Eddie was strapped four times on each hand. He didn't cry. The real pain he suffered back in class from the looks of his fellow students and on the bus when Eva ignored him.

A week later Joshua stumbled up the stairs at lunchtime, blood streaming down his face from a gash on his forehead. Mr. Latimer called an assembly. In front of the entire school, he loosened his tie and rolled up his shirt sleeves. As he picked up the strap and lifted it over his head, everyone became instantly quiet. He struck the table so hard that bits of paper floated in the air. Everybody, even the teachers, jumped.

"I will hunt down the people responsible for doing such a thing in this school. You mark my word," he said. He ranted for a half hour before ordering everybody back to class.

No one challenged Joshua publicly again, but the trouble didn't stop. It happened secretly through notes left on his desk or voices within a crowd. Joshua attended school for three months. Then one day he stopped coming. Eddie often wondered if Joshua thought of him the same way that he himself thought of Rodney Bell.

14

The first Saturday morning Eddie saw his mother in her bedroom dressed in her best clothes, putting on bright red lipstick, he wondered where they would be going. Maybe they would catch the bus to town and have a hamburger steak at the Silver Grill.

"Should I change, Mom?" he asked.

She capped the lipstick with a click and dropped it into her purse. Then she pulled out a pack of Du Maurier cigarettes. The red pack matched her lipstick. She looked pretty. Her eyes centred on Eddie. She pulled a cigarette from the pack and lit it with a match. As she inhaled the smoke, her right hand swung back and forth to put out the match. But the flame stayed.

"You're going to look after things today. You're old enough now. I have to get out of this place before I go crazy. There's stew in the pot and buns in the breadbox. Just don't bother your grandma, she won't like—Ow. Dammit," she said, dropping the match. "I'll be back on the bus at 10:30 tonight." She put her finger to her lips as she turned and walked out the door.

Eddie and Lewis stood at the picnic ground and watched as she hurried across the highway. On the shoulder she looked down the road in the direction of Falkland. No traffic was coming in either direction, and it was quiet except for the gravel rolling under her restless feet.

When she saw a Greyhound bus coming down the road, her body relaxed. She put out her arm and waved. Just before the bus pulled alongside, she looked over at them as if saying goodbye. Eddie wondered if he would ever see her again.

Eddie began to dread Saturdays. Neither he nor Lewis were keen on walking up to the highway to meet her. But every Saturday evening they were there early, standing in the dark, waiting. Lewis jumped at the slightest sound, so Eddie showed him the Big Dipper and the North Star.

"See those last two stars at the end of the Big Dipper's bowl? They point right to it. It looks like the dipper in the bucket at home. And the handle is bent like ours."

They could hear the bus even before they saw it. It was easy to tell the difference between the bus and the delivery and tanker trucks by the high whine of its tires. The loneliness Eddie had felt all day gave way to excitement when he saw the bus come around the corner with the three orange lights above its destination sign that read Kamloops. The bright headlights lit up the trees that seemed to stand taller, unafraid. After Grace stepped out of the bus, she and the boys walked home together.

But they could never be sure she would be there. Last week they watched the bus pick up speed and stood disappointed as the tires hit the bridge deck and the bus rocked up and down to the hiss of air ballasts. The tail lights faded into the distance, and the diesel exhaust swept into the trees and moved through the branches. They could smell the changed air as they walked back to the house under winking stars in the cold pitch dark. Sometime in the night Eddie heard her come into the house and stumble to her bedroom.

One Saturday Eddie and Lewis watched from across the road as Grace stepped into the Greyhound and walked down the aisle. When the driver leaned over and pulled on a lever, Eddie heard a light thump as the door swung shut. The bus eased back onto the road, belching black exhaust with a roar. It nodded and dipped as the driver worked his way through the gears. A woman sitting at the rear of the bus stared at the two boys standing under a tree. They watched the bus out of sight and walked home.

It was too hot to do much, so they sat in the doorway of the empty house, trying to think of something to do. Then they spotted someone walking down Range Road. The person turned down their driveway. It wasn't every day they saw white people approaching the house. Any that did stayed inside their cars with their windows rolled halfway down to ask directions.

Eddie saw it was Eva Cluff, dressed in cut-offs, leather sandals, and a red bikini top. As she came closer, Eddie realized there was something different about her. Maybe it was her clothes. Or the way she walked.

Eva joined them on the steps, and they talked for an hour until the sun drove them to find shade around the corner of the house. Eddie was surprised that Eva had taken the time to walk across the bridge for a visit. He wished there was a way for everyone to see her, to see how pretty she was. When it was time for her to leave, he would take her by Grandma's house. What would Grandma say? And he couldn't wait to see the look on Alphonse's face when he saw Eva walking with him down the path.

"I'm so thirsty. Can I have a glass of water, please?" Eva asked.

Eddie hurried inside the house and grabbed the dipper off the wall. He filled it from the water bucket, and when he turned around, Eva stood inside the doorway with a peculiar look on her face. After she took a sip of water, Eddie poured the rest back into the pail and hung the dipper on the wall. Puzzled by her expression, Eddie turned to see if she had seen a mouse run across the floor or maybe a spider. But he couldn't see anything out of the ordinary.

The kitchen table was cluttered with dirty cups and glasses stacked on top of plates and bowls. Large-eyed flies buzzed around the brim of the slop bucket, jumping over each other in a game of leapfrog. Eva approached Eddie's and Lewis's bedroom and placed both hands on the door frame as if afraid of being pulled inside by a dark force. The bed was covered in a layer of coats, clothes hung out of a dresser's half-opened drawers, and two bunches of socks and underwear—one mound dirty, the other clean—lay in the corner. Sometimes Eddie forgot which was which and just put on the cleanest-smelling pair.

Eva walked to the middle of the kitchen. "Do you boys want me to help you do dishes? I do them all the time when I'm at home. I like doing dishes and I like cleaning. My parents think I'm crazy because I always seem to be picking things up and wiping them off. Maybe they're right. I just can't sit still until everything is clean. Let's give your mom a surprise when she gets home. I think she'll really appreciate the effort."

She lifted the lid off the stove reservoir and saw it was half-filled with warm water from the morning's fire. "Do you have soap?"

Eddie reached under the water stand for the box of laundry detergent and bottle of bleach.

"Good. Now make a fire so we can heat up more water. You go ahead and do that, Eddie. Lewis can get the broom and sweep the floor. Just make a pile right in the middle of the room."

Eddie had a fire roaring up the chimney in no time. Eva emptied the buckets into the big kettle, took the stove lid away, and placed the kettle on the open flame.

"You better get some more, Eddie. We're gonna need plenty of hot water."

With a pail in each hand, Eddie set off for the river at a dead run and at first didn't see Alphonse and Grandma sitting in the shade at the back of the house. Grandma said something, but he didn't hear. On his way back she stood in the middle of the trail, blocking his way.

"What the hell is going on? Why are you runnin' around with buckets of water? I can smell smoke. Is the house on fire or something?"

"No. We're boiling water."

"What for?"

"For washing dishes," Eddie answered breathlessly.

"Washing dishes?"

"Yeah, we want to surprise Mom. She'll appreciate the effort."

Grandma looked at him as if she didn't hear right.

"What are you talking like that for? You're acting stupid like something funny's going on. Is there?"

"No. Mom said we had to clean the house. That's what we're doing. When she gets back, she'll be surprised."

"She'll fall over dead. That's what's gonna happen. Well, go ahead then. Just don't burn the house down."

Eddie ran up the steps into the house. Lewis had rounded up all the empty cans and cardboard boxes into one big pile. Eva was up to her elbows in suds, rattling the plates in the metal bowl Eddie's mother kept under her bed.

"This is sure a nice big bowl Lewis gave me. I can get twice the dishes in this one than in the other one your mom uses."

Eddie's mouth fell open when he saw the bowl. Lewis looked at Eddie as though he wasn't sure he'd done the right thing. Grace got angry if she got out of bed in the night to take a pee and couldn't find the bowl anywhere because they'd taken it.

"Take that slop bucket and dump it somewhere far away from here, Eddie. And I think you should leave it out on the porch. That way all the bugs don't come in the house and get into everything. When you're finished, rinse it with water and pour a little bleach in the bottom."

The plates were stacked in neat piles in the cupboard. Cups sat in straight rows in front of the saucers. The knives, forks and spoons were arranged in sections in the cupboard drawer. The damp floor looked new after Eva scrubbed out the grooves in the bare planks with a stiff brush. Even the stand where the buckets of water and the basin were kept had been washed with bleach. The black ring on the floor left by the slop pail was gone, and

Eva had pulled down the spider webs in the corners of the room with a broom.

Eddie and Lewis were given the job of cleaning up their bedroom and separating the clean clothes from the heap on the floor. Eva told them to take all the coats off the bed and hang them on the nails on the wall. Eddie didn't tell her that as soon as she left, the coats would go right back on the bed for blankets. Whenever the brothers finished a job, Eva found something else that needed doing.

Finally, one hour and four buckets of water later, Eddie and Lewis sat exhausted at the kitchen table. Eva wiped a damp rag across the backsplash of the stove, dropped it on the table and sat down. Eddie couldn't believe it was the same house. Sweat trickled down between his shoulder blades. He was hot and thirsty and couldn't wait to hear what his mother had to say. She was in for a big shock, especially after he told her Eva Cluff had done it all.

As they strolled down the hill toward Grandma's, Eva undid her ponytail and shook out her hair so that it fell around her face. There was a scratch on her forearm and her knees were dirty. Anyone could look good wearing clean clothes after a bath, Eddie thought, but nobody would look as good as Eva dirty and sweaty.

At the corner of the house Eddie saw his grandma and Alphonse sitting in the shade. Grandma sat up straight, her eyes locked onto Eva. Alphonse's gaze roamed up and down as if his eyes had suddenly become extensions of his hands. Eddie realized his plan had been a mistake. No one spoke.

Eva broke the silence by approaching Grandma. She held out her hand. "Hello. I'm Eva Cluff. My family lives just across the river. You must be Eddie's grandma that I've heard so much about. Pleased to meet you."

Grandma lifted her hand, her fingers hanging limp. Eva shook once. Grandma's hand fell lifeless on her lap. Then Eva leaned toward Alphonse as far as she could without taking a step and gave his hand a quick lift. For a second it looked as if she had to pull her hand away. She placed both hands out of sight behind her back. Seeing that Grandma wasn't about to speak, she looked at Eddie as if he would know what to do.

"Well, it's been nice meeting you." She glanced at Alphonse. "The both of you."

Eva walked up the road. As Eddie and Lewis fell in step beside her, Eddie looked back. Grandma's eyes moved off Eva to him. Eddie turned away but felt her stare burning his back.

"Your grandma scares me, Eddie. Why is she so quiet?"

Eddie had been embarrassed by her silence. "She doesn't talk."

"You mean she doesn't understand English?"

"No. It was an accident. She lost her tongue in an accident."

Lewis looked over at Eddie. Eddie gave him a warning stare.

"Who was that man?"

"Uncle Alphonse."

"Doesn't have much to say either, does he? Is there something wrong with him? Is he a little . . . slow . . . or something?"

"Yeah. I guess so," Eddie answered.

Eddie watched Eva rush across the bridge. It had been a great day and would have been perfect if only he had taken the road instead of going past Grandma's. He knew she was angry but couldn't see any reason. All Eva had done was to help clean the house. What was wrong with that?

"How come you said Grandma lost her tongue? I seen her licking her fingers lots of times," Lewis said.

"She did. But she got it sewed back on, and now she can't talk to white people."

"You're lying."

"Ask her if you don't believe me and see what happens. I asked her once, and she gave me a licking."

Eddie took the long way home down Range Road. Even though they were well out of earshot, he tried not to make noise walking across the cattle guard. If Grandma walked up a small knoll near her house, she could see through an opening in the trees up to a spot in the road. Eddie hoped the heat of the day would keep her in the shade. But when he peeked down the opening, he saw her waiting.

"Get over here," she called with an angry jerk of her arm.

They stepped through tangled brush and stood in front of her.

"What you bringin' a *summa* over here for?"

"I didn't. She walked over by herself."

"What for?"

"I dunno."

"Don't know. Don't know. What do you know?"

Eddie kept his eyes pinned on his grandma's eyebrows that were inching closer together.

"What did she mean, she heard about me? You been talkin' about me or somethin'? Huh? What you been sayin'?"

"Nothing."

"Nothin'. You don't know much and you don't remember nothin'. What's got into you? You think a girl like that gives a damn about you? All she wants to do is come and see how we live so she can go back and they can all have a good laugh at us. How long she been up there? What she been doin'?"

"I don't know," Eddie said weakly.

Lewis answered. "She cleaned the house."

"Oh, I bet it was good and dirty for her too. Well, I feel sorry for you guys when your mom gets home. She's gonna skin you like a rabbit. Now go on get outta here and don't bring any more *summas* over here."

Grandma would have said more but stopped and put her hand over her mouth to keep her dentures from falling out.

"Is it your tongue, Grandma?" Lewis asked.

"What? What did you say?" She looked around her on the ground for a switch.

Eddie moved away, careful not to do it too quickly; he needed just the right amount of humility in his walk. He heard the door slam shut but didn't look back.

"Hey," Alphonse called to them.

Eddie looked back as his uncle pinched the top of his nose, blew hard, and squeezed off the snot that hung down in a stretchy string. A flick of his hand sent it flipping through the air. He wiped his fingers on his pant leg.

"You never mind what she said."

Eddie thought for a moment he was being kind.

"Give that little girl a couple hot summers, and then she can come clean our house any time. I'll even let her give me a bath and wash my back," he said with a smirk.

Eddie walked away disgusted.

Grace stepped off the bus smelling of sweet perfume, stale beer, and cigarette smoke. She was unsteady on her feet, so the brothers each took an arm to help. She stumbled and laughed too loudly.

"You are good boys for waiting for me," she said, pulling them close, something she would never have said in the light of day.

When she walked inside the house, Eddie dreaded what she would say.

"Who done this?" she asked.

Eddie wanted to explain it slowly, but Lewis blurted out the story in one long sentence. Grace looked from Lewis to Eddie.

"She the one you always talked about?"

"Uh-huh."

Grace nodded her head as she swept her eyes around her clean kitchen. She pulled out a chair at the table and sat down. Five minutes went by before she spoke.

"She did a good job. But don't you bring any more *summas* over here again. And you done such a good job, this is something you both can do every Saturday from now on."

15

1964

Just as the logging truck rounded the bend, Eddie and Lewis took off running. They made it all the way across and up the bank to the fence before the truck even made it onto the bridge. The driver gave a blast of his air horn and the support timbers creaked when he crossed the bridge. The logs sticking out the back of the load wobbled like spaghetti.

They lingered to watch the cars go by. Eddie always found it hard to find anything fun to do after school. Plenty of jobs waited for him but nothing to hurry home for. He laughed when Lewis made faces at a staring woman. A Volkswagen bus filled with laughing girls and boys looked like they were having fun as they went speeding by.

The brothers stepped through a stretched square of page-wire and walked down the trail. When they topped the hill above Grandma's, Eddie was the first one to spot the car parked at the door. Lewis ran on ahead but stopped at the door to wait. Eddie tried to remember if he'd ever seen the car before. It looked like the one he had seen in a Yakima street when his mother had punched the driver years ago, but the car still looked new with its shining paint and gleaming chrome.

They walked in to see a man sitting at the kitchen table. He had long sideburns and greased hair that drooped down over his forehead in an Elvis-style waterfall Eddie had seen in a magazine. The man stood and jammed his hands into his pockets. His white shirt with upturned collar was unbuttoned down below his chest and tucked into blue jeans, and each of his brown shoes had a coin tucked into a strip of leather across the instep.

Grace came out of her bedroom. "It's about time, you guys. I told you before to get right back here as soon as you get off that bus."

She rubbed the back of her left hand with her fingers and nodded to the man beside her. "Anyway, this is your dad. This is Jimmy."

Eddie wasn't sure he heard correctly. "What?"

"I said, this is your dad."

Grace's arms were folded tightly, and she didn't look very happy. Eddie had imagined something a little more cheerful if he ever met his father. Lewis stepped forward. Jimmy gave him a bear hug. Seeing Eddie still hadn't made a move, Grace walked over and put her hand behind his neck, pulling him forward. Eddie lifted her hand away.

Jimmy laughed. His eye teeth looked like fangs. When Eddie didn't make any effort to greet his father, Grace gave a grunt and went to the stove. She lifted the lid and jammed wood inside.

"Everybody quit standing around. It's time to make supper. You boys go bring some wood in and hurry up about it," she said.

Eddie eyed the man sitting at the head of the table. He ate with his mouth open, and everybody could hear him slurping and gulping when he swallowed. Eddie knew that if he and Lewis ate like that, his mother would tell them to stop eating like pigs, but she ate quietly and stared at a spot on the table. Already he couldn't stand this man.

Jimmy finished with a loud burp. "I brought my phonograph and records but I saw you still don't have power yet. I thought you would've by now. I was wondering if I should bring it in or not."

"We got one of those big dry batteries hooked up to the radio. Can't we hook it up somehow so we can get music in here? You always been good at doing stuff like that."

"I'll give it a whirl. But I don't think that battery is strong enough. We'll give her a go as soon as I'm finished."

Jimmy wound wires around the battery terminals and fastened them to the record player plug, then wiped his hands on a rag and opened the box of records.

"What do you want to hear? I got some new ones. How about Elvis, or Fats Domino? Huh?"

"You know who I like," Grace said.

Jimmy took care to lift the record albums out one at a time before he slid them back down into place. When he found the one he wanted, he eased the record out of its jacket, placed it on the turntable, and clicked on the switch. The battery wasn't strong enough, so he put his finger on the turntable and spun it faster. They could barely make out the voice of the singer.

That night Lewis couldn't stop talking about his dad, but Eddie wanted to sleep and covered his head with a pillow. Lewis's voice pierced through the feathers.

"Dad said he was going to make me a soapbox derby racer. He said in the States they have races and they get prizes and even money sometimes. Dad said the little hill would be a good place to learn me all about it. Dad said you were probably too old to want one because you never said anything. Dad said—"

"I was sitting right beside you. I heard him. You think I'm deaf or something? Shut up and go to sleep."

Lewis's chatter had driven the sleep from Eddie. Long after his brother dozed off, he lay in the dark staring up at the ceiling, trying to sort out his thoughts. He had gone down to his grandma's after supper to tell her the news. It turned out Grandma hated Jimmy.

"I don't believe it. You mean he's up there right now? Damn him anyway. I thought I got rid of that bugger. What's wrong with that mom of yours? She used to swear every time she talked about him. She said she couldn't trust him at all. When they were together they'd get so stupid sometimes, holding hands and making eyes at each other. Maybe that's why he left. Maybe they both got sick of each other. God almighty. He's a no-good devil, that one. You watch. Soon as something happens, he'll leave again. But it sounds like they kissed and made up already.

"If I was you, I'd get back home and hide all your toys. He's probably up there playing with them right now. Makes me sick just thinkin' about him. He's lucky I'm not a man. Boy, if I was, I'd go up there right now and stand him on his head." She waved Eddie away with the back of her hand. "Go on. And don't come down here bragging about him to me. You go right back up there and give that good-for-nothing dad of yours a big kiss."

Alphonse looked up from his pocketbook western and snickered.

Maybe Grandma was right, Eddie thought in the dark. His mother had hardly talked about Jimmy in the past. The times that she had, she said they were better off without him. He'd even seen her chase after him and punch him in the face. If that was the way she felt, why was he here? As Eddie tried to make sense of it all, he heard squeaking bedsprings in his mother's bedroom.

The next morning Grace and Jimmy sat at the table blowing steam off cups of coffee. The woodbox was piled high with split wood and kindling. Condensation trickled down the sides of the full metal pails like rain on a window.

Grace filled two bowls with porridge and set them in front of Eddie and Lewis. She reached down to take Jimmy's plate away, but he put his arm around her waist and pulled her down on his lap. Her face turned red as she struggled to get away. Jimmy stuck his jaw into her neck and dug his fingers into her sides until she laughed and squirmed. When she pulled away, Jimmy finished his coffee, jumped to his feet, and picked up a dish towel. After the last plate was put away, he hugged Grace from behind and bit her lightly on the ear. Pushing him away, Grace threw the wet dishrag at him and he grabbed her by her arms. She threw back her head, laughing.

The brothers glanced at each other. Eddie couldn't stay in the house any longer to watch all the funny business going on, and he motioned Lewis to come with him.

Jimmy wheeled around. "Where you going, guys?"

"Outside."

"Hold on just a minute. I need you both to give me a hand."

Eddie saw his reflection in the car's paint as they approached. The fire engine red rims and chrome hubcaps were framed by wide whitewall tires. Black fender skirts on the rear wheel wells showed only the bottom part of the tires. A raccoon tail was tied to the aerial. Eddie reached out to the fender to see if it was as smooth as it appeared.

"Don't touch that," Jimmy snapped.

Eddie pulled his hand away. A slow heat rose to his face.

"You don't touch a paint job like that. Your sweaty fingers takes away the shine. What's wrong with you?"

Jimmy turned the key in the trunk, and it opened with a click. He pulled out two boxes and gave one to Lewis.

"Here, take this into the house and put it on the table. I'll be there in a minute," he said.

"Oh, it's so heavy," Lewis said with a smile.

"Here. This one's yours." Jimmy handed Eddie a long narrow box.

Jimmy pocketed the keys and put both hands on the trunk lid, palms out, and brought it down gently. He leaned forward to blow across the trunk at a piece of lint that had appeared out of nowhere. Turning to go back inside, he didn't take his eyes off his car until he reached the door.

The box made a scratching sound when Eddie placed it on the table and gave a hard shove. Lewis looked at his mother for an explanation, but she shrugged her shoulders.

"Open it up, Lewis, and see what you got there," Jimmy said.

Lewis pulled back the flaps. The box was filled with marbles. "Wow. These are all for me?"

"All yours. I stopped at my mom's and picked them up. I couldn't believe she kept them all these years. When I was your age, I won all these at school. I never had to buy one single marble in my life. We'll go outside later, and I'll show you how it's done."

"Holy cow," Lewis said.

"Open yours now, Eddie," Grace said.

Eddie looked at the way she was smiling at Jimmy. The ever-changing mood of the household was confusing. He pulled off the binder twine wrapped around the box that smelled of dried alfalfa. Pulling back the cardboard lid, he saw the stock and iron barrel of a single-shot .22 rifle.

The gun was old but had been well taken care of. Someone had kept the wood oiled so the grains wouldn't crack or dry out, and there wasn't a sign of rust anywhere on the polished steel. The only marks on the gun were notches carved into the butt. A shoulder strap was attached at both ends of the wooden stock. Tucked inside the box were a tin of 3-In-One Oil and a neatly folded rag. How could Jimmy have known that when all the kids at school wanted ponies and toys, all Eddie wanted was what he now held in his hands? He felt as if his insides were being tickled with a feather.

"Pick it up. It's the gun my grandpa gave me on my thirteenth birthday," Jimmy said.

The gun fit Eddie's hands perfectly as he lifted it from the box. His ears felt hot.

"Thanks," he said.

"See all the nicks there? Those are all deer kills. We ate a lot of grouse and rabbit for a while until Mom got tired of doing all the plucking and skinning. She said cleaning fish was easier. Tell you what. After I show Lewis a few tricks, we'll go up to the range and do some target practice. I got a eagle eye and a box of shells. You hang on to that gun. Don't let anything happen to it."

Jimmy dug a hole under the clothesline tree and showed Lewis how to toss the large cob. He leaned forward demonstrating how to use the bounce of his body. Jimmy made him stare at the pot until he had the location memorized and toss his shooter with his eyes closed. Eddie could hear the impatience growing in Jimmy's voice each time Lewis missed. Lewis didn't do well under pressure, and Eddie knew he couldn't hit the hole now if it was four feet wide. He wasn't even coming close. Lewis's nerves were obvious when his marble landed two feet past the hole.

"What's the matter with you? Are you even listening to me? Lean ahead like I told you. Come on."

Eddie glanced back and saw his mother standing in the doorway. He waited for her to say something, but she just stood and watched. Eddie turned away. He was angry enough that, even though he knew there would be trouble, he would tell Jimmy to lay off. But before he could speak, Lewis's marble fell into the hole.

"See, I told you. It's not that hard. You just have to practise more. Every night you're gonna come out here and sink at least five in a row. That's what I did. That's why you got all them marbles," Jimmy said.

Jimmy didn't want to take his car on the rough road up to the range, but Grace said the truck had broken down and nobody knew how to fix it. Jimmy brought out a metal case from his trunk and spread his tools out on the ground. He worked under the truck for so long that Eddie wondered if they would ever get going. Finally, Jimmy crawled out, put his tools back into the toolbox, and switched batteries with his car. After poking a stick into the gas tank to check for fuel, he told the boys to get into the back of the truck. Then he poured gasoline into the throat of the carburetor and turned the starter. The truck roared with a puff of smoke. Sputtering and backfiring, it chugged up the driveway and made the turn toward the range.

Since World War II the army had taken over a large corner of the range to train militia and cadets. Each summer, for as long as Eddie could remember, they returned to set up camps the size of small towns with tents lined up like a game of checkers. Popping and rattling gunshots could be heard from morning until late afternoon.

One summer, during a long period of hot weather, long lines of vehicles drove up and down the dirt road all day long until Eddie's house was covered in a layer of dust. That day, after going out to the clothesline to bring in the washing, Grace had had enough. For years she had written letters to the Indian Affairs office in town about the army vehicles going up and down the road and making a mess. But as with her letters about the bridge, she received no answer.

At noon that day Grace and her family drove over the cattle guard so fast they were airborne. Ploughing past a checkpoint, she barely missed the sentry before skidding to a stop in the centre of the camp. Eddie and Lewis were alarmed to see men with rifles approach the truck. An officer listened as she held up their clothes and told him they were dirtier than before she had washed them. Grace ignored several warnings to leave or face arrest by the military police, then drove away. Nothing was done about the road, but at the end of summer, when the army packed up to leave, a jeep drove to Eddie's house and dropped off boxes of food rations: canned fruit and vegetables, instant mashed potatoes, and powdered milk.

Now the truck sped uphill on an old track overgrown with brush and saplings. Jimmy manoeuvred the truck around fallen trees and washouts as the boys held on to the roof rain trough. They ducked when a low-hanging bough brushed across the top of the truck. The needles scratching the metal sounded like fingernails on a blackboard. Every so often they saw a sign written in oversized red letters nailed to a tree, warning of unexploded bombs and live ammunition.

Every year in late spring, when parts of the range turned bright yellow, Grace and the two boys walked up to see the unreal colours.

On Eddie's first trip as a four-year-old, he'd spent an afternoon hunting for flowers and fallen asleep under a pine tree. Awakened by sounds coming from the tall grass, he imagined snakes crawling everywhere. But when he looked closer, he saw only small birds fluttering among the grass stalks.

The truck was noisy, but Eddie could still make out the birds piping back and forth. A meadowlark rushed across the road with its wing hanging down, a trick meant to attract danger away from its nest. After the truck passed, the meadowlark stood up straight and folded its wings.

When the land levelled off and the fir trees gave way to scrubby pine, they came to a fork in the road. They could either keep right for an extra few minutes of bone-jarring travel or take a shortcut up a steep hill. The rising face of the hill was scarred by tracks of army trucks and motorcycles that had tried to make it to the summit. Each time Grace had driven past the spot, Eddie and Lewis had begged her to give the hill a try. She wouldn't try it even once.

Suddenly the truck veered left. Through the glass Eddie saw his mother's hand on the door handle as if she planned to jump out. With the motor revving a high-whining roar, they sped toward the hill. Twenty feet from the base of the hill, terror and excitement came over Eddie. At the steepest part, where the road seemed to go straight up, the tires kicked up rocks and dirt like a mad bull. It was almost impossible to keep from falling out the back. Eddie heard a shout from Lewis and saw him giggling with such a wild look that he feared his little brother might lose his grip.

"Hang on, stupid," he warned.

But his voice was drowned by the racing engine. Just as the motor was about to stall, the front end of the truck dropped down onto level ground. Jimmy had done it. He switched off the engine and stepped out of the truck.

"What do you think of that, boys?" he asked, beaming.

"Can we do it again?" Lewis asked.

"Better not. I think I scared your mom a bit," Jimmy said. "Anyway, Lewis, you go catch up with your mom while me and Eddie do some shooting."

Jimmy pulled the gun from behind the seat of the truck, slipped the shoulder strap over his head, and picked up a box that rattled with tin cans and bottles.

"Wait right here," he ordered.

Jimmy walked over to a spot fifty feet away and lined up the bottles and cans. As he walked toward Eddie, he dipped his shoulder and the gun slid into his hands. He smiled and winked. "Okay. First things first. This is a single-shot rifle and takes only one shell at a time."

Jimmy opened the box of shells. The brass and grey lead jackets of the rows of shells looked like soldiers. Jimmy jerked back the bolt, placed a shell into the chamber of the rifle, and pushed the bolt forward, locking it in place. With his thumb holding back the end of the bolt, Jimmy pointed the gun into the air and squeezed the trigger. The bolt slid forward and stopped.

"You see how I did that? I just put on the safety. That's the only way you got of not shooting yourself in the foot or somebody in the back. You make sure you do that every time you go hunting. That way you don't have to go digging around for a shell and miss a chance at a deer or something. After that you just pull back on the bolt slow until it clicks twice. Then you're ready. I'll fire off a few rounds to get it sighted."

Jimmy leaned against the truck, aimed at a target, and fired. The shell kicked up a spray of dust in front of a can.

"She's a little low."

He tore a strip off the cover of a book of matches and slid it under the rear sight, reloaded, and tried again. This time he was off to the right. He tapped the rear sight with a stone ever so softly, and Eddie couldn't see how it could possibly make a difference. He reloaded again. This time he shot over the top of the can. As the minutes went by, Jimmy fiddled with the gun, blaming it each time he missed. Finally on his fifth try he hit the can.

"Okay. It's good now. Your turn. Scoot yourself down on the ground. You'll be able to keep the gun steady that way."

Jimmy waited until Eddie found a comfortable position on his stomach before passing him the gun. He handed Eddie a shell and watched to make sure he loaded the gun correctly. Eddie smiled to himself but listened to instructions and did exactly what he was told. Lining up the dot of the front sight into the vee of the rear sight, he aimed at the centre of a bottle and squeezed the trigger. The bottle burst with a pop, scattering glass over the ground.

"Jiminy Crickets. Where'd you learn to shoot like that?"

Eddie shrugged his shoulders. Jimmy pulled the gun away. He ejected the empty shell and went down on one knee. He aimed at the target for a long time, held his breath and shot. The can spun away. He handed the gun back to Eddie. Eddie knew Jimmy thought that his hit was more luck than skill, so he took steady aim as if he were down to his last bullet, just as his mother had taught him.

Grace had her own way of teaching Eddie to shoot, with little money to spend on shells, and she'd used the old .30-06. It was a relic from World War I and had a kick like a horse. She wedged the gun between stones so there would be no movement and showed Eddie how to line up the sights on a target. After checking his aim, she gave him three shells. He had three chances to hit the target and wasn't to shoot until he was sure about his aim.

Now, as Eddie lined up his shot, he held his breath and pulled the trigger. The can flipped into the air. He passed the gun to Jimmy. As time went on, Eddie knew Jimmy was worried that he might be shown up, and he remembered how angry Jimmy had been after he'd touched his car. When Eddie lined up the sights again, for a second he considered missing the target on purpose. But he took aim and hit the can dead centre. Jimmy shook the empty box of shells.

"I guess that's it. We're all out of ammo."

They hurried down a narrow cow trail to a flat piece of ground on the slope where Grace and Lewis sat on an old tank turret. The three-inch-thick iron shell was speckled in shades of rust. Where the giant gun barrel had once poked through, knee-high grass now covered the opening.

"So you killed off all the cans and bottles? What a waste of shells," Grace muttered.

"Wasting shells? We had to get the gun sighted, for Pete's sake. What do you know about guns anyway?"

"Nothing. Nothing at all," she said.

Lewis and Eddie rolled a large rock over to where the hill dropped straight down. With a hard push, the rock rolled toward the bottom, bouncing and kicking up chunks of grass and dirt. Reaching the floor of the flatland, the rock rolled twenty feet before coming to a stop and tipped over on its side.

They sat looking out at the broad plateau that spread from the treed slopes in the east and the lakes in the west all the way to the southern skyline. The stubby bunch grass covering the plain looked like a deer hide spread over the land. The only object to stand out against the landscape was a single juniper tree in the centre. Most trees grew away from the wind, but the juniper leaned stubbornly forward. The tree had stood alone in the relent-less wind for so long that its trunk was twisted and crooked. Its sparse boughs drooped like umbrella spines.

"This place never changes," Jimmy said. "Like it won't let you change it. A long time ago, the chief of the Okanagans was asked by the cattle growers on the reserve to clear more land for grazing.

A lot of people had cows then. When *summas* were having a hard time in the Depression, our people did good. We had a herd that one family could look after for two years and they could keep the calves. Then somebody else had a turn. The chief said the range would be a good place to grow a newer, better grass so the cows would get fat and they could make a lot of money. Those guys started rubbing their hands together cuz they thought they were gonna be rich, so they met on the range in the spring.

"They started walking on the farthest corner with torches and set fire to the bunch grass. They all said that grass was good for nothing anyways. The tallest it ever got was half a foot high, and only the wild horses could graze it because it was so slow growing.

"The wind pushed them flames across that flat land until the smoke was so thick it was hard to tell the red sun from the sparks. Birds flew out of the grass, while all the little trapped animals were burned. Their bones popped like pitch wood. The wildflowers folded up to nothin', and the whistlin' gophers ran underground to wait for the fire to burn itself out. When that big flame reached the juniper, the heat lit the needles on the branches, and pretty soon you couldn't see anything but smoke. When the flames moved on, the men thought there would be only ashes left of the old juniper. But the tree was still standing. The wood at the heart of that juniper must be hard as iron.

"After the ground cooled off, the men walked in a line turning the handles of their seed spreaders. And when they finished, it rained and rained, and then the first grasses popped out of the ashes. Just what the chief and cattle growers hoped for. When the grass was a foot tall, the cattle growers released their cows onto the range, and they got good and fat.

"The next year the grass grew tall again from the spring rain, and all the cattle people came back with a bigger herd. But it didn't rain. No sir. Not until fall. That range was dryer'n a popcorn fart. There wasn't a drop fell that summer, and all that fancy new grass up and died. Well, the chief and cattle growers walked around with their bottom lips hangin' down because they didn't have money to plant the new grass. They spent it all."

Eddie laughed. That seemed to please Jimmy.

"So they rounded up their cows and took them home. The spring after that the rain didn't bring back the new grass, but the old bunch grass grew as tall as it was before the fire. And wildflowers came out of the ground again, and on the branches of that old juniper small buds showed up. And the bunch grass grew half a foot high, and only the horses could eat it."

No one spoke for a few minutes.

Jimmy jumped to his feet. "Let's vamoose, guys. Hop in the truck, and we'll go for a little tour. I ain't been up here in a long, long time."

Bouncing over boulders and jerking out of potholes, they drove off the rough ground onto an old road. The smoother ride allowed the brothers to kneel so they could look out through the windshield without the risk of cracking their kneecaps. Up ahead at the end of the road, on the other side of the reserve boundary where the upper high peaks met the range, stood an abandoned log cabin surrounded by poplar trees. The sod roof sagged in the middle as if it could cave in at any time. No one knew much about the cabin's history except that it was called the old Smith place. It had been there for as long as anyone could remember.

Jimmy drove through an opening in the barbwire fence and parked in the shade of the trees. When he switched off the engine, it gave a slow groan.

Eddie wanted to wash the dust from his face and eyes and have a drink from the creek that had the coldest, sweetest water he'd ever tasted. He raced around the cabin. But instead of the two-foot-wide flow he'd hoped for, he found only a small trickle at the bottom of a stony trench.

"What you looking for?" Grace asked, coming around the corner of the old house.

"I wanted a drink from the creek, but it's almost all dried up," he said.

"Yeah, we're a little too late, I guess."

"Shhh . . . quiet," Jimmy whispered loudly. He cocked his head to the side, straining to hear. "I remember that sound."

Below a steep rock cliff stood a column of ponderosa pine. The great trees swept at the clouds, creaking and groaning like ship masts. Heavy boughs waved and dropped cones to the ground where they spiralled away with a click. The wind washing through the needles made a calming hush. Eddie leaned back to watch the clouds race past, his body swaying with the trees.

"Hey. You guys hear something? What is that? Is it thunder?" Jimmy asked.

The ground shook with a drumming sound as if rising from the centre of the earth. "Look. Up there," Jimmy said, pointing.

Eddie saw running horses coming down the mountain like a vee of geese. As they came closer, Eddie spotted the lead horse, a bay stud, at the front of the pounding feet and bobbing heads. His long tail whipped the wind like a banner, and his feet kicked up saucer-sized chunks of earth that flipped in the air like pancakes. Closer and closer they came, twisting, turning, and plunging down the steep hill. Yearling colts stumbled as they tried to keep up, aware of the laid-back ears and bared teeth of old mares behind them.

At the base of the mountain, the herd turned to the right like a wave of sparrows and sailed over the single strand of drooping barbwire hanging between the leaning posts. With a quick turn of his head the stud swung to the side, spun around, and stopped to face the humans. The herd closed in behind him, and twenty sets of guarded eyes watched. Hot breath blew dust out of rattling nostrils. A mare answered a lost foal's whinny somewhere among the milling hooves. The stud pulled his head high, stamped his hooves, and pranced forward lightly as a deer. Stopping thirty feet away, the stud observed the people for a moment before he snorted, tossed his head, and pivoted around on his rear legs. He galloped away. The herd turned and broke into a run behind him.

"Jeez. You see that? He was giving us a once-over. Man oh man. There's only a couple dozen of the wild horses left now. Looks like they're going to water down at the lake," Jimmy said. "There used to be a hundred of them around when I was a kid.

"There was this stud we called Snowball. He was white with big hairy feet and a mane full of burrs, and his hide was covered in scars. If another stud even set foot on his ground, he would hunt him down and run him off or just kick the shit out of him. Me and Pop rode up here once looking for deer and we seen him chasing this little grey. It was something to see. That little horse was running for his life. I don't know how far they ran, but he was gone for quite a while. When he got back, he went after my horse and almost took a piece outta my leg. Then he turned around and starts putting the boots to us. Pop lets a shot go behind him and he just stands there. When we start to leave, well, the chase is on again. The old man said these horses were just left here, and they went kinda wild. Shitters, everybody calls them, because that's all they were good for. But you shoulda seen that old stud. He was something."

They watched the herd disappear over the hill.

"I don't know about you guys, but I'm getting hungry. My stomach sounds like a bear in heat. Let's skedaddle," he said.

A grey light began spreading across the range as the sun slipped out of sight behind Blue Grouse Mountain on the west side of the valley. They drove down the long road to the bottom, coasting the last quarter of a mile with the motor turned off. Fenders rattled as the truck drifted sideways on washboard corners. Rocks flipped from under the tires with a hum. Cool air floating back into Eddie's face made his eyes water.

The road curved alongside Madeline Lake, where Eddie saw fish surfacing for bugs. Only the wake of the ever-moving coots broke its smooth reflection of the valley walls. Dust behind the truck lifted from the road and rolled out across the water like smoke. Deep tracks in the mud at the lake edge left behind by cows gave the air a musky smell. Small twisters of no-see-ums swirled inches above the water. The truck clattered over the cattle guard and turned down the driveway to home.

Jimmy rested the rifle on two spikes he drove into Eddie and Lewis's bedroom wall. The gun was the last thing Eddie saw that night before he fell asleep and it was the first thing he saw when he awoke the next morning. His eyes wandered up and down the length of the gun as he lay with his hands behind his head, amazed at the feeling the gun gave him.

16

Eddie woke the next morning, surprised he had the bed to himself. Pulling the blanket over his nose, he smelled the milky aroma of sleep coming off his body, and he held his breath and squeezed out a fart. The house was quiet except for the sound of someone slurping hot coffee.

"Mom?"

"Nope. Only me," Jimmy said. "They went to visit the old battle-axe. Your grandma. Anyways, get outta that fart sack."

Eddie pulled on his clothes and walked into the kitchen. Jimmy held his cup in both hands. His chair was tipped back on two legs and his feet rested on top of the table.

"Pull up a stump," he said as he reached under the table with his foot to slide out a chair.

Eddie heard the plop of porridge cooking on the stove. Someone hadn't put the cover back on. Nothing was worse than overcooked porridge. A large bubble grew and grew until it popped, spitting ragged bits of oatmeal against the back of the stove.

"Better pull that pot away from there before she blows," Jimmy said.

Eddie walked to the stove and pushed the pot off the heat.

"Have one of your mom's buns."

Jimmy picked one off the table and banged it against his chair leg. "Real squirrel-killers, these things."

"There's better stuff than that," Eddie said.

The hinge of the breadbox let out a squeal as Eddie opened the door to pull out a loaf of bread. He cut off a thick slice with the butcher knife, slid the loaf back inside, and refastened the door. "It's good if you keep it in the box. If you don't, it gets so hard you can't even eat it."

He spread butter and jam over the bread and ate while Jimmy watched.

"How's school? You doin' okay?"

"Yeah."

"You like it?"

"It's all right."

"Good. That's good."

Jimmy pulled a pouch of tobacco and papers from his shirt pocket and quickly twisted up a cigarette. After lighting a match with his thumbnail, he sucked the flame deep inside the cigarette and blew smoke rings that floated toward the stove and disintegrated in the rising heat. Eddie watched the way he savoured each inhale as if it were candy. Wood popped in the stove.

"Why did you leave?"

Jimmy took a drink before setting his cup on the table. "Jesus, you sound like your mom."

He was quiet again. Eddie took a bite of bread.

"I came back for my pop's funeral. I never seen him for a long time. I was working down in Yakima when my mom got a hold of me. The miserable old coot. One of the last things he ever said to me was, 'Get outta here and don't come back.' What a thing for a dad to say to his kid."

Jimmy finished his coffee, stood, and placed the cup on the counter. Then he reached inside the cupboard and brought out a deck of playing cards. They were worn from years of use, and a few of the numbers were so faded they were hard to read. Sometimes a person had to count the clubs or spades and hearts and diamonds just to make sure. He shuffled the deck and laid out the cards for a game of solitaire.

"I'd never say something like that to you, Eddie. No matter what you done."

Eddie heard a sound in Jimmy's voice that made him look up. Jimmy brushed something out of his eye as he sat up straight and cleared his throat.

He slid a card out of the deck with his thumb, picked it up, and turned it over. Then he placed the red queen on a black king.

"The first thing I ever remembered about my pop when I was little was him yelling and swearing at me for not eating all the food in my bowl. I don't even remember what it was—cabbage, liver, something. Maybe I was full. I don't know. That's the first time I knew he hated me. And Mom just sat there and never said a word. All the years I was growing up he beat the hell outta me, and she don't even try to stop him. Not even once. It got so I couldn't be around Pop without him flying off the handle about something.

"Once he told me to dig a hole, and he gave me hell for piling the dirt on the wrong side. He never gave me no pat on the back for anything. I split and stacked two cords of wood when I was eight years old, and Mom told me I done a good job. He told her to shut up and quit treating me like a baby. You know, I always wished he'd just keel over and die. He walked around thinking he was better than everybody. No wonder nobody liked him.

"About the only thing good I ever got from him was an old truck he bought cheap somewhere. It took me a long time to get that thing up and running. But I did it my own self. He never helped me at all. Then me and some of the boys used to drive around on the back roads of the reserve. Sometimes we'd go to the bootlegger and get beer. There's nothing better than drinking beer and listening to the radio. I still like to do that sometimes. We liked coming up to this part of the reserve because on the highest part of the range, you can pick up Spokane if you play with the dial a little bit."

"Was he always mean to you?" Eddie asked.

"Always. There was one time I thought he was tryin' not to be such a bastard. All day long I waited for him to say somethin' like how stupid I was or how I didn't do a good job of getting water or anything. So that night when I crawled in bed, I felt pretty good. I was almost asleep when he walked in the bedroom. He had the slop bucket and he held it in the air right above me like he was goin' to dump it on me. 'You forgot to take out the slop bucket again, you useless little prick.'

"He just held it there starin' at me with his eyes open so wide they looked like they were gonna pop outta his head. And his breathin'. I'll never forget that sound of his breathin'. I remember thinkin' that's what pure hate sounds like.

"Anyways, on the way home from the range one night, me and the guys seen there was a dance down at the band hall, so we drove over to have a look. We stayed for a while, but there was too many old people looking at us sideways. We were almost outta gas and then we seen this car a little way from the hall, just out of the lights. When we found an empty gallon wine jug laying behind the car, it was too good of an invitation, so I was elected to do the honours.

"I crawled under and poked a hole in the gas tank with a screwdriver and filled up the jug. Maybe if we weren't so drunk we wouldn't have made so damn much noise, and maybe we wouldn't have got caught. Anyway, this guy steps outta the shadows and he sees us before we can get away. I stayed at my friend's place, and the next morning that guy told Pop that he owed him a new gas tank. Nobody liked him except for Pop. They were the only friends either one of them had. I guess God made 'em and he matched 'em.

"Old Pop got so mad he took it out on my poor mom. When I came home, I can't find her. I look everywhere—in the shit house and the woodshed. Then I hear her calling my name, but I don't know where the hell she's at. Finally I look up, and there she is, crawled up a tree. That bastard hung a beating on her and might have killed her if she didn't get away. Here all this time I'm feeling bad because I can never please the old bastard, and he does something like that.

"After that I started talking back and getting even more beatings. One thing I'll say for him, though, he never once hit me with his hand. He always used a strap or a stick. He might give me a kick but he never raised a fist to me. He was good that way. Anyway, he corners me about something, and I can see what's gonna happen. He's got the strap all wrapped around his hand and then he starts whipping me and whipping me, and I ask him, 'Is that how you beat the shit outta your underwear? Go ahead. Swing harder. That don't hurt.'

"That gets him all fired up, so he starts using both hands. I just stand there looking him in the eye, watching him swinging like he's going for a home run. All the time he's doing it, I don't blink, not once, and after a while, I can't even feel it no more. And it really gets under his skin. Pretty soon he's arm-tired. Then he just quits. He stands there with his legs spread, breathing hard like a winded old cow. That's when he tells me to get out and never come back. You know how old I was? Sixteen. I told him right then and there that someday I'm gonna be bigger than him and I'll get him back. Before that day I found my mom up that tree, I don't remember him ever laying a hand on her. Maybe he waited until I was outta sight, I don't know. My mom said he never done that to her before, but she was probably lying."

"She was up the tree all night?" Eddie asked.

"Oh, you bet she was." Jimmy nodded his head. "I moved in with a buddy of mine on the far end of the reserve. We did some logging and fencing, and I stayed there a couple years. His folks felt more like family than my own. It's something when you wish you were born to different family.

"One day years later we headed into town on a Saturday night, starving for a Chinee meal at the Lotus Gardens. When we got there, I seen in the window my pop screaming at my mom, calling her down. She's just sitting there taking it. Too scared to even cry.

"I pushed back the doors like I was Gene Autry his own self and stepped right in front of my pop. He's drunk, and he's got spit hanging from his mouth. When he sees it's me, he starts to laugh.

"I grab him by the front of his shirt and drag him out of the booth. Mom doesn't say a thing. He scared the words right outta her. For all I know she might crawl up that tree every night just so she can get a good night's sleep. Who knows what else he did all the time I was gone?

"I haul him out in the street, and he's still laughing, so I put a boot halfway up his ass. He tries to get away from me, but I just keep on putting the boots to him. I never hit him, though. I just use my feet. Finally he starts beggin' for mercy. But I just keep kicking. Then he starts to bawl like a baby.

"Everybody in the café is watching, but nobody tries to stop me. Finally, I let go of his arm, and he curls up on the sidewalk. I stand there looking at him while he tries to get up. My mom is standing beside me, and she's telling me he's had enough. But I'm so mad I want to kill him. Pop is almost on his feet when I push him back down again. He starts bawling all over again, so I say to him, 'Kiss my feet.'

"He's on his hands and knees, shaking his head side to side. Boy, it feels good seeing him like that. I tell him if he don't kiss my feet real quick, I'm gonna give him another shit-kicking. 'Go on, kiss my feet. Kiss my feet,' I said." Well, you know what? He kissed my feet. After that I told him if I ever heard of him touching my mom again, I'd come looking for him and I'd kill him.

"I never saw him again. Not until the day I seen him in his coffin last week. And you know what's the funny thing? My mom was cryin' like she really missed him. I couldn't believe it. I don't know how she could do that. But me, I didn't feel a thing. Know what I said when I found out he died? I said, 'Good. Take him up to the hills and leave him there. He had enough poison in him to kill a hundred coyotes.' I buried the meanest old man a kid could ever have, and it was wrong that we didn't get it arned out. I wished I could have asked him what made him so damn mean. Eddie, if you ever got something bothering you about me, well, we'll put our heads together till we come up with somethin'. We'll get it figured out somehow. Okay?"

Eddie nodded.

"You asked me why I left. You're too young to understand, and if it was anybody else, I'd say it was none of your business. But you're my son, so I'll tell you. I used to have this habit of running away all the time when things went bad. I'm not gonna do that anymore. I'm here to stay. Looks like I come back just in time too. Things look pretty grim around here."

He put down the deck of cards and leaned back in his chair. Looking up at the ceiling, he rubbed his chin with his palm. "First thing I'm gonna do is go into town and get some insulation. Yep. Needs insulation."

He walked over to the dish pantry. "Then I'll get rid of this old thing and put in some real cupboards."

He turned around and opened his arms. "We can put the sink right here with water taps so you don't have to haul water out of the river anymore. But the first thing we have to do is get some power in here. Goddamn. You guys been living in the dark ages too long. You know people in London, England, been riding trains underground for a hundred years?"

Eddie smiled as Jimmy wandered around the house, sharing his plans of what needed to be done.

"We can even get a television. An eighteen-incher, soon as we get Indian Affairs to pull their thumbs outta their asses and get us some power. Won't it be nice to switch a light on instead of pumpin' up gas lamps every hour? Huh?"

The front door opened with a bang. Lewis ran inside holding out his hands. "Look, Dad! I found these nuts. Want to come back and get some more?"

"What did you guys do all the time we were gone?" Grace asked.

Jimmy turned to Eddie and gave him a wink. "Nothing," he said. "Just talking."

17

The snow was a foot deep. Eddie stepped around the corner of the house and pulled a cigarette from his coat pocket, the last of the three he had taken from his mother's pack. He pulled a match across the asphalt siding, sucked hard, and inhaled. It felt good to smoke without coughing. Two cigarettes ago he would have choked and wondered how long it would take before he would be a real smoker.

He blew smoke out through his nose and thought about Jimmy's return a year ago. It was turning out to be anything but a dream come true. Eddie wished his dad hadn't shown up at all.

It started when Grace told Jimmy she was going to have a baby. She looked surprised when he laughed and said it was good. He found a job at Hoover's Sawmill on the reserve. The extra money lifted everyone's spirits. Jimmy even bought a new radio and dry cell battery, and no matter where you were in the house, the music was always in the background.

Even though the mood had improved, sometimes Eddie walked into a room to find Grace and Jimmy looking miserable and not speaking to each other. It wasn't always that way, which gave him hope that everything could change and their lives would get better.

All day long at the mill Jimmy pulled rough-cut lumber off a conveyor, then sorted and stacked it into piles. When he came home, Grace rubbed horse liniment on his shoulders until the house filled with Jimmy's groaning and the smell of his sweaty work socks and the eye-watering liniment. But it wasn't the job that slowly began to wear Jimmy down. It was the other men from the reserve, his workmates, that constantly ribbed him and teased him.

"How was it?" Grace asked after his first day, sounding like a mother talking to a child on his first day of school.

"Know what the guys call me? Hollywood, because of my sunglasses," he said laughing.

But weeks later, when Grace asked him again about work, Jimmy didn't laugh.

"Indian men. Hah," Grace said. "You're all the same. It's funny at first, but you keep on going until somebody gets mad. Now you know how it feels."

Jimmy ignored her and looked out the kitchen window with his bottom lip sticking out as if he was pouting.

With each passing week, Jimmy's bad mood grew and grew. Fridays were the worst, as if he had been saving his anger all week for the time when he walked in the door. Usually Fridays for Eddie meant a weekend away from school, but lately, as he and Lewis walked across the bridge and turned up the trail to home, a slow feeling of dread began to grow inside him.

Eddie flicked the cigarette onto the snow and was about to go back inside the house when he recognized the grumble of Jimmy's mufflers as his car turned off the highway. He heard the tires bump on the cattle guard; then the mufflers roared as the car picked up speed. Jimmy didn't let up on the gas pedal, and the car slid sideways as he turned down the icy road. Eddie could tell he was playing now as the car switched from one side to the other before sliding to a stop. Eddie waited until Jimmy opened the trunk before he opened the door and stepped into the kitchen. Lewis was at the window, looking out the curtains at Jimmy.

"Get away from there before he sees you," Eddie said.

Lewis backed away from the window as Jimmy closed the trunk. Just before Jimmy came inside, Eddie and Lewis glanced at each other. Lewis looked scared.

Jimmy carried a case of beer and a brown paper bag tucked under his arm. He tossed his hard hat, lunch kit, and jacket on the floor and closed the door with his foot. He sat on a chair near the door.

"Get over here and untie my laces," he said to Lewis. Eddie watched Lewis scramble to his knees and struggle with the tight knots. Jimmy looked over at Eddie, but this time, Eddie didn't look away.

I'm fifteen years old and I'm not scared of you or anybody else. I'll fight you anytime.

Jimmy smirked at Eddie as if he read his thoughts.

Lewis backed away. Jimmy pulled off his boots and stood. He searched the room that was dark except for a sliver of light inside the coal oil lamp.

"I hate this place. Always so goddamn dark in here and stinks like shit. Like living in a chicken house. Where the hell is your mom?" he asked.

"Went to town with Alphonse," Lewis said.

Jimmy kicked the chair, sending it tumbling across the room. Then he went to the kitchen table and set down the beer and paper bag. "You know what, the hell with her. More for me," he said, opening a beer with his belt buckle.

An unfamiliar boldness rushed over Eddie, and he could hear the blood roaring in his ears.

Jimmy turned the knob on the side of the lamp and the room brightened. He took out four cans of smoked oysters from the grocery bag, opened them all, and laid them out in a row in front of him. He took a long guzzle of beer and began gulping down the oysters. He even tipped up the tin to drink the oily dregs. When Lewis made a face at the smell, Jimmy saw his reaction.

"Come over here and have a taste," he said to Lewis as he held out the can.

"Looks like turds in a can," Eddie mumbled softly.

Jimmy looked over at him. "What did you say?"

Eddie shook his head. Jimmy eyed Eddie carefully as Lewis picked out a small oyster and put it in his mouth. He made a face, swallowed, and immediately threw up on the floor. "Jesus Christ. You useless little shithead. Clean it up. Now."

Lewis picked a rag from under the wash stand and wiped the floor. Jimmy picked up a beer and drank until the bottle was emptied. He let out a watery burp and slammed the bottle on the table. He noticed Eddie staring at him. "What are you lookin' at?"

Eddie shook his head.

"I asked you a question."

"Nothing."

"Bullshit. You're always giving me the eye when you think I don't see you. Don't you start gettin' high-toned with me, or I'll slap that nose right off your face."

Jimmy brought out a pack of cigarettes. "Get me a match, shithead," he said to Lewis.

Lewis took a match from the holder on the wall and held it out. Jimmy snatched it out of his hand and scraped it across the table. He held the match to the tip of his cigarette as he stared at Eddie.

"Now open me a beer," he said as he slid the case toward Lewis with his foot.

As Lewis bent down to pick up the last bottle of beer, Jimmy blew out the match and touched it to Lewis' neck. Lewis screamed in pain and jumped back, dropping the bottle on the floor. It exploded with a pop, spraying beer onto the wall. Eddie saw a spiral of smoke from the matchstick in Jimmy's hand.

"You little bastard. You did that on purpose."

Jimmy jumped to his feet and went for Lewis. Eddie put his head down and charged. Jimmy looked surprised as if he couldn't believe Eddie would ever think about fighting back. Jimmy stepped aside to avoid Eddie and pushed him head first into the wall. Eddie was stunned.

Jimmy grabbed him by the ankles and jerked him up in the air and began swinging him from side to side like a pendulum. Eddie felt about to pass out when he saw the steel poker leaning against the wall by the stove. He grabbed the poker and swung with both hands, striking Jimmy on the ankle. Jimmy yelled out in pain and dropped Eddie on the floor.

Eddie got to his feet and moved quickly toward Jimmy, but he was back-handed across the face. He fell awkwardly into the woodbox, feeling a burning pain in his spine. Just as he stepped toward Eddie, the door flew open. The doorknob made a perfect round hole in the paperboard wall. Jimmy turned wide-eyed to see Alphonse coming through the doorway.

Alphonse floored Jimmy with one punch. Then he dragged him outside feet first and sat on his chest and began slapping him. Eddie's uncle was tireless. He laughed while he hit Jimmy over and over.

The next morning Jimmy sat at the table drinking coffee, miserable and bruised. And later that day when he called Grace "darling" and "sweetheart," Eddie couldn't understand how she could smile at him like nothing happened.

Weeks went by, and Jimmy's bruises finally healed. He seemed happy most of the time, and when he began to sulk and act as if he might make trouble again, Alphonse showed up for a cup of tea, and Jimmy settled down again.

18

Jimmy reached out his hand and helped Grace up the steps into the house. It was her third trip to the toilet in an hour. She was sweating as she sat down at the table holding her large belly in her hands, breathing hard. Jimmy handed her a cup of water that she drank; then she handed the cup back for more. Her breathing settled down, and she leaned back on her chair.

"I'm not going anywhere, specially to town with all the noise and smells. You take Eddie and get a few things. Don't take too long either. I can't eat anything at all. My stomach is so sore. All I can think about are them cheese slices wrapped in plastic and some loafs of sliced bread. And a bottle of Canada Dry. Oh, that sounds good. Better get something for the kids, then. I'm not sharing with nobody."

On the road shoulder just before turning left onto the highway, Jimmy jammed down on the gas pedal as if he were trying to push it through the floorboard. The loose gravel bounced off the back of the car and rattled against the rear fender walls. The tires squealed, and blue smoke pushed ahead of them by a light breeze drifted inside smelling sweet and hot. When Jimmy speed-shifted into second, the rear tires barked, and when he shifted into third, they were going fifty miles an hour. By the time they reached Moccasin Lake, Eddie watched the speedometer needle edge past ninety. Jimmy smirked; he thought he was scaring Eddie.

The road signs whipped past them so fast they made a sound. When they reached the bottom of St. Anne's Hill, Eddie looked at the speedometer. It was so far down on the gauge it couldn't move any more. Because of the bumps and dips in the road Jimmy had to use both hands on the steering wheel as he struggled to keep the car from going out of control.

As they rounded a bend, Eddie saw the four road signs that always drew his attention with their strange message. Lit up at night by headlights, they stood by the roadside like four square-headed ghosts.

If you drive
When you're drunk
Carry a coffin
In your trunk.

In Vernon Jimmy parked the car behind the Kalamalka Hotel. He handed Eddie a five-dollar bill and a key.

"Get the groceries and put them in the trunk. This is my only spare, so you better not lose it. And don't stick your head in the beer parlour looking for me. Just sit in the car and wait. Keep the change and get something to eat. Just make sure you're here when I'm ready to go, or I'll leave without you. Prob'ly not comin' out till closin' time."

Eddie placed the bags of food in the trunk, closed it, and pocketed the key. Then he hurried to the corner of the hotel and turned down Main Street. This was one of his favourite things: just walking up and down the street with nothing to do but watch the people who came from all parts of the country. The Okanagan Valley was becoming a tourist spot. The beaches around Vernon were crowded with people swimming and waterskiing in summer, and some came for the Winter Carnival or for the skiing at Silver Star Mountain.

After walking all the way along Main Street looking in the store windows, Eddie walked back the way he'd come in case he'd missed something. Then he decided to go to the museum—he hadn't been there in a while. He grinned at the stuffed bear that had scared him when he was younger, but now it had dry cracks on its nose, and its hair was beginning to fall out.

Eddie quickly grew bored. His stomach growled, but he wanted to wait as long he could before spending his money, at least until he needed to go to the bathroom, so the restaurant manager would see he was a paying customer.

The bus depot had the best French fries in town. For fifteen cents you could get a brown paper bag overflowing with golden fries. The bag would be wet with vinegar, and the waitress would finish it off with a big shake of salt. He would sit in the corner of the café eating his fries and drinking a Coke, watching the Band Box. When someone dropped a nickel into the jukebox and the little curtains parted, the puppet musicians seemed to come alive.

After delaying for as long as he could, he headed for Nick's Kandy Kitchen. It was a small café where the owner, his wife, and her twin sister sold handmade chocolates and peanut brittle, and they had the cheapest hamburgers in town. Just one hamburger patty on a bun with mustard, ketchup, and relish, no extras like lettuce or tomato, no pickle sticking out both sides. But for under a dollar, with a Coke and a bowl of tomato soup made fresh from the can, it was the best deal in town. He was about to go inside when he noticed Eva Cluff on the other side of the street.

At first he wasn't sure it was her because she had a yellow kerchief wrapped around her head to cover rows of large curlers, and she was smoking a cigarette.

Eddie sprinted across the road and stepped in front of her. She was surprised to see him.

"Oh, I look a sight, don't I?" she said, trying to hide the curlers with her hands. Eddie thought she looked beautiful.

"What are you doing here?" Eddie asked.

"I live here now. For the summer anyway. Then I go back to UBC. Oh, it's so good to see you again, Eddie. I've been thinking about you a lot lately."

To Eddie's surprise, she threw her arms around him and hugged him. She held him for so long that people walking by stared at them. Eddie placed his hands on her back and was about to return the hug when she pulled away. She reached out and cupped his face with her hands. Eddie didn't know what to think. He had always liked Eva—a lot—and dreamed of them being together, kissing and looking into each other's eyes like people in the movies. He couldn't believe what was happening.

"Why don't you come back to my place? You can meet my roommates, Misty and Dawn. We're carhops at the North End Drive-In. I told them all about you, and they'd be thrilled to meet you. I think you'll like them. Okay?"

"Sure," he said. "You know, when I saw you smoking, I thought, that can't be her."

Eva laughed. "Now that I've left home, I get up to all sorts. Anyway, it's my turn to do the shopping. It's not too big a list. I used up the last of the shampoo, and they're waiting for me, so I should get going. Come on. Hurry!"

The basement suite was dim, and the only light came from two small, grimy windows that looked out across a weedy lawn. Three single mattresses lay side by side on the floor, and clothes were piled high in a corner of the room. A metal shower stood to the side of two steps leading up to a toilet perched on a stage. The privacy of anyone using it was guarded by a flimsy curtain.

"The place is a bit messy from the little party we had last night, and we're all feeling a little under the weather. The landlord wasn't happy with us at all. He said he thought we were all good church girls, and if he had known we were hippie partiers, he never would have rented the place to us. We just batted our lashes at him and smiled and said we were so sorry."

Eddie noticed an empty bottle of Baby Duck sparkling wine, Mateus Rose, and two cases of beer empties in the corner.

A girl with a bobby pin in her mouth walked over. She had gathered her long dark hair on the top of her head and pushed the last pin in place. Eddie was surprised that she was in her bra and panties and wasn't shy about it. She was so pretty. When she saw Eddie, she smiled and looked into his eyes.

"Hi," she said softly. "Well, well, Eva. Who is this?"

"This is Eddie. I told you all about him. Eddie, this is Misty, the only one here with a car and driver's licence. She's so much older than us," Eva said.

Eddie didn't know what to do or say when Misty reached out and shook his hand.

"Pleased to meet you. Any friend of—"

A blond-haired girl wrapped in a towel that was too short to cover her up completely stepped out from behind Misty. Eddie was stunned. She looked like a *Playboy* centrefold. "It's about time, Eva. I've been waiting and waiting. Is that the shampoo?"

As she reached over for the bag in Eva's hand, the towel fell away from her sides and Eddie saw the full outline of her body. When she noticed Eddie, she quickly pulled the towel under her neck, leaving her legs, hips, and shoulders bare.

"Oh!" she said in surprise. "Who is this?" She smiled and bit her bottom lip.

Eva pulled the shampoo from the bag. "This is Eddie. You get in the shower, Dawn, before you freeze to death."

Dawn grabbed the shampoo and turned away, showing her bare backside. "Glad to see you, Eddie. I bet you're glad to see me."

"Oh, you are such an exhibitionist," Eva said.

Dawn threw her head back and laughed. Eddie couldn't look away and didn't dare blink. This was almost too much for him. He could get aroused simply walking into a brisk wind, so he had to be careful.

Eva stepped in front of him. "Hey. Put those eyes back in your head."

Eddie felt suddenly embarrassed and his face flushed. "I—I—"

"I was teasing, Eddie. She is so shameless. Come into the kitchen and sit down while I get ready. Do you want something to eat? How about a hamburger? We have a fridge full of them from work, but we all hate them now. Would you like one?"

"Yeah, sure," Eddie said.

Eva's roommates took turns in the shower, washing and shampooing their hair. They walked about in their bras and panties as easily as if he weren't even there.

"Come on, you girls," Eva said. "Put some clothes on. What's Eddie going to think with all these half-dressed females parading around in their underwear?"

Dawn laughed. "Oh, come on, Eva. He's living a boy's dream. Even if he told everybody at school that he was locked in a basement with three nymphomaniacs and all the hamburgers he could eat, nobody would believe him anyway."

Eddie sat in the kitchen for an hour, not wanting to be anywhere else in the world, until Eva stood in front of him in her carhop clothes.

"It wasn't much of a visit, was it? Next time we can sit and talk, away from the distractions," she said, pointing to her waiting roommates. "Okay?"

Eddie nodded and went to the door while Eva looked for her change purse. Her yellow kerchief hung from a coat hook. He pulled it down and stuffed it into his pants pocket.

Eva waved from the front seat as Misty ground the gears of a smoking 1960 Corvair. From the back seat Dawn blew him a kiss and smiled. He couldn't believe he had spent time with three such beautiful girls.

"You're right, Dawn," he said out loud. "Nobody would believe me."

Later Eddie stood outside Dye's Billiards. Should he play here or go to Al's or just keep walking? Eva had given him a hamburger, so he had enough extra money to play pool for hours. He fingered the change in his pocket for a moment and went inside.

The place was packed, and the cigarette smoke was so thick he couldn't see the tables at the back. Someone tapped him on the shoulder. It was Otto, the flunky who cleaned the tables with a whisk broom and racked the balls after a game.

"You can't be in here by yourself until you're sixteen. You know that," Otto said.

"My dad's coming. He went to the car for his wallet," Eddie said.

Otto walked away. Eddie bought a bag of potato chips and a pop just to show he had money and sat under the large-print sign that said No Vagrants. He munched on chips and sipped his grape pop as he watched the pool players milling around in the blue haze of smoke.

Dye's wasn't where Eddie normally went to play pool; it drew a certain clientele of people with money jingling in their pockets. They dressed well and followed the rules on the sign above the counter: No swearing. Use the ashtrays. No minors allowed. If any school-age kids showed up on a weekday, Vern Dye warned them, "Get back to class before I call the school."

Eddie walked around Dye's place. Usually he went to Al's Pool Hall near the end of Main Street and down a steep set of stairs. The dark place with no windows made him feel he was deep underground. The games didn't cost as much, and the pop and chips were cheaper. All the troublemakers and hooky-players who'd been kicked out of Dye's ended up at Al's.

It was also where Eddie and other Indians could hang around and kill time, and people left them alone. The Indians were mostly from an area of the reserve called Six Mile because it was six miles from the main highway. Six Mile Indians, Eddie called them. They didn't bother him the first time he showed up, but they watched him out of the corners of their eyes.

The Indians always played on the tables at the back of the pool hall while the *summas* used the tables toward the front. Eddie got to know one of the Six Milers, an older man called Hank. When he first approached Eddie, his face was so stern that it frightened him.

"Hey, Salmon River. Shoot some pool?" he asked loudly, as if challenging Eddie to a fight.

Eddie stared at the man, not sure what to do.

Then Hank broke out in laughter. "Come on, uncle. What you doing hanging around up here? Come back and join us," he said, polishing his pool cue with a cloth.

Hank was a skilled player who seldom paid for the table because of the loser-pays rule. All the times Eddie played Hank, he didn't come close to winning, but he began to play better and came to know a few of the Six Milers. There was no big hello when they met, just a "lo" or a nod.

Here at Dye's this evening there were no empty tables. Maybe Eddie should go to Al's. He downed his pop and tossed the empty chip bag into a garbage can, then wound his way around the packed tables toward the street. If he played as well as he thought he could, he might have money left over for the next time he was in town. And instead of stealing cigarettes from his mom's purse, he could buy his own.

Just as he neared the door, Hank walked inside. Eddie almost didn't recognize him. Hank was clean-shaven with his hair Brylcreemed straight back, and he wore black dress pants and a new white shirt buttoned up to the neck. He carried a skinny wooden case under his arm. People seemed to know him.

"Uh oh. Looks like the pickpocket is here."

"You might as well just hand over your wallets, boys."

"Yeah. He's got that look."

"You can tell he's a shark the way his mouth hangs."

Hank laughed at their comments. Eddie was surprised when the *summas* reached out to shake his hand and pat him on the back. Hank stood at the table that was covered with a white cloth. It was the money table where only the best were allowed to play. Hank opened the case and pulled out two sections of a pool cue. After he screwed them together, he rubbed the cue with a cloth. Otto peeled back the cover on the table and turned on the overhead light.

Hank chalked his cue and looked at all the people gathering around the table, revelling in the moment. When he saw Eddie, his expression changed.

"Hey, uncle. Sit over here," he said, tapping the chairs just out of the triangle of light above the table. "You're my good luck tonight."

For two hours Eddie watched Hank beat player after player. He couldn't help but smile at the way Hank called out each shot loudly and pointed to the pocket with his cue. After a close game Hank had only the black to sink. He pointed to the corner and lined up his shot. Then he looked back at Eddie.

"Whaddya think, uncle? Am I gonna make it?"

Eddie nodded.

"I dunno," Hank said with a grin. "You'd have to be pretty good to make a shot like this." Without looking back at the ball, Hank hit the cue ball hard. The ball banged into the corner pocket. Hank held the pose as his cackling laugh drained the last bit of confidence out of his opponent.

A few spectators clapped and waved at Hank as they headed toward the door. Hank stuffed two five-dollar bills into his pants pocket. He took his cue apart and gently placed it in the box, then turned to Eddie.

"Nothin' I like better than takin' money from *summas*. Anyway, I'm goin' over to the Kal for a kielbasa hot dog and a beer. Ya never know. Maybe I'll get lucky and find me a dance partner tonight. What you gonna do?"

"I'm going to Al's and shoot some pool," Eddie said.

Hank reached over and shoved a two-dollar bill into Eddie's shirt pocket.

"Thanks, Hank. Jeez," Eddie said.

"Just don't lose it all at once," Hank said.

"How's about a game there, chief?" A man approached and laid down a five-dollar bill on the table. Tall and hunched over like a crow, he swayed as his bloodshot eyes fixed on Hank. Anybody could see he'd had too much to drink. When he glanced around to see if anyone was listening, Eddie could tell the man didn't like Indians and was looking for trouble.

Hank looked at the man and smiled. "Just headin' out the door, uncle. Nex' time."

The man placed his hands on his hips, took a wider stance, and faced Hank squarely like a gunfighter. "What's the big hurry, chief? You scared they're gonna run outtta horse cock and beer at the Kal? Or you just scared to play somebody good? And don't call me uncle."

"Oh no, they always get extra beer when they hear I'm coming. That all you got? Five bucks? I just played for ten," Hank said with a smile that didn't waver. "And don't call me chief."

Eddie felt his own anger begin to spread as he sized up the man. *Dumb-looking bugger. Looks like Ichabod Crane. Hah. He's so drunk I can get a couple good shots at him before he does anything.*

Just then there was loud banging on the back doors leading out into the alley. Otto limped over and unlocked the door. Hank, Ichabod, and everybody else turned to see the cause of such a commotion. "You're not supposed to come in this way," Otto said.

A big man stepped inside. He towered over everybody at the back tables. He had an enormous bald head and a long bushy beard. His T-shirt was sleeveless, and his biceps bulged and unbulged when he swung his arms. "Then what are we doing here?"

Players, open-mouthed in amazement, backed away to let him through. Eddie saw two more people that at first he thought were the big man's children. Then he realized they were men but shorter than any he'd ever seen before.

Ichabod placed his hand over his mouth as if he couldn't believe what he was seeing. "Hey, everybody. Look who it is. It's the midget wrasslers. Ain't that somethin'?"

Then he laughed and pointed as he staggered toward them, holding out his arms to greet them. "Damn. It's the midget wrasslers. I don't believe it. You guys are the funniest things I ever seen. And you. You're the Big Bopper. Well, ain't that somethin'. The Big Bopper and the midget wrasslers. I was in the arena just a little while ago watching you, and now here you are. Ain't that somethin'. Jeez, I love watchin' wrasslin'. You know some folks think it's all phony. But I don't. No sir. No siree."

Hank turned to Eddie. "I've seen these little guys before. They're gonna save us the trouble. If he keeps it up, that poor bugger is going to get his ass handed to him," he said.

The two short men ignored Ichabod, but he wouldn't shut up. Finally, one of them had heard enough. "Shut your yap and leave us alone, or I'll tie your tongue in a knot."

Ichabod's face turned red. "What's the problem? I like you people. What's the matter, anyway?"

"I'm not gonna tell you again. Just turn around and walk the hell away from here."

Ichabod looked at the Big Bopper.

"Don't look at me," he said.

"You little short-ass bastards. Don't you tell me what to do."

The Big Bopper jumped out of the way as both wrestlers charged at Ichabod, tackling him to the floor. One sat on Ichabod's chest and pinned his arms to the floor while the other rained down punches. People were too afraid to stop them.

Otto pushed his way through the crowd. "What the hell is going on here? Stop that before I call the cops."

The wrestlers left Ichabod groaning and bleeding on the concrete floor as they went back to their game. Otto pulled the man to his feet and helped him out the door. Otto closed the big doors with a bang. "All right. Closing time, everybody. Let's go."

Eddie looked at the clock. It was eleven. He had no idea that it was so late. Al's would be closed now too. Had Jimmy gone without him like he said? Eddie walked quickly up the street and around the back of the Kalamalka Hotel. It was a relief to see the car was still there.

He felt tired. Jimmy wouldn't be out for an hour and he could sleep in peace until then. As he reached for the door, he saw movement in the back seat. Looking closer, he saw Jimmy was on top of a woman and was going at it hard. Eddie stepped back into the shadows and waited. Ten minutes later, Jimmy and the woman got out of the car adjusting their clothes. The woman went inside through the Ladies and Escorts entrance, and Jimmy entered through the lobby.

Eddie fell asleep in no time. It was midnight before Jimmy came out of the beer parlour. Eddie could tell right away he was drunk. When they drove out of town, he wandered across the white line as he looked for the ashtray. Neither of them spoke. They both knew what was waiting for them back home. As the car turned down the road, Eddie saw his mom standing at the window. She must have been watching for hours because before the car came to a stop, she came outside yelling at Jimmy. She was spitting mad and even took a swing at him. He ducked just in time. It was the maddest Eddie had ever seen her. She screamed at Eddie. "You're another one."

"What did I do?"

"Just get into the house and go to bed." They were still arguing when Eddie fell asleep.

It took Grace a long time before she was able to speak to Jimmy without raising her voice. Jimmy eventually gave up shouting back, and he let her go on and on until she ran out of swear words.

Grace didn't trust Jimmy from then on. The next time she needed groceries from town, they all piled in the car and went together.

19

Eddie pulled up his coat collar and started down the trail to Grandma's. Rain had been falling for three days and nights, washing away the last snow on the high mountains, but it was finally slowing to a drizzle. Trembling beads of water hung from the clothesline and fell into the grass. The soaked black stumps looked like the remains of a forest fire.

He saw Alphonse still hadn't finished Grandma's front steps. She'd been after him because she was having a hard time getting in and out of the house. He had gotten as far as taking the old steps away, but now Grandma had to step twice as high. Eddie opened the door.

"Anybody home?" He was about to step inside when someone shouted behind him, and he felt a jab in his ribs.

"Hey!" He almost fell as he stumbled backward into Lewis.

"Damn you. What are you doing here?"

"Why? What are you doing?"

"Nothing," Eddie said.

The rain flattened Lewis's hair except for the rooster tail at the back of his head that bounced up and down when he moved. Water dripped off the end of his nose, and the cold had turned his ears red as strawberries. Eddie pulled the door shut, and the window rattled in its frame.

The brothers stopped at the trail and looked down at the river. Brown water rushed only inches below the banks. As they walked down the trail, the river boomed in their ears and the ground shook. The wind created by the fast flow sprayed water onto their faces. Keeping close to the bank, Eddie pushed through knee-high undergrowth. In places water washed over the bank onto the ground in front of them. If they stepped too close to the edge, clumps of sod dropped into the water where the river undercut the bank.

They climbed the trail up the steep slope and sat down on the ground. In the middle of the chocolate-coloured river, water spun in whirlpools. An unearthed poplar floated close to shore; the silvery underside of its leaves looked white like the bellies of dead fish. Suddenly the river choked with broken trunks and branches of trees from a breached logjam upstream somewhere. Debris bunched together until an impassable dam formed. When there was nowhere for the water to go, the river turned toward the Cluffs' field. Through an opening in the trees, Eddie saw cars driving across the bridge but couldn't hear them over the racket. The cottonwoods on the far bank where the Cluff cattle took cover from the summer heat now stood in a foot of water.

Lewis pointed below the logjam where the water level was two feet lower. Eddie saw in front of the logjam that a part of the river had begun to turn in a clockwise direction like a large wheel. A birch sapling drifted into the centre and disappeared. A large stump headed toward the logjam like a battering ram. Twenty feet away, the stump joined the rotation, held briefly, and was sucked under. Then, with a great underwater crack, the logjam broke. Eddie and Lewis felt the ground shudder beneath them. Within minutes the water withdrew from the Cluffs' field.

Yellow foam had gathered in a quiet spot close to shore. When the froth built up too high, a gust of wind lifted part of it up and carried it away. That's when Eddie noticed something square among the sticks and bark drifting in circles around the foam. It reappeared for a second and then was gone. He stared into the lather until he spotted it again and slid down the bank. Reaching the bottom, Eddie hurried to where he had last seen the object. It looked like a small box. When he bent down to look underneath the foam, he saw it nodding up and down with the movement of the water. He tried to pull it closer with a stick but only managed to knock it farther away. He took a quick measurement of the depth of the water with the stick and guessed it was about four feet deep.

Motioning Lewis to grab the end of the stick, Eddie stepped into the river. The icy water reached his chest and took his breath away. He bent over to grab the box, but it was just out of reach. Fearing he would lose it this time, Eddie felt blindly around in the foam until his fingers closed around the box. He hurried to shore.

"Let's go," he said, shaking with cold. They walked to the door of Grandma's house. "I just want to have a quick look at what's inside."

The box fit perfectly in the palm of his hand and felt heavy for its size. The grey cloth covering was in shreds as if it had been in the water for some time.

"Open it! Quick!" Lewis said.

Holding the box tightly, Eddie pried it open. Tucked inside a fold of fabric was a ring with an enormous clear stone. Eddie pulled the ring out of the box and rubbed it on his shirt. The stone seemed to send out brilliant sparks of light.

"What is it? A ring?" Lewis asked.

"Course it's a ring."

"What's that writing on the back?" Lewis asked.

"Where?"

"On the back of the cover."

"I don't see any writing."

"Right there." Lewis pointed to the faded lettering stamped on the inside of the lid.

Eddie looked closer. "It says 'Cartier.'"

"What does that mean?" Lewis asked.

"I don't know, but I think this is a diamond ring. If it is, it's worth a lot of money."

"How much?" Lewis asked.

"I dunno. Lots." Eddie was shivering hard. "I don't even know for sure if this is a diamond ring. I seen in the movies that if you rub it on glass and it makes a scratch, it's a diamond."

Eddie stood at the window and rubbed the ring across the glass. There was a sound like the scraping of ice.

"Jesus. It is a diamond," Eddie said. His jaw and legs were shaking and his ears ached. "Let's go up to the house before I freeze to death."

Eddie could barely feel his toes. All he could do was point his feet in the direction of the house and stumble forward. At the top of the hill they saw Jimmy's car was nowhere in sight. Lewis held the door open, and Eddie went inside. He took off his clothes and stood close to the kitchen stove.

"B-b-blanket," he stuttered.

Lewis came out of the bedroom with a quilt and wrapped it around his brother. It took a few minutes before Eddie felt warm enough to move away from the stove and change into dry clothes. He pulled the kettle from the side of the stove onto the heat, and when the water came to a boil he poured water into two coffee mugs and added a spoonful of cocoa and three spoonfuls of sugar in each one. He sat in a chair pulled close to the stove, sipped the cocoa, and held the cup in his hands until his fingers began to tingle.

"Are we gonna tell Mom and Dad about the ring, Eddie?"

"No."

"Why not? They'll know what to do," Lewis said.

"Listen to me. Don't you say a word to either one of them. I'll figure out something. But don't you tell them about the ring. Okay?" Eddie snapped.

"Okay," Lewis answered.

When he went to the outhouse that night, Eddie placed the ring box inside a plastic bread bag, stuffed it in one of his mother's old nylons he found under her bed, and tied it into a knot. Then he reached down inside the opening and hooked the nylon onto a nail under the seat by the outside wall.

20

Eddie patted Lewis on the knee and smiled at his brother. "You have fun with the lovebirds today." He grabbed the shopping bag holding his clean set of clothes, stepped out of the car, and hurried away.

"Hey," Jimmy yelled after him. "Be here around three."

Hah. Fat chance. Seeing Eva today. You think I'd rather go home with you yahoos than be with her?

"I got a ride with one of the guys," Eddie called back over his shoulder. "He lives at Silver Creek." He didn't know any such person, but it was none of their business.

Lewis's look said he wanted to be with his older brother. Eddie smiled as he turned away. Lewis would have to figure it out for himself, just as Eddie had done. Their parents would give him just enough change to get a pop and bag of chips while he wandered the streets and stared into the store windows. Then he would sit in the lobby of the National Hotel for hours trying to avoid the mean stares of the lady behind the long desk. Lewis would wonder if the day would ever end. He would fall asleep, and Grace would shake him awake to go home. He should have stayed home with Grandma. Eddie broke into a run.

At the Kalamalka Hotel he swung to the right and slowed to a fast walk until he came to Polson Park. Then he turned up an alley and came to the old flatbed truck resting on its axles. It was packed with trash sticking out of its busted windows. Rusted doors and fenders were piled high on the back.

Each little house backing on the alley had at least one wrecked auto that was stripped of its parts and left to the elements a few feet from the front door. It looked more like an auto wrecker's yard than a place to live. Over the years the soil had become so saturated with grease and oil that it was unable to absorb liquid of any kind; whatever landed there sat on top of the ground in inky pools. Even though the air had a foul stench, a woman with a clothespin in her mouth hummed as she smoothed out sheets on a clothesline that ran from her front door to an outhouse tucked inside thick brush. The colourful flowers overflowing the window box stood no chance of ever having their fragrance appreciated. A cat sunning itself on a caved-in roof swatted at a bee.

As he turned the corner, Eddie came across two men working under the hood of a car unbolting an engine from its mounts. With eyes blinking out of blackened faces, they looked like creatures from the tar pits.

Surrounded by all the trash and filth, Eddie couldn't have been happier. This was the second Saturday he'd worked splitting shakes for Henri Larouche, a man he'd met at Al's Pool Hall. Henri had looked desperate as he walked from table to table asking the players if they wanted to work, only to be ignored or answered by a shake of the head. At first Eddie responded like the others, but with barely enough change in his pocket to pay for more games, he ran after Henri and asked about the job.

"How much money would I make?"

"Up to you. How hard you want to work?" Henri answered in a thick French accent.

A few Six Milers laughed at Henri and at Eddie's new job. "How the hell can you work for that crazy bugger? Workin' all day over in Dogpatch humped over a cedar block, using a piece of wood for a hammer. Like a goddamn caveman."

"I didn't say I was going to work for him. Just wanted to know about the money. That's all," Eddie said.

But when he showed up that first day, he saw two Six Milers hammering away at a large piece of cedar with a metal froe and a mallet made out of a block of birch. All three had a good laugh.

Today Eddie was the only one there.

"Where are the other guys?" he asked Henri.

"After you leave, they ask for pay and tell me they not come back. Work too hard, they say. Only you and me now. Gonna be hard day. We make taper shingles. I show you," he said.

Henri made it look easy the way he set the froe in place on the block. Then he lifted the mallet over his head and brought it down hard twice. "Only twice. Not ten times. Too slow," he said.

The shake dropped to the ground and he flipped the block end over end. It took Eddie a few tries, but he soon had shakes springing off the cedar block until there was a good pile at his feet.

Eddie brushed the cedar dust off his shirt and pants the best he could, then washed his face in the cold tap water. He wiped his face dry with his sleeve. After changing, he placed his work pants and shirt in the bag and put it on a shelf just inside the outhouse.

The Frenchman placed dollar bills in Eddie's hand as he counted them out. "Un, deux, trois, quatre, cinq. There. Five dollar."

Eddie shoved the bills in his pocket and rushed out of the cedar lot. He jumped over a dark puddle and raced up the street.

He didn't stop until he came to Eva's place, five city blocks later. When he knocked on the door, she appeared with her coat draped over her arm. "I didn't think you were ever going to get here," she said.

Eddie let out his breath. The long week he had been away from her was finally over. "What do you want to do?" he asked.

"This is the only Saturday I have off for a long time. I've been stuck inside all day and I just feel like going for a walk. Okay with you?" she asked.

"Sure." Eddie had been on his feet all day and would have liked to just sit in her basement, eat cold hamburgers, and talk. But if she'd asked him to walk home and back again, he would have done it willingly.

They strolled Main Street and looked in the store windows, something Eddie had done many times by himself but enjoyed more now. They went into the Hudson's Bay store because Eva wanted to browse through the jewellery section. Eddie watched how her eyes widened and she smiled when she saw a piece she liked. When she pulled on his arm to show him sparkling earrings, she sniffed at his shoulder.

"You smell so good. What is that?"

Eddie laughed. "Cedar. And sweat."

"My dad doesn't smell like that. When he comes in from the fields, it's all I can do to keep from throwing up."

Eva leaned over to draw in his scent, and Eddie noticed their reflection on the mirrored panels behind the glass shelves. He couldn't believe what he was seeing. He had a strong desire to kiss her on the forehead but resisted the urge.

When they passed Dye's Billiards, Eddie saw Hank watching them with a pool cue in his hand. His big grin seemed to fill the doorway where he stood. Eddie wondered how long he'd been watching.

"Who is that?" Eva asked.

"Just a guy I play pool with," Eddie answered.

"You're a pool player? Oh no. You're not one of those juvenile delinquents that smoke and wear leather jackets with big zippers and chains and ride motorcycles with a gang, are you? Is it true you have to kill someone before you can join? My parents warned me about guys like you. First it's hubcaps or car batteries, then you steal a girl's heart. Is that what you plan on doing? Huh? You gonna steal my heart, Eddie?"

Suddenly tongue-tied, Eddie felt his face flush.

"I'm only kidding," Eva added with a laugh. She leaned her face on his shoulder and squeezed his arm as they walked on. "Oh, you're so funny, Eddie. I didn't know I could make you blush so easily. You are so much fun to be with. The more time I spend with you, the more thankful I am to have you as a friend."

A light sprinkling of rain was making her hair wet, so Eva bolted away from Eddie and rushed inside the National Café. When he went to join her, she grabbed the door handle and shook her head at him. "Nope. No. You can't come in. No motorcycle guys allowed."

Eddie was puzzled at her serious look. When he tried to push his way in, she laughed at his effort. When she finally let go of the door handle, she put her arms around his neck and hugged him hard, laughing in his ear.

When she stood back, Eddie looked at the beautiful, unpredictable girl in front of him and shook his head. "You're crazy."

They shared a plate of salty French fries soaked in vinegar and ketchup. He had a Coke, and she drank a chocolate milk through a straw, and they dropped dime after dime into the jukebox selector at their table. He could hardly hear the music over the noise inside the café, but it didn't matter. Eddie had never expected to be sitting in a booth in town with a girl so pretty that guys walking by stared at her and looked at Eddie as if they couldn't believe he could have a girl like that. He watched a couple sitting close in a booth. They were so happy. It made him feel good that he was a part of something like that.

They lost all track of time until Eddie read the clock on the back wall. It was getting close to the time the Greyhound would be leaving the depot, headed for his home.

They hurried back to Eva's. At the door, as Eddie was turning to go, she looked as if there were something she wanted to say.

"What?" he asked.

"I just wanted to tell you what a great time I had tonight. When we first met, I knew you were different from everyone else. Even then, when you were six, I just knew you could be a lot of fun. You looked so cute and mischievous. That's all."

Then she touched Eddie's face. Her fingers felt soft against his skin. She leaned over to plant a kiss on his cheek. Eddie's stomach fluttered, and he couldn't stop himself. He turned his head and kissed Eva on the lips.

Eva stepped back. "What do you think you're doing?"

Eddie was stunned.

"Oh, Eddie. If I ever gave you the impression that we were anything but best friends, then I am sorry. I couldn't possibly think of you any other way. But I'm so disappointed that you're just like all the other boys after all. Being nice so you could wait for a chance to do something like that."

Eddie opened his mouth to speak, but she interrupted him. "Don't you read books or watch movies and figure out how friends act with each other? They kiss each other on the cheek and hug and tell each other secrets, and it doesn't mean anything except a close friendship. They certainly don't ambush each other. But— but—why did you have to ruin everything?" She opened the door and rushed inside.

Eddie stared at the door a long time, not understanding what had just happened. Finally he gave up and walked away. Just then the eleven o'clock bell on the town clock sounded out the hour. He had missed his bus. Now he would have to walk home. All twenty miles.

He'd made it to the outskirts of town when a car pulled over to the shoulder. A man stepped out and waved him forward. It was Hank. Eddie ran up, opened the car door, and slid onto the seat. Hank jammed on the gas, and they sped into the cold dark night. Eddie could feel Hank's curious stare but acted as if he didn't notice.

They had gone a mile before Hank spoke. "Jesus. Did that pretty girl go and kick your ass out the door? Already? Gotta be.

No other reason. What happened, anyway? What the hell did you do? Try and sneak a kiss?"

Eddie turned to Hank with a look of astonishment.

"You did, didn't you?" Hank said with a laugh. "You tried to get in the pants of that little *summa*, and she didn't like it. I don't blame you, though. Damn, she's good-looking. She looks a little older than you."

"Two years," Eddie said.

"Hah. You like your women older. Not me, boy. I like them younger than me. Now that's what you call white-tail. Damn, I bet she even squeaks when she walks."

Eddie flushed but didn't reply. If he did, he wouldn't be able to stop himself from saying things he would regret. And worse, he'd get kicked out of the car.

21

Days after Jimmy's and Eddie's late-night return, the house was still tense. Grace had been avoiding Eddie. She acted as though there were nothing wrong, but when she spoke to him, she couldn't look him in the eye. And Jimmy always held him in a warning stare for a moment before turning away.

On Friday night after supper, when Eddie went to empty the slop bucket over the bank, he saw Jimmy leaning against the car, smoking a cigarette. He was staring at the faint glow of the lights of Vernon reflected in the night sky, twenty miles away.

"What you doing?" Eddie asked.

Jimmy didn't answer.

At the bottom of the steps Eddie turned the slop bucket over to drain. Reaching for the doorknob, he looked back just as Jimmy drew in on his cigarette; the red glow lit up his face, and the smoke curled down from his nostrils.

Inside Lewis sat at the table fingering through the pages of his spelling book. Jimmy came inside and joined Grace, who relaxed on the couch listening to the radio. Eddie felt like an outsider. It wasn't right that they should be mad at him. If Jimmy couldn't be nice to him, then why should he keep his secret about the woman in the back seat? Why should he get the blame for something Jimmy had done?

Eddie saw a mouse stick its head out of a small hole in the bottom of the wall. Its nose waved in circles, sniffing at the air. Tiny eyes shimmered like teardrops. Under the stove where she lay dozing, the cat spotted the mouse and her tail curled and uncurled like a beckoning finger. The cat rose to a crouch and inched her way along the wall. At the corner she stopped. Her sweeping tail became motionless when the mouse moved out a little farther. The cat went stone still as the mouse took one more adventurous step. The cat pounced. Eddie heard a soft squeak. The cat walked to the door with the mouse dangling from his mouth. Eddie slid off his chair, opened the door, and the cat hurried outside.

Grace and Jimmy sat next to each other, but they were barely speaking or even glancing in either's direction. This was how it was, day after day, and it made living together in the small house so uncomfortable that Eddie couldn't stand it any longer. He went to the outhouse, reached down, and brought out the stocking. He pulled out the box and stuffed it into his pocket. At the front door, Lewis stood blocking the way.

"Are you telling them?"

"Move."

Eddie shoved him aside and marched into the living room. His sudden approach surprised Grace.

"I found something in the river." Eddie brought the ring case from behind his back and held it out to her.

Grace turned it over in her hand. "What's so special about this?" she asked, looking up at him.

"Open it."

She looked at the case. When she opened the box, the fold of skin between her eyebrows pinched together as she focused on the ring. Thinking it was a joke, she took out the ring and held it up to the light. Bright, thin points of light swam across her face. "What is this? A Cracker Jack prize?"

"Let me see that," Jimmy said.

Grace handed him the ring with a shrug of her shoulders. "It's just a toy. Throw it in the stove," she said.

Eddie wasn't surprised at her reaction. That was her way. She didn't like to get her hopes up about anything.

Jimmy looked it over carefully. "Boy—you know what?"

"What? What is it?" she asked.

"It's a ring," Lewis said.

"I know that. You think I'm stupid?" Grace snapped.

"No. It's a diamond ring. Eddie scratched Grandma's window with it. Only a diamond can do that."

"You scratched your grandma's window, Eddie?"

"It's the only way to tell if it's a diamond or a fake. I saw it in the movies. And it was just a tiny scratch."

"Look at the back of the box. There's a name on it. It says Cartier," Lewis said.

"Cartier—what?" Grace said puzzled.

Jimmy took the case from her hand and peered closely inside. "Cartier. It says Cartier. Holy sufferin' Moses. This is a Cartier diamond, Grace."

"What's that supposed to mean?"

"All the times you been reading those movie star magazines you never heard of a Cartier diamond? It means it's worth a whole lotta money. That's what it means. It could be worth hundreds of dollars maybe. Thousands even."

The mood in the house changed quickly, and the brothers listened as their parents talked about what they should do with the ring and the way it would change their lives.

"Know what I'd like to do?" Jimmy said. "Get a new paint job for the car with flames on the front."

"Hell, I can put flames on your car for you. And they wouldn't be the painted ones," Grace said. "No. The first thing I wanna do is go to the store and ask how much the grocery bill is. And when that old bag May tells me, I'm going to hand it over to her and listen to her stutter. Every time I go to the store, she always has to say something. Once I wanted to buy some cheap toffees, and she stuck her big nose out and said to me, 'You think you should be spending your money on candy with your bill getting so high?' I couldn't say a thing."

"We should just buy all the candy in the store so she wouldn't have none to sell. That'd really make her mad," Lewis said.

Grace laughed and patted him on the head. "I bet if somebody locked you in a roomful of candy, you'd eat your way out."

The next morning Grace and Jimmy disagreed about what they should do with the ring. Jimmy wanted to go to the pawnshop, where the cash would be quick and there would be no questions asked. Grace wanted to take it to the jeweller; it was the only way for her to find out the diamond's true worth. The pawnshop would be the worst place to go, she said; she didn't trust the owner to give them a fair deal.

After Jimmy and Grace drove out of sight, Eddie and Lewis went down to the river and tossed rocks at a log. Then they went back to the house to wait for their parents' return, anxious to see what they would bring home.

When they heard the car pull up in front of the house, they saw two downcast faces as their parents walked up the steps. Grace went into the bedroom. Jimmy plopped down in his chair. Neither said a word to the boys.

"Didn't you bring us anything, Dad?" Lewis asked.

Jimmy shook his head.

"We didn't sell the ring. Not yet," Grace said from the bedroom.

"Your mom's big idea didn't work. Tell them, Grace. Tell them what happened."

Grace went to the kitchen stove and filled it with wood. She took the dipper off the wall, filled a pot with water, and began peeling potatoes.

"What about the ring, Mom?" Eddie asked.

Grace peered out the window while a long potato peel unravelled to rest in a coil on the table. "We won't know. For thirty days."

Jimmy gave a loud snort. "Know what your mom went and done? She took the ring to the jeweller to sell it. I told her if the ring was stolen, we'd get in a lot of trouble. Mounties don't like Indians. She knows that, but she had to do it her way and take it to the jeweller. Well, I was right when I said it was a Cartier diamond. And it is worth a lotta money. You know how much he said it was worth? He said it could be worth as much as five hundred dollars. Then he took it. He took it and said that somebody must have lost it and the police would want to know. But I think he thought we stole the damn thing."

"He said it's the law that if somebody comes into the store and tries to sell something that expensive, he has to tell the police," Grace said.

"You don't know that guy. He'll probably tell the cops that he found it. Christ, he might say that after thirty days somebody come along and claimed it. I bet that's what's gonna really happen. And you're too stupid to know it."

"I thought you said he was going to tell the cops that we stole it?"

"You know what I mean. We'd have money right now if you listened to me. The guy at the pawnshop would have given us a hundred and fifty bucks right then and there. Now we might get nothing. Nothing at all."

"Anyways, Eddie and Lewis, don't get your hopes up," Grace said. "The police have the ring. After thirty days, if nobody comes to claim it, then it's ours. Or if somebody did lose it and they prove it's theirs, the jeweller said, there might be a reward. But I don't want to hear about the ring anymore today, so you guys go do something and stop dreaming about rings and money."

Eddie grabbed his coat and warned Lewis not to follow him. He wanted to be alone. Setting off down the road toward Heart

Lake, he hurried across the soft mud onto firmer ground to a knoll beside the lake. He crawled on his stomach to the top and saw the beaver lodge rising out of the water. A canal stretched back into the woods where the beavers dragged trees to dam the creek that flowed out to the connecting lakes. The beavers, like the army, were tidy. Sharp-pointed stumps underwater showed that the lake level had risen two feet.

A stick snapped, and a beaver appeared out of the trees, dragging a sapling in its mouth. The tree got stuck, but the beaver kept tugging and finally pulled it free. Eddie watched the beavers for hours as they waddled back into the darkness for more wood. Each seemed to know what the other was doing and worked with a plan. Eddie lost track of time, and it wasn't until he heard his mom's voice calling that he realized it was getting dark. Walking back to the road, he came upon his own footprint in the soft ground. Placed squarely on top was a fresh bear track. He walked quickly home.

Grace made a face and sat down to hold her round tummy with both hands. Eddie's biggest fear was that she would have the baby when they were all alone. There was an air of danger about the birth of a baby, and Eddie wanted to be far away when it happened.

Once, while he helped her make supper, she grabbed his hand and pressed it to her stomach. Eddie was alarmed to feel the baby kick, and he jumped back and looked at her.

"Smarten up, Mom."

Grace had held her tummy and laughed.

Four weeks passed. Arguments still broke out whenever the ring came up. Even though Grace had said she didn't want to hear another word about the ring or money, Eddie often saw her just before bedtime sitting at the kitchen table looking through the Simpson-Sears catalogue. She started at the front of the book and worked her way back, sometimes placing a piece of paper between pages as a marker. If she came upon something interesting, she took her hands from the table, placed them on her lap, and nodded her head as if agreeing with herself, then looked around the room to see if anyone had noticed.

One evening after Eddie and Lewis had gone to bed, Jimmy pulled out a chair and sat at the table with Grace. From the darkness of his room, Eddie moved onto his stomach to watch through the open door.

"I got a idea about the money. But let me talk first before you say anything."

Grace closed her eyes and took a deep breath. "What's your big idea?" she asked tiredly.

"Don't say nothing until you heard it all. You're gonna like it. I know you will. This guy I know, he's got a stock car, and he goes all over the States to these big races. Him and two other guys, his pit crew. They start in spring and go until the end of summer. He doesn't work or nothing, he just races. And he makes good money too. He said he made twenty-five hundred dollars last year after he paid all the bills. Jeez, Grace, twenty-five hundred dollars. At the end of the year I could pay you back and you could do whatever you want with it.

"This guy started out with one car that he bought cheap. Now he's even got a spare in case one breaks down. Well, he's thinking about getting a new one, and he said he'd sell me the spare. Grace, we could make a lotta money stock car racing. You know what a good driver I am. Hell, there ain't a cop that can catch me when I floor that pedal. He said he'd throw in an extra set of tires and even a trailer for hauling the car. All he wants is two hundred and fifty bucks for the whole works. That's half. My half. The first race is in January. He said he could have the car here as soon as we want. Think for a minute about how nice it'll be having enough money so you didn't have to worry no more. What you say, Grace?"

Eddie saw his mother take her time before speaking, as though she knew there would be an argument as soon as she finished. But

Jimmy thought she was taking too long and pounded his fist on the table. Lewis jumped awake.

"Say something, dammit. Quit sitting there thinking up all the ways of telling me it's a dumb idea."

"Don't you go getting tough with me, Jimmy. I'm not scared of you. You or any man. I'll tell you what I think, but you keep quiet and you let me talk now. You make it sound real good travelling all over the States, going from one town to another with me and the kids sitting and cheering you on while you get to do what you always wanted. But what about us? What about the kids' school? You want to do what you been dreaming about for a long time. You used to talk to me about that when we first got together. I even said to you, 'Sure, let's do it,' but you never done a damn thing. Even after I found out I was knocked up, we still could have done whatever we wanted. Do you remember what Mom said when I told her? She said, 'What you gonna live on? Love?' You got mad when I told you and you said, 'I'll show her.' But you never did. I thought that was what you were doing all the time you were gone. What the hell have you been doing all them years?"

"You told me to take a flying leap. Remember? I didn't want to go nowhere. So don't go sayin' I took off because I wanted to. I'd a never left," Jimmy said.

"You make it sound like I didn't have a reason. Did you forget about the floozy you was running around with?"

"What you bringing that up for? I thought we weren't gonna talk about that no more. Here I'm trying to tell you about a way to make us some money, and all you want to do is win another damn argument. That's always been your way. You stick what happened somewhere in the back of your mind so you can just bring it out and slap me in the face with it. Am I right or am I wrong?"

"Boy, Jimmy, if you think it's easy for me to just up and forget about what happened, then I don't know. But let's talk about what you said. You tell me how we're going to do it if you got everything figured out. I want to hear what you're gonna do about the kids' school, where we're gonna sleep, and how we're gonna eat. I'll just sit here and listen and I won't say a word. But before you say anything, just tell me one thing. Did you even get your driver's license yet?"

For a moment Jimmy didn't speak. Then he pushed back his chair and stood. "I been living here for a while now and I let you say anything you want even though I know you got it all wrong. But don't you go looking down your nose at me. And don't take that tone neither. You say one more word, Grace, and I'll slap the living Jesus outta you."

They glared at each other. The lamp cast a shadow on the table that sat between them like a black hole. The bitterness that had been perking for some time between them was about to bubble over.

Jimmy walked around the table as Grace stood. "You heard what I said. One more word outta you and you'll be sorry."

Knowing his mother wouldn't be told to be quiet, Eddie slid out of bed and pulled on his pants.

"Your half, my ass," Grace said with a sneer.

Jimmy shook his head. "I told you."

He punched Grace hard in the stomach. She doubled over with a sharp cry and went down to her knees. Eddie ran out of the bedroom. Grace made a sound that was between a cough and a choke. Eddie didn't know what to do. Should he find a club and beat Jimmy to death with it or look after his mother who looked in so much pain?

Jimmy turned to Eddie. "What you gonna do, boy? You come at me, and I'll beat the shit out of you too."

Jimmy grabbed his coat and slammed the door behind him. The car roared, spraying stones against the side of the house. Eddie took Grace by the elbow to help her into a chair. Grace was shaking. She took deep breaths until she was able to sit up. She put an arm around Eddie.

"It was my fault he got so mad. Go on, get to bed."

22

Thirty days after the ring had been handed over to the police, at last the family left for town to find out if it was now theirs.

Grace parked the truck two blocks away from the police station. As they passed by a small engine repair shop, three men carrying chainsaws came out the door and blocked the sidewalk in front of Grace. She grabbed Lewis's hand and stepped onto the road to go around them. Eddie looked back at the men glaring back at him.

"Why did those guys do that, Mom?" Lewis asked. "Why did they make us walk out on the road?"

"Never mind," Grace said.

Grace opened the door of the police station, and Eddie and Lewis followed her in. Somewhere in the office a typewriter clattered and a phone rang. They stopped at a shoulder-high desk where a steely-eyed constable looked down at them.

"Yes?"

"My name is Grace Toma. I came in to see about a ring."

"What ring?"

"The ring my boys found in the river. The one the jeweller brought in thirty days ago. Has anybody come in to claim it?"

With a sigh the constable turned. "Hey Bill, know anything about a ring some Indians found?"

A man walking by looked them up and down, shook his head, and continued on his way.

"Sorry, Mrs. Toma. Nobody knows anything about a ring. I'll ask around. Why don't you come back in a couple of days? Maybe it'll turn up by then."

Grace pulled the boys with her to a bench by the door and sat down. "That ring's been here for a month. If nobody's claimed it, then I'll take it with me. You guys were the ones supposed to be looking after it. But if you lost it and think I'm just gonna go away and forget about it like I'm stupid, well, you thought wrong. I know how much it's worth. The jeweller told me. I'm not going anywhere. I'll wait right here while you go and look for it or make me out a cheque for five hundred dollars."

The constable walked away and returned holding a piece of paper.

"It looks like somebody came and got it first thing this morning. His name was James Alvin Toma."

Grace rose from the bench and leaned on the desk. "What? You gave that sonofabitch the ring? He didn't find the damn thing. My boys did."

"Don't use that kind of language in here. We're only steps away from the cells, you know."

"He stole it, then. I want to press charges. I want you to find him and bring him back."

"You said your name was Toma, right? Is James Toma your husband?"

"He's my husband. But he had no right to take it. What's the matter with you guys? I told the jeweller that the boys found it. It belongs to them, not that—asshole."

"Okay, I told you before about your language. Now you keep that tongue in your mouth or—"

"Or what? What you going to do? Throw me in jail? You don't care what happens to us. You let a man just walk out the door with the only thing we ever had that was worth anything. So you go right ahead. Lock me up. You're big and tough. Come on. Put your handcuffs on me."

Grace turned around with her wrists joined together.

"Mom, let's go," Eddie said, pulling on her arm.

Grace pulled away and stuck her wrists higher.

"I'm not going anywhere. I'm going to keep on swearing until they drag me into the back and beat me up with their clubs. I guess swearing is pretty bad if they lock you up for it instead of a person that robs a mother and her kids. Am I right? You dumb bastards. You assholes."

Eddie and Lewis were frantic. Three more officers came to the desk. An older man with a flat-top crew cut nudged the constable aside.

"Ma'am, nobody is going to arrest you. I know you're upset, and you're saying things you don't really mean, but you're only embarrassing yourself and scaring your kids. The law is the law. If you wanted to be the one to sign for the ring, you should have said so. Because he's your husband, there's nothing we can do. We're sorry, but what's done is done."

Grace turned and faced the row of policemen. "If I was a white woman, you would have made damn sure. You would have checked with her first before you handed it over to anybody who just walked in."

"It says right on the form you don't have a telephone. How are we supposed to check with you if you don't have a phone? Smoke signals?"

The other officers chuckled.

"I don't have electricity neither. Why don't you have a laugh at that too? We were going to pay for the power poles ourselves. Now I guess we'll just go home and sit in the dark. You're supposed to be helping people, not laughing at them."

"Mrs. Toma, we sympathize with you, but our hands are tied. If we had a little more co-operation from you people when we need your help, then maybe we could do something."

"You people. You people. That's what you call us, isn't it? Well, I'll tell you what. I'm never going to trust a cop again. Next time I see that man you call a husband, I'll put a bullet in him. And you'll know it was me, because I'll put it right between his eyes. From now on, I'll take care of my troubles myself so I won't be a bother to you people anymore."

Grace, Eddie, and Lewis walked out the door.

That night Grace gave birth to a stillborn baby girl.

23

Eddie pushed through the school door as the school bus pulled up to the wooden sidewalk. Near the bus stop people were gathered around the marble pitch.

Why didn't they rush inside the bus as usual to find the best seats? Eddie walked over to find out.

Lewis was obviously winning, by his bulging pockets, but his opponent made Eddie stop and stare. It was Rodney Bell, tongue sticking out the corner of his mouth in concentration on his next shot. Something bad was about to happen.

Rodney's steely fell short of the hole just as the bus doors opened and students began filing in. Now it was Lewis's turn. Eddie watched nervously. He hoped Lewis would miss the hole, lose a few marbles, and Rodney would go away happy. Lewis tossed his cob, and it bounced and rolled straight into the pot. As Lewis stepped forward to collect his winnings, Rodney grabbed him by the coat collar and threw him to the ground. Rodney and the other boys filled their pockets with his brother's marbles.

Eddie dropped his books on the ground and ran. "Hey!"

Rodney barely had time to drop the marbles in his hand before Eddie crashed into him. They flipped over and rolled to a stop against the rear tire of the school bus, locked in a bear hug. A crowd quickly gathered. Rodney pushed Eddie away and pulled his arm back to strike. Eddie made a grab at his sleeve and missed but ducked his head away just as Rodney's fist went past his face.

Eddie waved his arms in front of him, trying to block Rodney's punches. He managed to grab Rodney's jacket, but it wasn't a good grip, and he could feel it slipping out of his fingers.

Then two strong hands pulled them apart and lifted them to their feet. It was the bus driver, Willy Krebbs. Rodney kicked at Eddie. Eddie kicked back.

"Stop it. Both of you," Mr. Krebbs said.

He was a tall, broad-shouldered man with large, strong hands. When he tightened his grip, Eddie felt his jacket stretch across his back. Willy's knuckles banged against Eddie's chest as he swung the two boys back and forth.

"What's going on here?" It was the principal, Mr. Latimer. "I should have known. You can't seem to stay out of trouble, can you, Bell? The two of you are lucky it's Friday and Toma has a bus to catch. But I want to see you both in my office Monday morning sharp, all right?"

"Yes, sir."

"Yes, sir."

"Send them on their way, Mr. Krebbs. And keep a close watch on Toma."

The principal walked back up the sidewalk toward the school entrance.

"Get out of here," Willy said to Rodney, pushing him away. Then he motioned to three girls sitting in the front seat to move. "This boy gets to sit up here with me for a while."

Someone handed Eddie his books. The bus driver watched in the mirror as the door clapped shut and the bus pulled away from the sidewalk. There was a thumping sound on the side of the bus. Eddie saw Rodney motioning to open his window. He slid down the glass.

"You and me behind the gym Monday after school," Rodney said. Then he jumped up and down and bobbed his head in a mock Indian dance. Someone in the bus laughed. Reflected in the bus mirror Eddie saw Lewis in the seat behind him, watching to see if he reacted, looking disappointed when he sat still. A tingling heat spread across Eddie's neck and scalp.

Behind Rodney, egging him on, were Sid Mullen and his brother Sam, who followed Rodney around the schoolyard. On their own they weren't so tough. Sam Mullen especially always made sure there were people around before he called Eddie names and ran away. He was always too fast for Eddie to catch.

One day while Eddie was sitting out in the hall for talking during class he saw Sam coming out of the classroom. Eddie slipped unnoticed into the boy's washroom, went into a stall, and stood on the toilet seat to wait. Sam huddled close to the urinal. Even though he thought he was all alone, he still covered up his privates with both hands. A sudden push from behind caused him to wet on his pants. Eddie remembered the surprise in Sam's eyes when he turned around. Eddie punched him just once in the stomach, but it was enough.

Sam doubled over as Eddie pushed him out into the hallway. Wiping away the tears with the back of his hand, Sam opened the door to go back inside the classroom. Just before he stepped inside, he turned to Eddie and said, "Squaw man."

Now, protected by Rodney and the bus walls, the Mullen brothers shouted out insulting names as fast as they could think them up. Eddie turned away, slumping in his seat. He looked in the mirror and saw Lewis watching him as if he expected him to do something. Eddie knew better. He'd seen what happened to a person who tried to fight back against so many people.

Eddie didn't mind going to school. Usually life would go along so smoothly that he forgot about the bad parts. He even tried letting the names roll off his back as Joshua had done, and most of the time it worked. Sometimes the name caller would move on to something else, except for one person: Rodney Bell. Eddie couldn't understand why Rodney hated him so much. He always stayed out of his way, and whenever he had no choice but to fight, he ended up on the bottom taking a beating.

The last time they had a fight, the last week of school before summer holidays, Eddie had been the one that started it.

Eddie and Rodney were playing soccer on opposite teams, and both ended up going for the ball. Eddie didn't back away this time. They kicked the ball at the same time, sending it straight up in the air. Before the ball hit the ground, Eddie and Rodney were rolling on the grass, hitting each other until some older boys pulled them apart. Rodney was so angry that he kicked one of the boys between the legs.

In the fall when school resumed, Eddie readied himself for the moment when the bus pulled up to the school sidewalk and Rodney was there waiting for him.

Over the summer he'd taken on all the hard work given to him so he could build up his body. He cut down trees below the house with an axe to widen the clearing, ran to the range and back many times a day without stopping, and piled rocks in the river to make the swimming hole deeper. Any job that needed heavy lifting, he'd jumped at the chance to do it. When Grace said that he'd grown two inches and put on weight, he felt confident and ready for anything Rodney had up his sleeve.

But Rodney had taken so long to make his move that Eddie wasn't so sure of himself anymore.

Leaning his head against the window, Eddie looked out at the leafless trees along the road. They looked dead in the cold air of fall. The front yards of the houses were covered with dry grass and weeds. Pieces of rusty tin plugged holes where shingles had completely rotted away on a sagging roof. Blistered, peeling paint that exposed the nails to the elements now wept in a pencil lead gray down the clapboards. A dog waiting at the corner began chasing a car and suddenly squatted and dropped one, two, three black steaming turds on the ground.

As the bus stopped next to a house, Eddie saw an old man staring out through the dirty windows. His eyes looked vacant, like the eyes of a fish that has been out of water too long. Inhaling on a hand-rolled cigarette until his cheeks caved in, he squinted to keep the smoke from getting into his eyes. The bus jerked forward. The old man didn't notice; he exhaled the smoke through his nose. The bus sped away, leaving Falkland behind.

24

At fifty-five miles an hour the truck began to shake, and the steering wheel wobbled back and forth. Grace stepped on the gas. At sixty miles an hour the shaking stopped.

On the outskirts of town they passed by a large sign that read Welcome to Vernon. In a trailer park tucked under weeping willows to the right, the trailers in neat rows all looked the same. Eddie wondered if anyone had ever walked into the wrong one by mistake. At the front of the trailers people sat on decks that looked more like corrals, each deck facing the back of the trailer in front of it. The people seated in white high-backed chairs seemed to have everything they needed.

Lewis said, "Look at them, Mom, they all look the same. I wonder if anyone goes into the wrong one by mistake."

On the street Eddie thought was the prettiest in town, they drove past old Victorian homes with lilac hedges between them. In spring when the lilacs were in bloom, the air would be filled with a scent that reminded Eddie of honeysuckle season. Some of the homes were so huge they looked like palaces. He wondered how many rooms were inside. And there were so many different kinds of trees. Walnut, horse chestnut, and red maple grew along sidewalks leading to wraparound porches. Most of the leaves had fallen, but some sheltered trees still held a few bright colours of autumn.

At the end of Main Street a parking lot sloped down toward the street. Grace backed the truck between two cars, pointing its nose downhill so she could start the truck in case the battery died. Stepping off the running board, Eddie saw the wide main street was already busy. A few stores had their neon signs turned on. Even in broad daylight their colours were bright.

Mannequins in store windows displayed expensive clothes, hats, and shoes. The smell of a bakery somewhere mingled with car exhaust, and leaves gathering around storm sewer grates smelled wet and musty. Tall chimneys on rooftops spewed out smoke and steam. A car speeding by honked its horn. Everywhere people were moving about, talking and laughing. A bicyclist rang a cheerful bell. A dog barked. Tires screeched. Doors banged shut. Someone hammered on lumber. Music filtering down from the record shop mixed with the sounds of the street like a movie score.

Grace muttered under her breath, "Sometimes I hate this noisy, smelly town."

Eddie found it hard to walk on the sidewalk with mobs of people coming at him. No one wanted to move aside, but Lewis smiled as he ducked in and out of the crowd. They passed the city park that was always lively with chirping sparrows and swallows swooping from tree to tree. Old men in wrinkled suits and stained fedoras sat at picnic tables playing cards or checkers while others smoked cigarettes or drank coffee out of thermoses. A few read newspapers.

Lewis pointed. "Hey, look at that guy over there with his pants leg tied in a knot."

Grace said, "Don't point! He'll come over here and hit you with one of his crutches. A lot of guys came home like that from the First World War. If you get too close, they'll swear at you and tell you to keep the hell away."

Across the street the barber shop, with its ever-turning candy cane pole at the entrance, had a sign that read "Six chairs, no waiting." Every Saturday proved the sign wrong; each chair was occupied while more men waited their turn.

At Dye's Billiards Eddie and Lewis looked in the window at ornate boxes of cigars with names like El Producto, Old Port, and White Owl. Leather wallets, combs, and pipe tobacco were displayed under a grimy glass counter alongside hair restorer tonics. Eddie looked inside for Hank but couldn't make him out among all the pool players milling inside a cloud of smoke. The loud smack of a cue ball breaking a triangle of red snooker balls made Eddie want to go inside.

There was Vern Dye himself, handing a foil-wrapped cigar to a man who immediately placed it under his nose. Closing his eyes, the customer ran his nose along the cigar's length and nodded in approval. Eddie wondered how he could smell through the wrapper.

After handing over a fifty-cent piece, the man stepped outside. He peeled back the wrapper, slid the paper ring off the cigar, and tossed the wrapper in the direction of the garbage can beside the door; the paper ring floated down to the sidewalk. Lewis quickly retrieved the ring, placing it on his finger. Pulling a small pair of scissors from inside his waistcoat, the man snipped the end off the cigar. The Zippo lighter in his hand glinted in the sunlight as he flipped the top open, and it made a tinny sound. The man took deep puffs until the cigar glowed red and crackled, and the flame disappeared somewhere inside the cigar. Snapping the lighter shut, the man brushed by Eddie, leaving him in a cloud of sweet smoke that smelled of coffee, chocolate, and leather. He blew smoke out of the corner of his mouth as he walked down the sidewalk with a swagger.

"Come on, you guys," Grace called back to them.

Lewis ran ahead, but Eddie held back so he wouldn't be seen with his mother and brother. They crossed the street and went into the Hudson's Bay store. The thick glass doors opened easily, perfectly balanced, and their brass hinges and door handles gleamed like gold. Inside the warm air smelled of perfume and floor wax.

Eddie saw the jewellery display where he and Eva had spent time as if they were a real couple.

Hearing footsteps on the mirror-like floors, Eddie looked up as a lady in high heels came toward him. She was so beautiful that he couldn't help but stare. Her skin looked smooth and perfect like the mannequins in the windows. Her long legs swung through the folds of a fur coat. She wore a small black hat with a veil draped over one eye. Eddie stared at her red shoes and up to her silky stockings and a dress of the brightest red. His gaze brushed past her pearl necklace and stopped at her eyes. She looked directly at Eddie as she glided past as if floating on air. Eddie looked away. When he heard the doors close, he turned around for one last look. Just before she disappeared into the crowd, the lady looked back and smiled.

Grace picked out socks, underwear, pants, and shoes for Lewis and Eddie. From the men's section she bought underwear for herself. "They're warmer than women's."

Two hours later Eddie'd had his fill of shopping, but Grace needed to buy a few more things for Lewis.

"I'll wait outside." Eddie walked away before she could answer.

Between two large windows the concrete was warmed by the sun. It was a perfect spot for him to lean back and watch people go by. He wouldn't have much time. Taking a bent and flattened cigarette out of his pants pocket, he straightened it as much as he could, scraped a wooden match on the wall, and took a long draw.

Most people tried to avoid eye contact. They walked by with their eyes locked onto the sidewalk ahead as if they were looking for dropped change. Three types of people looked another person in the eye: the friendly ones smiled back, the nosey ones tried to figure a person out—what they were up to and if anyone was looking at them the same way—and a few looked for trouble. Every so often someone noticed him but looked away before being caught staring. A couple stopped in front of Eddie, almost stepping on his toes. They argued until they saw they were being watched, then hurried away.

When the traffic light turned red, cars and pickup trucks of every age and condition rattled to a stop. Engines roared when the light changed, and the vehicles surged ahead. Someone honked at an old man with a cane when he took too long to cross the street. The old man stopped and waved his cane at the car. When the honking stopped, he put down his cane and continued his long journey to the curb. As the light turned green, the driver shouted out to the man.

"You old fart!"

The old man turned around to look at the car speeding away down the street until it was out of sight. He turned to go but looked back one last time before shuffling away.

Eddie dropped the butt to the sidewalk and ground it out with his heel. He was hungry, about to go back inside to see what was taking so long, when he saw three girls walking toward him. The striking blonde in the middle looked familiar. He turned up his jacket collar, crossed his arms, and waited. She looked at him and smiled. It was Dawn, Eva's friend who looked like a *Playboy* model.

"Hi, Eddie. Whatcha doing? Girl watching?" She walked over and leaned against the wall so close that Eddie stepped back.

Boys and men who walked by looked her over from head to toe with obvious longing. She had more confidence than anyone Eddie had known, pushing herself in front of him as if taking control. When she crossed her arms, her breasts swelled under her jacket. For all Eddie knew, he could be dreaming, and the sexy girl he thought he was seeing, the one with ocean-green eyes and blond hair, wasn't real. Maybe he was picturing her just the way he imagined naked girls in his bedroom in the dark.

She smelled so sweet and warm that Eddie's body tingled. *You and me all alone on a desert island.*

"Aren't you going to ask me about Eva?"

Eddie swallowed. "No? Why should I?" He quickly moved away from Dawn into the street.

"Hey! Watch where you're going," a woman said, stepping around him.

"She's gone back to UBC. She said that you did to her what she was always afraid of. You broke her heart."

"I don't care," Eddie shot back.

"Why did you do it? She said she thought you were different. But you're just like all the boys. Toe jam. You guys only have one thing on your mind. Don't you? Huh? Look at the way you're looking at me right now. I'm wise to you guys and the rise in your Levis. So I better get outta here and head for home before I get knocked up." Dawn and the two girls laughed so hard that people passing by smiled at them.

"Oh, Dawn. You are so terrible," one said.

Eddie felt his face flush with embarrassment. He walked away and left them giggling and hooting. He was about to go into the store when Dawn ran up to him, still trying to catch her breath from laughing so hard.

"Wait. Wait, Eddie," she said grabbing his arm. "I'm only teasing. I really don't think Eva knew what she was doing. Just in the little time we saw you both together, Misty and I thought you were a couple. And when she told us what happened, we both told her that she was leading you on.

"She said you were too young, and her folks would have a conniption if they found out. That's the way Eva is—an old-fashioned farm girl. She doesn't mean to, but it has happened before. I guess she's so darn lovable. So, don't hate her. She knows she treated you badly. You wait. She'll smarten up. All you need is a couple hot summers under your belt and she'll come running. Anyway, I have to get home. You take care, and maybe we'll see you around."

She joined her friends and the laughter resumed as they disappeared into the crowd.

Eddie heard a loud "hey" and yelled when he felt a jab in his back.

Lewis was giggling and pointing at him.

Eddie grabbed him. "I told you before what I'd do to you if you didn't stop doing that, you little shit."

Lewis smiled and tried to hold back a chuckle. Eddie shook his brother hard. Lewis rolled his eyes in circles, let his body go limp, and laughed. Eddie knew it was pointless to go any further. He shoved his brother up against the wall and let him go. Lewis smiled.

Eddie walked twenty feet, found a new spot, and slumped against the wall, trying to get his mind off Dawn and the shrinking lump in his pants. A woman wove in and out of the crowd tapping her unopened umbrella on the sidewalk with every third step and smiled at no one in particular. Just as Grace came out of the store, the woman stopped in front of Lewis, reached inside her purse, and held out a fistful of change. Lewis looked up, not sure what to do.

"It's okay, son. Take it," she said as she dropped the money into his hand. She patted him on the head and walked away.

"What's going on here? What are you doing?" Grace rushed over. She rapped her knuckles on Lewis's head as if testing melons. His head sounded hollow. "Get out of here." She herded Lewis down the street and pushed him into an empty doorway. "Boy, I can't take you anywhere. What do you think would happen if somebody from the Indian Department seen you standing on a corner begging for money. Huh? They'd take you away. God, I hope nobody from the reserve seen you either. Gimme the money you got in your pocket. You're damn lucky we're not at home right now, or boy oh boy, I'd give you a damn good lickin'. And is that what you're doing too, Eddie, standing around waiting for a stranger to give you money? Huh?"

"Yeah. All the time," he said dryly.

Lewis handed over the change, and it fell clinking into her hands. "We'll go to the restaurant while you take these to the truck," she said to Eddie.

"I want to go to McKenzie's Men's Wear and look for Lee jeans. I'm not going to wear Cowboy Kings. They're for kids," Eddie said.

Grace shook her head. "They cost twice as much, and Indian Affairs only gives us twenty-five dollars apiece for a clothing allowance every year. That's all."

"But they last twice as long," Eddie claimed.

When Grace saw Eddie's stubborn look, she handed him a ten-dollar bill. "Jesus, seven dollars for a pair of pants. Just don't take all day, then."

She spun Lewis around by the shoulder. Lewis glanced back at Eddie. Grinning, he opened his hand to show two nickels in his palm.

When the light changed, Eddie crossed the street to McKenzie's store. After finding jeans with his waist and leg size, he paid the cashier and walked out the door toward the Top Hat Restaurant.

The traffic light at the Hudson's Bay intersection was taking forever, and he was ravenous. Directly across the street a woman stood with a baby carriage. She had dark skin, but Eddie couldn't tell if she was Indian. She looked tired, shifting her weight from one leg to the other. His eyes skimmed past her to the pigeons gathered on the electrical cables. He was always amazed that no two pigeons looked alike and there were so many different kinds.

When he looked back to the stop light, he noticed a figure next to the woman was staring at him. His heart almost stopped when he recognized Rodney Bell. He had completely forgotten about Rodney. Now, when the light changed, they would meet in the middle of the street. But whatever Rodney wanted to do, after Dawn and her friends made fun of him, Eddie was ready. He would fight Rodney in the street if he had to.

The woman was impatient, her eyes focused on the traffic light as though pleading for it to change. The light turned green. Rodney smirked at Eddie, and the woman quickly pushed the buggy off the curb.

Someone shouted a warning. Then a horn beeped and tires squealed. The buggy seemed to explode out of the mother's hands, knocking her off her feet. A pink bundle flew out of the buggy and flipped end over end in the air as the buggy crashed upside down onto the road. A small wheel rolled under a parked car. Bits of metal rained down, ringing like pennies. A large motorcycle slid on its side with the rider bouncing and rolling behind. With metal grinding and orange sparks showering everywhere, the motorcycle ran over the bundle, ripping away the pink wrapping, revealing a baby's arms and legs. Someone screamed.

A man in a suit ran toward the baby. He knelt and pressed his ear to the baby's mouth. The mother tried to stand. An older couple near her helped her to her feet. More people approached.

Eddie stood still, too stunned to move. The man took off his jacket to cover the baby that hadn't stirred.

The motorcycle rider who wore a helmet buckled under his chin and goggles sat up and looked at the people gathered around the baby. He put his head in his hands and rocked back and forth.

The mother pushed away the helping hands to go to her baby. Kneeling beside the man in the suit, she gently touched the tiny, still face. Two policemen appeared, and the man in the suit said something. One policeman positioned himself between the mother and baby, slowly moving her backward, while the other tried to push back the crowd. Caught in the surge, Eddie was carried along. The woman couldn't move her eyes away from her child lying on the cold asphalt. She said nothing. She hadn't uttered a single word. Someone recovered the pink blanket. The man in the suit placed the blanket over the baby's face and body. The mother began to shake. She closed her eyes and opened her mouth to scream. All Eddie heard was a loud whisper, like a brush moving across a blackboard.

"No," she mouthed. But there was no sound.

Eddie was confused until a voice in the crowd said, "She's a deaf mute."

Someone tried to help the rider to his feet, but he pushed their hands away.

The crowd began breaking up. Eddie pushed his way through the horde of people and ran toward the restaurant, searching the faces for Rodney.

At the restaurant he saw Grace and Lewis in a booth with plates of food on the table. Grace waved him inside. As he slid into the booth, Grace pushed a plate of French fries and a cheeseburger across to him. The aroma of the vinegar coming from Lewis's plate smelled sweet, but food didn't appeal to Eddie.

"What took you so long? You're white as snow, and your hands are shaking. What happened?"

Eddie couldn't answer.

"Eddie."

"I saw . . . it was an accident."

"A car accident?"

"No."

"Well, what then? Eddie. You tell me now. What's the matter?"

"It was a car accident."

"But you said—"

"I'll tell you later."

"Why? What happened?" Lewis asked, putting down his fork.

"Never mind," Grace warned.

"Why won't he tell us, Mom?"

"I said, never mind."

Eddie took a bite of his cheeseburger. Frustrated that he couldn't eat, he placed it back on the plate, leaned back, and watched the kitchen workers rushing through the swinging doors.

They pushed carts filled with dirty dishes, cutlery, clinking cups, and saucers. A waitress appeared carrying large plates of steaming food. She held a plate in each hand, with two more balanced on her left arm. Eddie wondered how she was going to set them down without dropping any on the floor. She placed the plate in her hand down first, then the others, one by one, as though dealing cards.

The doors to the kitchen were constantly swinging open and closed. There were near misses, but not a plate was broken or a drop of coffee spilled as they wove in and out of each other's way like square dancers. Eddie closed his eyes and took long breaths. But with so many comings and goings through the kitchen door, someone dropped a stack of plates, breaking them all. Eddie jumped and banged his knee under the table.

Lewis sat in the corner of the booth turning the flaps of the jukebox selector on the wall. Grace watched Eddie while slowly sipping her tea.

"I gotta pee again," Lewis said.

Grace set her cup down on the saucer. She slid out of the booth.

"Wanna come, Eddie?"

"I seen you pee before."

"Just get going before you piss your pants," Grace said.

Lewis hurried toward the bathrooms.

Grace placed her hands on the table and leaned toward Eddie. "Jesus. You almost jumped outta your skin. What the hell's the matter with you? What's going on?"

"I told you. I saw an accident."

"A car accident?"

"No."

"What was it then?"

"Mom."

Lewis stood at the edge of the table.

"Now what," Grace snapped.

"There's somebody in the bathroom. The door's locked."

"Use the ladies' then."

"I don't want to go into the ladies' bathroom."

"You will if you know what's good for you. Now get in there before you wet yourself."

His face screwed up in a last protest.

"Go."

Lewis walked away.

"Okay. Now tell me what happened, Eddie."

The story rushed out of Eddie so fast that he stuttered and had trouble putting it in order.

"Calm down, dammit," Grace said.

He told her everything that happened, except that he had seen Rodney. Grace didn't speak for the longest time.

"I don't feel like town anymore," Eddie said. "Let's go home."

"No. Not yet. You're gonna take Lewis to the show. You're always saying you want to go to the theatre. We're here now, so you're gonna go. I'm going to have a few beers with some people I haven't seen for a long time. All I ever do, day after day, is look after you two. I need to have some fun too, you know. After the show we'll go home."

She wrapped the cheeseburger with napkins. "You can eat this at the show."

They sat in the booth in silence.

A lady with blue-grey hair in a yellow dress and white sweater walked slowly up the aisle between the rows of booths greeting the diners. "How are you folks today? Don't you just love this time of year?" Just before reaching Eddie's booth, she turned back to the kitchen. She glanced at him over her shoulder. The corners of her mouth were drawn down.

Grace saw Lewis hurrying out of the bathroom.

"Now you listen, Eddie," she said quickly. "You forget about what you saw or you'll make yourself sick. Just think about you and your brother and how nobody would give a damn if it was one of you lying on that road. You remember that and don't go feeling sorry for somebody you don't even know."

Grace paid the bill, and the three walked out of the restaurant. The single bite of the cheeseburger sat on the bottom of Eddie's stomach like a rock. The dark sky seemed to match his mood. The sight of the baby lying on the street wouldn't go away. All he wanted was to go home where he could be alone.

Rain hitting the tops of their heads made them walk faster. Soon larger drops tapped the sidewalk in front of them, splattering onto the concrete like bugs on a windshield. By the time they reached the Capitol Theatre, the clouds had let loose. People stepping out of cars pulled up their collars before heading toward the yellow rectangle of light beaming out from the theatre. Crouched figures ran for cover. Eddie and his family raced to join them. Everyone crowded together under the canopy.

Eddie heard a car door close and footsteps splashing through puddles. A man and woman hurried across the street under the man's topcoat used as an umbrella. Inside the theatre entrance, the man brushed drops of water from the woman's hair as they stared into each other's eyes. She reached up to wipe a raindrop from his cheek, and Eddie realized it was the lady he had seen at the Hudson's Bay store. The man draped the coat over her shoulders like a cloak and smoothed the wrinkles from the fabric. Faces stared at the two people who looked as if they'd stepped off the movie screen. He was handsome. She was beautiful. The blinking overhead lights reflecting off her teeth sparkled like glitter when she smiled. Eddie couldn't help staring again. The man approached the ticket booth while the woman browsed the posters. People gawked at her, but she ignored them. When she saw Eddie, her admirer, her mouth eased into a smile.

"Hello," she said softly.

Eddie's hair prickled. "Hello." He tried to sound as if beautiful women spoke to him all the time.

When the man returned with the tickets, the lady placed her hand on his arm and they went inside the theatre.

Grace leaned over to Eddie. "Who the hell was that?"

"I dunno."

"Why did she say hi to you?"

"I dunno."

"Maybe she's in love with Eddie," Lewis said, fluttering his lashes.

"Shut up," Eddie said, giving his brother a shove.

Lewis watched a woman lean down to two children. "You look after each other. When the show is over, I'll be right here waiting."

"Okay," they answered.

She ran, holding her purse over her head. She looked back. Her children waved. "Goodbye, Mom!"

"Goodbye. Have fun!" She waved by bending and unbending her fingers as if it were a secret code between them.

Grace shoved dollar bills and change into Eddie's hand. "This is a long movie. It's almost three hours. It'll be dark when you get out, so you guys meet me at the truck as soon as the show is over. Don't you go fooling around either. Just get in the truck and sit there. And don't go poking your head in the hotel looking for me." She stepped out into the rain.

"Mom," Lewis called.

She stopped to look back.

"Goodbye," he said, waving.

Grace scowled and hurried away.

Entering the theatre, Eddie felt hungry when he smelled popcorn. He bought a large box with extra butter and two large Cokes and they made their way down the centre aisle. Sinking down in the plush seat, he gave Lewis a pop and two sticks of liquorice. Lewis reached into the box of popcorn on Eddie's lap and immediately spilled some on the floor. "Jesus, Lewis. You're always doing that."

With a clash of music a cartoon appeared on the parting curtains, looking transparent. A loud cheer came from the children. Eddie went to the theatre every chance he could, no matter what was showing. Even the musicals were enjoyable, despite the singing and dancing. The title of the main attraction, *The Great Escape*, appeared on the screen.

"This is such a good show," a girl sitting behind him told her friend. "But I saw it months ago in Vancouver. You guys up here don't get the new ones right away, do you?"

"No," the other girl said. "I've heard that before—"

"Shhh." The usher put his finger to his mouth and shook his head.

The movie ended too quickly. Eddie'd had enough popcorn and pop-flavoured ice water to last him awhile. When the lights came on and the curtains began to close, people headed for the exit sign beside the screen. Emerging from the warm theatre, Eddie saw the mother standing near the coming attractions posters waiting for her two children just as she'd said. After giving each of her children a hug, they walked away together in the light rain.

The street was the quietest Eddie had seen all day. Businesses were dark and locked up solid. A few had display windows lit up by a weak light while some had drawn shades. Passing a long, echoing alley, Eddie felt a chill when he heard a tomcat yowling in the dark like a crying baby. A man and woman across the street yelled at each other. The taxi stand was occupied by a lone dispatcher.

Eddie searched the parking lot and was surprised to see Grace sitting in the truck with the engine idling. He'd expected her to be in the beer parlour until closing time, something she'd been doing more frequently each time they came to town. He and Lewis had often gone to the hotel and poked their heads inside the Ladies and Escorts door to look for her. She would leave the table and smoke and chatter to find out what was the matter, embarrassed by her sons' appearance. It only took once or twice before she came out and they went home.

Eddie closed the door and Grace put the truck in gear.

"How was the show?" she asked.

"Good," Eddie answered.

"I bet it wasn't as good as the show I saw. Everybody arguing and crying. I couldn't stand it anymore and got the hell outta there," Grace added.

Lewis leaned against his mother and fell asleep.

That night the house was still except for the crack of firewood smoldering in the heater and the ticking of the clock. Eddie lay in bed and stared out the window at the moon breaking through the clouds.

25

At breakfast Eddie poked at his bowl of porridge, unable to shake the sight of the baby with its tiny fingers and toes lying on the pavement.

One time he'd sat up at the highway watching the traffic go by, and someone had tossed a doll out of a car. It rolled down the road before rocking to a stop on its stomach. When he bent down to pick up the doll, its eyebrows, lashes, and ears looked so real that he threw it down. Suddenly his body jerked in his chair as if he were trying to pull himself back from the edge of a cliff.

"Want some more?" Grace asked.

"No. I'm full." He pushed away from the table. Outside thick fog rolled off the river through the trees. "I'm going fishing. By myself. Make sure Lewis doesn't follow me. I looked after him enough yesterday."

He picked up his coat and was out the door before Lewis had a chance to argue. Eddie only glanced at his fishing pole leaning against the house as he walked past. Grace watched him from the kitchen window until the fog closed in around him.

The fog stifled the chatter of the birds, and the traffic that normally sped across the bridge now drove carefully. Eddie turned onto the trail to the river behind his grandma's house. Smoke from a new fire spiralled out of the chimney before dissolving into the fog. Her back door opened with a loud squeak. Eddie stepped behind a tree. He watched her reach around the corner and place a package wrapped in brown butcher's paper into the apple box nailed to the wall of the house. It was the cold box where she kept her eggs, meat, and lard. Alphonse called it an "Indian refrigerator." Eddie pulled his head back as she turned toward him. She went back inside, banging her door shut.

Eddie followed the narrow path that looped in and out of the trees at the edge of the river. He squeezed past a large cottonwood that had fallen where the river had collapsed the bank. He hiked along the river for two hundred yards, stepping over deadfalls and a clump of spiny devil's club. When the fog became so thick that he couldn't see where he was going, he had to rely on his memory to find his way. He felt as if the ground under his feet moved like a conveyer belt while the fog held him still. It was like walking inside a dream.

Quickly he walked along a hidden trail that others wouldn't have noticed until he came to the cedar log that reached out halfway across the river. Its large roots were anchored to the shore. Stepping carefully on the slippery bark, Eddie walked out to the end of the log, where he sat dangling his feet over the water. The mist rose off the surface like smoke as a gentle wind began to move the fog off the river. The sun broke through in places and burned away the haze until a last clump of fog came speeding down the river straight for Eddie. As the fog touched his face, he opened his mouth to inhale it. A school of minnows darted back and forth under the cedar log. A single crow cawed from somewhere up in the trees.

Thankful for the calm, he sat for a long time thinking about the next day at school until he heard a noise coming down the trail. He wondered how he could have forgotten to bring the gun. It wasn't a bear by the amount of noise it made. There was nothing he could do but wait and listen as the tramping of feet through the undergrowth came closer and closer. Then his mother stumbled out of the brush. Eddie could tell right away that there was something on her mind. She slipped on the uneven path but didn't slow her pace until stopping at the foot of the cedar log.

"You get over here right now."

He stepped off the log and stood in front of his mother.

"I want to know what's going on. What's the matter with you anyway?"

"Nothing."

"Look, I know you saw that baby die yesterday, but there was something bothering you before that. Since you came home from school Friday, you hardly said a word. What's wrong with you? Are you in love or something?"

Eddie hated her special way of saying the word "love" by using the deepest part of her voice as if a person in love were the stupidest person in the world.

"No." Eddie glared at her.

"What is it then?'

"Nothing. I don't know what you're talking about."

"Well, maybe somebody at your school knows. If you don't tell me, I'll get on that bus with you tomorrow and I'll sit beside you all the way to school. Then I'll go to your classroom and I'll ask your teacher right in front of everybody. And if your teacher doesn't know, then I'll go to the principal, who I'm getting to know pretty good by the letters he sends me. I know about your fights at school. Funny how he never writes to tell me what a good student you are. I bet he thinks it's my fault too. Well, I don't want those kinds of letters anymore, so you tell me right now." She had the same look that came over her whenever she cut down a willow stick for whipping when he was little.

Eddie told her everything—about Rodney, the beatings, and how it started on his first week of school. He told her about Lewis, the marbles, and his fight after school on Monday. She didn't interrupt him once. It was the first time for as long as he could remember that she listened.

"I'm going to fight him tomorrow, Mom. If I don't, he'll start on Lewis. I'm not scared of him."

Grace stood quietly for a minute, then asked, "Does Rodney have a sister named Susan?"

"How do you know?"

"Did you see Rodney in town yesterday?"

"Yeah."

"I knew his mother, Theresa Bell. That was her baby that was killed yesterday. Alphonse just came back from the store and told me. I don't know how that storekeeper finds out about these things. Me and Theresa, we went to the school on the reserve together. I knew her husband too. Ellis Bell. Fifteen years ago they got married and lived in a little place by a sawmill up in Westwold where Ellis worked. They had two kids, Rodney and a girl—that must be Susan. I heard a while ago she was expecting another one. Ellis got thrown in jail seven or eight months ago for selling stolen car parts. I never seen her since the time she got married. Ellis made sure everybody stayed away from her." Her voice lowered as she looked down at the ground.

"Now I wish I did see her. I could have seen her new baby. Ellis Bell. Huh. He was a bad one. Him and Theresa's two brothers had a gang. They followed behind him and did all his dirty work. Everybody was scared of them. And for some reason they took after your Uncle Alphonse. I know you don't think too much of him, but if you seen what they did to him then maybe you'd know why he is the way he is.

"They used to go around in this big car with no mufflers. You could hear them coming a mile away. Sometimes they came into our place all drunk and feeling tough and did power turns around the yard of our old house. Well, for a long time, days and weeks, we never heard from Ellis Bell and had no more bother from him. We thought they took off somewhere. Maybe they found something better to do or somebody else to pick on.

"Then one night I woke up and heard that car rolling down our road, idling. They stopped at the front steps and sat in the car, roaring their motor. Boy, the sounds those pipes made under the car, crackling and backfiring in the dark. They must have known Mom was down in the States and it was only Alphonse and me at home by ourselves. We had to just sit and wait to see what they were going to do next. Then they came up the steps and started pounding on the door, yelling for Alphonse to get outside. They said they were going to kill him.

"They started kicking the door trying to break it down. Alphonse was going a little out of his head he was so scared, and he kept telling me to do something. Well, that did it. I wasn't going to let them get away with this no more. I remembered the rifle on the gun rack was loaded and ready to go. So I took it down and went into the kitchen. The noise from the car covered up the sound of me opening the window beside the door. But when somebody switched off the car and it got real quiet, I cocked the gun. They didn't do anything right away. Maybe they weren't sure if they heard right or not.

"When I stuck the gun out the window and pulled the trigger, a long flame came out the end of the barrel. You should have heard them take off down the steps and scatter like chickens. They got in their car and took off. There was rocks and dirt hitting the house. I opened the door and put a bullet into their back window. The glass exploded. Damn lucky I didn't hit one of them. I put one more in the trunk for good measure. Something to remember me by.

"They never came around our house again. And pretty soon everybody got fed up with them. People started catching them one by one when they were alone and beating the hell out of them. It took a long time, maybe a year, before they got chased off the reserve. They went into town to try their luck there, but it didn't work, so the gang finally broke up. But Ellis, he stayed. He started working for a living as if he was trying to be respectable or something. But men like him don't change. He was the one I told you about when you were little. That if I gave you a signal, you were to go to Cluffs' and call the cops. I always thought he would come back and do something to me or your uncle or your grandma.

"Anyway, the next thing I knew, Theresa was knocked up, and they got married. She knew what he was like, but she married him anyway. It didn't take long before she was walking around with black eyes and bruises. That poor woman never had much of a life. I figured with Ellis locked up she'd have some good times ahead of her. Now this. Her boy sounds like a chip off the old block. The one thing you don't know is Rodney Bell's mom is from the same reserve as us."

"Rodney's an Indian?"

"Part Indian anyway."

"But he hates Indians."

"Maybe that's the part he hates. Or maybe his dad told him about me chasing him off, and he's blaming us for his miserable life."

"Us?"

"Us. The reserve and everybody living on it. He's ashamed of who he is. Or he thinks it's easier fighting a few of us than a whole school of white boys. Kinda like what you're doing now."

"I'm not fighting everybody. I got some friends. I don't know what the principal writes in those letters, but I like going to school."

"You sure?"

"Yeah. Ask Lewis. He'll tell you the same thing."

"I moved to this end of the reserve so you kids could go to a white school. You need to know what it's like out in the world. It would have been a lot easier to go to school on the reserve. You wouldn't have had to face the real world until you finished, but then it would have been too late. That's why some people never leave here, Eddie. Like Alphonse. I just didn't want you to end up living here because you think it's easier. But it's not so easy anymore, and you need to go to school so you can fit in.

"The one thing you need to do is get that boy somewhere all by himself. That was how people got Ellis. When he has nobody to cheer him on, he'll have a hard time trying to hide how scared he is. You gotta stop that boy, or he's gonna be just like his dad. Some people don't like it when they see others doing better than them. They think you're getting high-toned. So every chance they get, they'll do anything or say anything to put you back into your place. He'll never leave you alone no matter how old you are, and you'll be waiting for him just like I did for his dad. And you'll be the one that tells your kids to be on the lookout for Rodney. This could be your only chance."

She turned and walked back up the trail, stepped through a thick clump of river grass, and was gone.

The next morning, when they ran to catch the school bus, Eddie and Lewis saw BC Hydro trucks parked by the cattle guard to install power poles. Eddie hoped by day's end he would be able to think about something else besides Rodney. Lewis hurried to the back of the bus. Eddie sat behind the driver. Even though the seat was a place of punishment, Eddie was glad to be alone. He looked out at the trees whizzing past the window as the bus picked up speed, hurrying to school, to Rodney.

Eddie went directly to the principal's office. He peeked around the door and saw Mr. Latimer sitting at his desk, reading a piece of paper. The principal motioned to him to come in. Eddie stepped inside the office.

"Now, what is all this business between you and Bell?"

"Business?"

"Why are you two always at each other's throats?"

Eddie found it hard not to notice the strap hanging on the wall.

"Why don't you like each other? And I don't have time for twenty questions."

"I don't know why we don't like each other. We just don't."

"I know what happened on Friday. I was there, remember? I know you were protecting your brother, but we can't have people fighting whenever they feel like it. We can't have total anarchy. This isn't Russia."

"Yes, sir."

"I don't think you're telling me everything. Be honest with me. I'm not just here to give out the strap, you know." The principal put his hands behind his head and began rocking back and forth in his chair.

"He just hates me."

"How do you know that?"

"He told me. He told me he hates me."

"But why? For what reason? Why the fighting?"

"I don't want to fight him. But I don't like getting beat up all the time either. When he hits me, what am I supposed to do?"

"Don't justify your behaviour to me. I'm telling you right now, Eddie, that I'm going to give the both of you one last chance. The first one that starts a fight will be expelled. Simple as that. I'm going to get order back if I have to strap every single student in this school. You understand?"

"Yes, sir."

"All right. Now get down to assembly."

The principal put a hand on Eddie's shoulder and walked him to the door. "Remember what I said. The first one that starts a fight will be expelled."

His hand felt hot. "Yes, sir."

Monday morning assembly in the school auditorium was a perfect time-waster. After singing the national anthem, all grades, one through eight, listened while teachers took turns reading announcements. The principal walked up and down the aisles, his hands behind his back, patrolling and watching. Eddie looked in all directions for Rodney. He couldn't see him anywhere. His little sister wasn't sitting with the sixth-graders either.

Rodney didn't come to school the next day or the day after that.

"They'll probably be away for a few days because of the baby's funeral. But you keep quiet about what you know about Rodney and his sister. You let everybody find out for themselves," Grace said.

On Wednesday afternoon the teacher was at the blackboard writing out an arithmetic problem when a slip of paper landed on Eddie's desk. He picked it up.

"Susan Bell was killed in a car accident," it read.

At lunch hour Eddie heard a group of students gathered in the hallway talking about Susan while a head lifted from the huddle to look for teachers.

"All I heard was she was killed in a car accident."

"Where did it happen?"

"I don't know."

"Who told you?"

"I heard the teachers talking in the staff room."

"She was so pretty."

A teacher appeared. "Stop plugging up the hallway. Move along."

Eddie knew it wasn't Susan who'd died. On the bus ride home he thought of how she was so different from her brother, how nice she was. Once he'd walked past her on the stairs and she'd smiled at him. He'd seen her around the schoolyard with her friends, talking and smiling, while her brother tried his hardest to look mean and scary.

26

Lewis and Eddie ran to the house just as the electrician's truck drove away. There were lights on the ceilings and outlet plugs in the walls.

"Is the power on, Mom?"

"Not yet. He said maybe a week or two."

Eddie flipped the light switch on and off just to make sure.

On Friday morning the students sat at their desks waiting for the morning bell to ring. Their chatter still centred on the death of Susan Bell, but the talk was interrupted when Anna Moore rushed into the room to make a breathless announcement to the class. "I saw Susan Bell in the principal's office."

"Who was it that said she was dead?"

A finger pointed to red-haired Paula Lowry sitting in the back row.

"Well, that's what I heard," Paula said.

"You made it up, didn't you?"

"No. I told you I heard the teachers talking about it."

"You're such a liar."

Eddie knew if Susan was at school, so was Rodney. He wondered if anything had changed, if he still wanted to fight. He got his answer in the bathroom while hunched over the urinal trying to drill a hole into the hockey-puck-sized drain cleaner. A pair of dirty runners moved up to the station beside him. A zipper was lowered. Liquid began flowing.

"Still wanna do it, Eddie?" It was Rodney.

"You?"

"I sure do."

"I know all about your little sister. And your mom and your dad."

"What?"

"I won't tell anybody, as long as it's just you and me behind the gym. If anybody else is there, I'll tell the whole school what a coward you were for running away from the accident. Then I'll tell them about your mom and your dad. How he's in jail and she's an Indian. That means you are too. Wonder if your friends will sing you an Indian song like they did for me?"

Rodney clenched his fists. "You shut up. Okay, then, just you and me." He turned and walked away.

What awaited Eddie behind the gym? Would Rodney be alone or would he bring his followers? Eddie hoped to take away Rodney's advantage and couldn't wait to see what he would do after he was hit and there was no one there to cheer him on.

The high gymnasium walls blocked out the sun, and the frost on the walls thickened as the freezing afternoon air added another sparkling layer. The grass-covered ground between the gym and the barbwire fence of a farmer's field would be their boxing ring. The sun-bleached fence posts leaned inward like tombstones. Bent metal and pieces of wood sat piled in a corner where scrap paper burned in a barrel; its smoke hung in the air overhead. Eddie thought how peaceful and undisturbed it was out of view of the teachers and watchers.

Then Rodney stepped around the corner, a cigarette in his mouth, and he was all alone. Eddie wondered if the fight could be stopped, if they could both turn and walk away. No one but them would know. But Rodney didn't walk away from fights, and the time for hoping was over.

Tossing his coat to the ground, Rodney approached Eddie and took a long draw from his cigarette. He took the cigarette from his mouth as he exhaled. Then he flicked it at Eddie's face. Eddie ducked and moved in.

Their fists came up, and they began circling each other. The smallest sound became exaggerated: the frozen stalks of grass brushing against their pant legs, the bang of the fire barrel and their rasping breath. Rodney's nose was red from the cold. His arm was shaking. The smoke floated over them, making Eddie's eyes burn. He blinked, but it didn't seem to help. His eyes blurred until he could only see Rodney's outline. Aiming his fist straight for Eddie's jaw, Rodney swung and missed. His punch landed on Eddie's throat, dropping him to his knees.

Eddie's throat felt crushed like a tin can. He grabbed at his neck, gagging and sucking for air. He couldn't breathe. His face felt hot. Tears poured out of his eyes. He was a sitting duck. But Rodney stood with hands on his hips, waiting. Eddie took deep gulps of air, stood and pulled his fists under his eyes. He rushed at Rodney and landed a good punch to Rodney's face. Rodney touched his lip. Shocked at seeing his own blood on his fingers, he charged forward with his head down like a bull and banged Eddie on the jaw. Eddie's mouth slammed shut. His teeth clicked and his head flew up as his back rammed into the wall of the gymnasium. His feet slipped out from under him on the slippery grass.

Rodney was on top of him immediately. Eddie heard Rodney's teeth grinding as they rolled across the grass. Eddie made it to his feet and swung for Rodney's jaw. But he ducked, and Eddie hit him on the forehead. His knuckles throbbed, and the back of his hand ached with a hot burn. Just as Rodney threw a wild haymaker, Eddie hit him hard on the nose. Now the tears were in Rodney's eyes.

Rodney grabbed Eddie's shirt, tripped him, and fell on top. Eddie's arms were pinned down by Rodney's knees. Blood bubbled out of Rodney's nostrils as his fist slammed down on Eddie's face. Shooting stars floated off in different directions in the sky behind

Rodney. The blood tasted salty in Eddie's mouth. Rodney struck Eddie on the cheekbone. He raised his fist to hit him again, but before the punch landed, Eddie arched his back and sent Rodney over his head.

Eddie rolled over until he was on Rodney's back. He grabbed him by the hair and pulled with all the strength he had; if the older boys had been there, they would have separated them to start over again. But there were only the two of them, just as Eddie wanted.

Rodney kicked wildly but Eddie clenched his teeth and pulled harder. Rodney slowed down until he went limp. Eddie let go and came away with chunks of hair in his fingers. Suddenly Rodney turned over and hit Eddie on the ear. Eddie lay on top of Rodney and wrapped his arm around Rodney's neck, tucking his shoulder against Rodney's jaw. This time he wouldn't let him up. Rodney pounded Eddie's back with his fists, but Eddie hung on as blood dripped from his nose onto Rodney's face. It wasn't until Rodney began making gurgling sounds that Eddie loosened his hold.

"Okay. I quit," Rodney gasped.

Eddie released his grip and stood. Rodney looked away. Eddie spat out a mouthful of bloody saliva. He couldn't believe it was over. He had no feeling of victory as he'd always imagined. As Eddie turned to leave, he saw faces at the corner of the gymnasium and wondered how long they'd been watching. With his blurred vision he couldn't identify anyone until he was ten feet away. He thought he could make out the smiling face of his brother.

Then voices yelled, "Look out!"

Before he could react, Eddie was struck on the left side of his head. With a strange sensation as if he were tipping over like a falling tree, he landed flat on his back. He was dazed but alert enough to know he needed to get up. Rodney came at him swinging a piece of lumber. Eddie rolled away, but Rodney kept coming. Someone stuck out a foot and tripped Rodney. By the time Rodney caught his balance, Eddie was up. Hoping his shaking legs could support him a little longer, he jumped on Rodney and hit him with as many punches as he could.

Rodney struggled. Eddie didn't let up. He had let his guard down once, but it wouldn't happen again. He sat on Rodney's chest, throwing one punch after another. Shouting voices urged him on until he couldn't feel his swinging arms. His movements became loose and natural like bouncing a ball from one hand to the other. He couldn't feel his punches connecting but knew they must by the smack of flesh on flesh and the thump of bone on bone. Even in the rage of the moment, a thought came to him about what would happen after the fight was finished. Would it really be over? For good? He knew Rodney would be teased, especially by the older boys, and it would build and build in him until he found another way to get his revenge.

Eddie understood exactly what his mother had told him; this might be his only chance to put a stop to Rodney. Whether he was out in the schoolyard or just walking around the grounds, he always had to be watchful. Yesterday he had been so afraid but today he, not Rodney, had the upper hand. As he thought of all that Rodney had put him through and that its end was so near at hand, he drove his arms downward, punching and pulling back—punching—pulling back. His ears popped as if he were falling off a steep hill. He heard himself grunting with effort. One moment everyone was cheering loudly; the next they went quiet. Eddie looked up as the principal stepped through the crowd.

Each time the car hit a bump on the road, Eddie's head hurt, but he wondered if the entire school had heard by now that he had beaten Rodney Bell. People would be less afraid of Rodney now, and some would call him a coward for hitting from behind with a club. Eddie didn't care what was ahead for him, what the consequences would be, even though the principal was driving him and Lewis home so he could tell his mother to her face that Eddie was in a lot of trouble and most likely expelled. Everyone would know within a week, the principal had said. But that was next week. As far as Eddie was concerned, his troubles were over. Nothing else mattered. His head rested on the seat with his eyes closed. The car shuddered over the cattle guard.

"I don't know what your mother is going to say after I tell her, but you brought this on yourself. I gave you a warning, but you went right ahead and did it anyway."

"You said whoever starts the fight would be expelled. I didn't start it. He did."

"So you say. But it doesn't look good for either one of you. You might have ruined your chance at a good education at a great school. I know your mother thought it was important that you go to our school. Now I don't know what to do. If I expel you, will you end up in a residential school somewhere away from your family? I don't know if I can put your mother through that. But there is one thing I do know, and I've said it before, I won't put up with students beating each other senseless. Jesus, Eddie. You looked like you were trying to kill him."

In the final moments of the fight Rodney had begged him to stop. What would have happened if the principal hadn't showed up? What would have happened in another minute or two? The car turned down the driveway to Eddie's home.

"Is there something going on at your house?"

Eddie sat up. Vehicles he didn't recognize were parked on the side of the driveway. He saw a woman carrying bags of groceries as two small children followed behind, laughing and pushing at each other. The woman turned and said something. To the right of the house a group of men sat on blocks of wood around a fire, talking or just staring into the flames.

Mr. Latimer stopped the car and stepped out. All eyes turned to watch.

"Go find your mother," he said to Lewis.

A man who had been watching with the others by the fire stepped out of the circle. With his hands stuck into the back pockets of his jeans, he walked toward Eddie and the principal. Mr. Latimer jingled the keys in his pocket. Eddie wondered what the man was going to do. He stopped in front of them with an odd look on his face and withdrew his hand from his pocket. "I almost didn't recognize you without your ball uniform on."

Mr. Latimer smiled at the man and shook his outstretched hand. "This is the uniform I wear at work."

"Where is that? In a hotel, slingin' beer?"

"I'm the principal of Eddie's school."

The man looked down at Eddie. "Jesus. What happened to him? He get dragged behind a horse or somethin'?"

"I need to speak to Grace. Is she here somewhere?"

"Here she is."

Grace hurried toward Eddie. She held his jaw in her fingers, turning his face one way, then the other. "You wait here a minute."

Eddie leaned against the car while his mother and Mr. Latimer walked away from the staring eyes. Grace listened to the principal, nodding her head, but didn't speak. She waved Eddie over.

Mr. Latimer put his hand on Eddie's shoulder. "I'm very sorry, Eddie."

Mr. Latimer gave a wave toward the fire, climbed into his car, and drove away.

"What did he say to you, Mom?"

"Doesn't matter what he said. You listen to me now. There's something I gotta tell you. Your grandma died. After breakfast this morning she didn't feel good and went back to bed. Alphonse came and told me, and when I went down, we found her. She fell asleep and never woke up."

It was dark when a pickup with Alphonse and two other men inside backed up close to the fire. The glare from the single brake light turned their faces bright red. The tailgate was unlatched, and firewood rolled out onto the ground. A few men helped stack the blocks onto a pile. Alphonse threw a four-foot block onto the blaze sending sparks spraying upward, lighting up the faces of people sitting in a half circle away from the smoke. Alphonse looked surprised to see Eddie sitting outside with people he didn't know. He walked over and sat on a block of wood next to him.

"A bunch of us are goin' down to the graveyard tomorrow to dig the hole. You wanna come help?"

Eddie kept his eyes on the burning wood. "Yeah, okay."

"You sure?"

"Yeah," Eddie said.

"We're gonna be leavin' early. Real early. Long as you know that. I'm not gonna drag you outta bed. If you're not ready, we'll leave without you. And you gotta work too. You're not gonna stand around like a sleepy-head and watch."

"I'll be ready."

"Is that right you beat the shit outta that Bell kid?"

Eddie nodded his head.

"Too bad you didn't kill the little bastard when you had the chance. You're crazy if you think you seen the last of him."

Alphonse walked up the steps to the house and went inside. A light wind swirled the smoke into Eddie's eyes. The men coughed and moved away. Seeing Eddie hadn't stirred, one of the men called to him. "Sit over here. You never played musical stumps before?"

Eddie went around to the other side of the fire but kept his distance. He jabbed at the glowing coals with a stick. He didn't feel like talking to anyone; he'd only come outside to get away from the women. It didn't feel like his home anymore, the way they pushed back the furniture so they could set up the chairs someone had brought. On a small table in the corner of the living room, lit up by the light of a single white candle, was a photograph of his grandma that Eddie had never seen before. People sitting on the chairs viewed the picture in silence.

Eddie was hungry. When he went inside and sat in a corner, someone handed him a plate of food. As he ate, he saw an old lady sitting across the room watching him. He was sure she was over a hundred years old. In her wrinkled bony hand was a tree branch she used as a cane. She rapped twice on the floor to catch his attention. Eddie tried to ignore her but he could feel her eyes on him. She said something to him in the Okanagan language. Eddie stopped chewing to see if she was talking to him. When he didn't answer right away she repeated herself in a gruff voice. Eddie looked helplessly around the room.

A grinning woman sitting next to the old lady spoke up. "She wants to know what happened to you."

Eddie swallowed and cleared his throat. "I got in a fight— at school."

The woman translated for the old lady. The old lady spoke again and other women sitting nearby giggled. The old lady put down her cane and shook her fists at Eddie. The room broke into laughter. Eddie's face flushed. The old woman flashed her gums in a wide smile and let out a screeching laugh. Eddie left his plate and hurried out the kitchen door.

People at the fire left him alone. He hoped his black eye, swollen cheekbones, his scratched nose, and puffy face made them think he was a fierce fighter. Or maybe he was just too ugly to look at.

Lewis handed Eddie a piece of cake. Even in the dimness, Eddie could tell by the crumbly texture what kind it was. It was matrimonial cake, the cake Grandma liked best because the ingredients didn't spoil and she could eat the cake without her false teeth. The toasted oatmeal and sweet date filling reminded him of her.

They had been digging for an hour before the sun broke over the ridge. It started out as a serious affair, marking the grave and turning the first shovels of sandy soil, but after a while the men began to joke and laugh. Each digger kept a fast pace as if trying to outwork the next man. If anyone showed any sign of slowing down, a hand reached out to tap him on the shoulder. Whenever a newcomer joined in, it seemed to revive them all, and they worked harder, their breath in the cold air floating up and out of the hole to roll eerily across the graveyard.

An old man with long grey hair walked to the edge of the hole and looked down at the sides. He walked around the hole a few times until he was satisfied. "Looks good. Except that one side is a little crooked. You guys are starting to go sideways. Any more and you would've dug up Uncle," he said.

The men passed around a tin of snuff and tobacco and papers. The way they told jokes and laughed too loud made Eddie feel uncomfortable. He didn't like being in the graveyard while they acted so casually, so he waited in the truck for Alphonse.

Looking around the cemetery, he remembered the times he had been here before. The first time had been after Gregory died. A girl had been killed in a car accident. He hadn't wanted to go to the funeral of someone he didn't know, but his mother said he had to, that it would show up the family if he didn't. There were many people crying at the funeral that day. Since that first funeral Eddie noticed there were a lot fewer tears if it was someone old or someone that had been sick for a long time, as if a long journey had finally come to an end. Everyone seemed to be affected more by the death of children or a parent leaving behind children. Lewis had stood on top of a grave and jumped up and down until people yelled for someone to take him away. Eddie expected to see a hand reach out of the dirt to grab Lewis by the leg and pull him under. Grace dragged Lewis away while people shook their heads at such a poorly behaved child.

The drive home was quiet. They were a mile from home before Alphonse spoke. "You did something a lotta guys wanted to do to that kid's dad. That's what we was just talkin' about back at the graveyard. Ellis Bell."

"I know. Mom told me about him."

"She did? You know, I tried. We all tried to fight him. But he never went anywhere without his sidekicks. Did his kid have people around him all the time? You know, ones that did his fighting for him?"

"Rodney did his own fighting. He didn't need people to do it for him. They just made him think he couldn't lose."

"Are you going after them when you go back to school?"

"I might be kicked out of school."

"What? You might get kicked out for stickin' up for yourself? Really?" Alphonse's head swung back and forth from Eddie to the road.

"I won't know until next week. The principal told me to stay home and heal up."

"*Summa* bastards. You know what then, Eddie? Fuck 'em. Fuck 'em all. Them sonsabitches. I hope you do get kicked outta school. Darn rights. We can go hunting and fishing whenever we want. Who needs school anyways? Look at me. I never finished school and I turned out all right. Huh? Right?"

Two days later, Alphonse, Lewis, and Eddie sat at the table eating. Eddie was ravenous and finished off his plate in no time. He was about to go for a second helping when everyone stopped what they were doing.

"They're here," someone said.

Eddie walked to the window. Looking toward the road, he saw the hearse turn in to the driveway. The vehicle swayed from side to side like a boat on rough water, while vehicles with headlights on followed behind. When the hearse idled past the side of the house, whispering children were silenced by a loud shush.

Eddie motioned Lewis to come outside with him. By the time they were able to push their way out the door, the waiting men had opened the rear door.

Six men, three on each side, formed a line at the back of the hearse. Practice had trained each person what to do. Two men stepped forward pulling out the casket, as two more stepped around to pick up the middle. Two men went behind and picked up the end. At the top of the steps they handed the casket over to others who had been waiting. It was a tight fit getting through the doorway, but there were many hands to help. The crowd in the kitchen parted to let the men through to the living room. Someone had lined up wooden sawhorses as a base for the casket. Placing the coffin down, one of the men asked that it be moved forward a little so it would be balanced correctly. After a few adjustments, everyone stepped away.

The man with long grey hair shuffled up to the casket and looked back at Grace and Alphonse. With her hands on Eddie's shoulders, Grace steered him toward the coffin. Eddie tried to pull away, but she held on to him firmly. The man waited for Grace to give him a sign, but she hesitated. The clock in the kitchen ticked away the seconds until Alphonse gave a nod. As the man lifted the lid, there was a sound of an inward rush of air as if someone had taken a deep breath. Eddie saw movement of a single lock of his grandma's grey hair. Grace turned away.

An old woman began to wail. Everything seemed unnatural to Eddie: the chalk-white cloth under Grandma's head, the satin padding lining the inside of the grey coffin, the hinges that were too shiny. Her rouged cheeks and skin made her look like she was covered in a thin layer of wax. The syrupy smell from a bouquet of lilies made him want to throw up. Grace pulled Lewis and Eddie back, and they sat in chairs and watched people file past the coffin.

Women sitting in a corner of the room hummed prayers and fingered rosary beads. Their eyes were closed as if reading braille on a string. Eddie couldn't look away from the coffin. He remembered that his grandma could always tell when he was staring at her, even if she was walking away. It wouldn't have surprised him at all if she suddenly pulled herself up, looked at the people gathered around her, and asked, "What the hell is going on?"

In the silence a fly flicked against the window. The kitchen door opened and closed as people came in and out. Floorboards creaked under shifting feet as people moved around, trying to find a place where they could see.

For four days a steady stream of people went in and out of the house and stood at the coffin to see Grandma one last time. Men held their cowboy hats in their fists. A few women murmured and made the sign of the cross. It wasn't until dark that the crowd thinned out when people returned to their homes. Some stayed to keep the fire going day and night. Women replaced the candles and made sure the body wasn't left alone. Alphonse had taken men with him up to the range, and they brought back a large pitch stump. They cut a thick slab off the front of the stump with a chainsaw and carved Grandma's name and her dates of birth and death.

A week after she died, the priest finished saying prayers. The coffin was closed and loaded into a pickup truck, and the pallbearers sat on the sides of the truck box. The truck made its way out to the road with Eddie, Lewis, and Grace following behind in someone's car. Eddie looked back to see a man tossing Grandma's clothes onto the fire.

As they crossed the cattle guard, Eddie saw a policeman standing in the middle of the highway to stop traffic in both directions so the procession could go through. The men in the back of the pickup slid down to the truck deck.

When the pickup turned onto the dirt road to the church, the pallbearers sat up on the sides of the truck box. Eddie looked back at the vehicles rounding the corner, their windshields and grills coming out of a half-tunnel of churning dust. As the road crested, the church spire seemed to rise out of the glittering water of Okanagan Lake. The hills to the left were speckled with red dots of grazing Herefords. A man in the truck stood to a crouch to look over the roof to the church, his shirt flapping, the wind blowing back his hair.

The truck pulled up in front of the church. More people had been waiting at the church. Men leaning against fenders of their vehicles stood and dusted off their pants. Curious eyes shifted about as people watched the family.

As the men eased out the casket, Eddie heard the rustling of the wheel pulley in the spire just before the bell sounded; its rolling clash stilled even the most restless children. After the casket was taken inside, the bell stopped. There was only enough room in the church for the closest of relatives. Everyone else gathered close to the open door.

Eddie's head began to ache. He closed his eyes hoping to shut out the voice of the priest that seemed to go on and on without pausing to take a breath. He put a hand over his mouth and nose to block out the sickening smell of the incense. Then he felt an elbow poke him in the ribs. Grace gave him a disapproving stare, so he placed his hands between his knees and tried to concentrate on the casket. He lifted his finger to wipe away the moisture in his eyes so people wouldn't think he was crying. Eddie was determined not to cry.

Even after the church emptied and the bell's vibrating gong travelled deep into his chest, even in the graveyard when the only sound was the stretching and creaking of the ropes as men lowered the casket into the grave, even when the wailing of the old women sent a shiver through him, even when the men stood at the four corners of the grave with full shovels so people could toss a handful of earth onto the casket, even as the grave was filled by men lined up behind each other, spelling each other off when they became tired, even when Eddie lay on his bed and Grace covered him with a blanket and shut his door, he didn't cry.

27

Eddie sat under the bridge tossing stones into the water. It was one of the places he avoided because it made him feel creepy. Empty skins of caddis fly larvae covered the support timbers that reeked of creosote and tar. Behind the pilings, Eddie saw toilet paper stuck on the ground waving back and forth in the breeze, left by a traveller who had come down from the road because the nearest bathroom was miles away. The endless banging of tires on the uneven approach was unnerving. When semi-trailers rumbled overhead, the wood cracked and shook so much that Eddie expected the bridge to come crashing down. But it seemed the only place left for him to get away.

Two days after his grandma was buried Eddie'd had enough of people bothering him and looking at him and clicking their tongues. All he wanted was for everybody to stay away from him, at least until the ugly bruises on his face went away. His headaches were easing, and the swelling had gone down enough so that he could go to school the next day for a meeting with the principal.

His rock broke the surface of the river with a splash. Eddie was hungry but wanted to wait a little longer before going back home just to make sure their company of the last week would be gone.

The old woman who had laughed at him was to be picked up at 12:30. She was related to him somehow, a cousin of a cousin or an aunt of an aunt. She didn't speak a word of English. He was tired of always being on the lookout for her. She had a habit of coming upon him in the dark, and when she saw she had frightened him, she let out a screeching laugh.

The day of the funeral Eddie had come home exhausted after staying up late for three days. It was almost dark when he had awakened. There didn't seem to be anyone else at home, and he thought he should go to the toilet while it was still daylight. He went through a box of movie star magazines someone had left for them until he found one with a photograph of Elizabeth Taylor on the cover. She looked beautiful with her freckled cleavage practically spilling out of her low-cut dress. He walked toward the toilet flipping through the pages and found more photos of her at a Hollywood party.

Just as Eddie was about to turn in to the toilet he heard a noise from the garbage pit. It was two squirrels running across rusted cans. As he watched them scamper away, he undid his pants, pulled down his underwear, and began backing into the toilet. When he came to the doorway he put his arms behind him to feel his way inside. The moment his foot stepped onto the floor of the toilet he heard a frightened squawk, and something hard poked him on his bare behind.

Swinging around he saw it was the old lady sitting on the toilet jabbing at him with her cane. Her lisle stockings resting on top of her shoes looked as if her skin had dropped to her feet. She screamed. Eddie let out a yell. When she saw it was him, she cackled with laughter as he ran away.

At supper the old woman poured her cup of tea into her saucer, then bent her head down and sucked at it. When she saw Eddie watching, she spoke to Grace in Okanagan. Grace laughed. Lewis wondered what was so funny.

Eddie tossed another stone into the water and ran up the trail to the road. He couldn't spend another minute under the bridge. Surely the old woman would be gone by now. Maybe he could walk past Grandma's and sneak up to his house to look for car tracks. But it was too soon to walk by her window and not see her sitting in her chair. He couldn't remember if he'd closed the rail gate, so he would return the way he'd come, over the cattle guard. Grace and Alphonse had told him to always keep the gate beside the cattle guard closed; more and more people were using the back road. Even though it was on Indian land, people stopped at Madeline Lake and left garbage spread all over the ground. Most people used the gate because a new cattle guard had been built, but the rails were spaced too wide and a vehicle needed to crawl across to keep from bottoming out on the wood. The chief and council had a sign installed on the gate that read "No trespassing on Indian Reserve. Trespassers will be prosecuted." Someone had crossed out "prosecuted" and written in red letters "scalped."

Stepping up onto the shoulder, Eddie noticed how quiet the highway was now that new pavement was being laid five miles down the road toward Vernon. The traffic could be bumper to bumper one minute and empty the next as the flaggers let cars through.

Just as he was about to step through the page-wire fence, someone called his name. He turned and saw Eva waving to him on the road above her house. As she ran toward him, he wished he had slipped away sooner. She was the last person he wanted to see. She wore blue jeans with the leg bottoms rolled up and a sleeveless yellow blouse. She held her arms tightly crossed against the cool air as she stopped in front of him, out of breath and smiling. Eddie could see the glint of a filling in her back teeth. Her eyebrows furrowed, and she drew in a sharp breath.

"Eddie. Oh, my goodness." She touched his face. Her fingers felt soft and cool. "Albert told me what happened, but I didn't expect it to be this bad. Do you have any broken bones or missing teeth?"

"No."

"Well, that's good. I wouldn't want to see your good looks spoiled."

The horn from a passing car honked, and a man stuck his head out the window and gave a wolf whistle.

"I'm so glad I saw you. I heard about your grandmother and I was hoping to see you before I went back to the coast. I'm so sorry, Eddie. When my grandmother died, I was so sad. The world felt empty without her, and I miss her terribly. I know how you feel."

Eddie shrugged his shoulders.

"Where are you off to?"

"Home."

"For lunch?"

"Yeah."

"Why don't you come over to my place? Mom and Dad are coming home from church, and I made a nice lunch for them. You won't even see Albert. He stays in his room until just before we eat and he's going horseback riding anyway. What do you say? After we eat, maybe we can go somewhere and talk. I have so much to say to you."

"No. Mom's waiting for me."

"Oh, come on, please. You don't have to stay long. As soon as you eat we can leave. I'll tell my parents not to stare and ask you all sorts of nosy questions. They're really glad I came home for the weekend, so I can ask them for practically anything, and they'll give it to me. Come on, Eddie. It'll be fine. I'll look after you. Nothing's going to happen."

"No."

Eva stepped forward and took his face in her hands. Eddie's heart raced as she closed her eyes and kissed him softly on the lips. She stepped back and reached for his hand, but he pulled away. He couldn't get out of his mind the Saturday they spent time together walking around town and laughing like they were a real couple. He would have loved it if she had kissed him then.

"I know what I said before. I wouldn't blame you if you told me to take a flying leap. But I've been thinking about you ever since then. I know now that I was wrong. I do like you. A lot. And I hope we can start being friends again."

Eddie stared at her, speechless and confused.

"I don't blame you for not trusting me. Misty and Dawn told me I was so bad to you. I didn't mean to be. They're certainly on your side. Anyway, when they heard I was coming back home for a few days, they told me that if I saw you that I had to say hi. So, hi there, Eddie Toma." She grabbed his hand. "Do this one thing for me, and if you don't ever want to see me again, I'll understand."

He felt uncomfortable walking through the gate onto the sidewalk. Going into the house without her parents being home didn't seem right. Eva sensed his uneasiness and smiled as she ushered him inside.

Eddie had always wanted to wander around inside her home and look into all the rooms to see how they lived. He had been inside a few times to buy potatoes but hadn't even stepped off the doormat. Eva kicked off her shoes. Eddie untied his laces and set his shoes neatly by the door. The rooms were smaller than he'd imagined. Even though the linoleum flooring was worn through in spots, it was clean and smelled of lemon. A tall lamp with a large white lampshade sat in the corner of the room. Two chesterfields faced each other from opposite sides of the room. He took a close look at the wall tapestry of elk with snow-capped mountains in the background and reached up and ran his fingers lightly across the fabric.

"Isn't that the ugliest thing you've ever seen? I tried to talk Mom and Dad into taking it down so I could paint the room a nice yellow. It's so dark with that thing drawing all the light out of the room. But they wouldn't hear of it because it's a wedding present from Grandma and Grandpa. They wouldn't even let me take it outside so I could at least air it out. That thing is over twenty-five years old, and it's such a dust collector. When I came home the other day, the first thing I could smell when I walked through the door was the tapestry."

Eva took a platter of sliced roast beef from the refrigerator and placed it on the kitchen table. There were bowls for soup, a stack of white bread on a plate, salt and pepper, a sugar bowl, and a chrome paper napkin dispenser. Eva filled the glasses with water from a porcelain pitcher and brought out plates of bread-and-butter pickles, dill pickles, and cheese she had sliced from a large orange block. Eddie wondered if they ate like this every day.

Albert Cluff came in through the back door. He looked surprised to see Eddie standing in the kitchen. Eva stepped away from the sink.

"Hi, Alley-Walley. You know Eddie, right?"

"Course I do. I go to school with him. And quit calling me that stupid name."

"Oh Albert, no matter how big and tough you think you are, you'll always be my little Alley-Walley."

"I need to get out of here before the old man gets home. I don't need another lecture about missing church. Make me a sandwich. Is that soup ready?"

"Yes, it is. Sit down and have a bowl."

Albert took a bowl off the table and reached into the bottom of the pot with a long ladle to bring up a steaming scoop. Fat ran down the sides of the metal dipper. Sitting at the table, he blew on the soup while turning it over with his spoon. He looked up at Eddie.

"I heard you got expelled. Karl Duncan said he was outside the staff room at lunchtime on Friday. He heard a teacher arguing with the principal about it."

Eva placed two sandwiches on a plate in front of her brother. "Are you sure about that, Albert?"

"Hmm-hmm."

Eva looked at Eddie. "I don't think any person can be one hundred percent sure about something they've heard second-hand."

"Why would I make something like that up?" Albert looked over at Eddie. "I saw the fight, Eddie. And I couldn't believe you gave a bigger guy what he deserved. So I did hear the teachers talking, and I heard you were going to be expelled."

Eddie believed him.

Albert looked past Eva, to where a blue station wagon had turned down into the driveway. "Aw, Christ. What are they doing home so early?"

"Go out the front door when they come in the back. They won't see you," Eva said.

"It's too late. They probably spotted old Blue saddled up and tied to the gas tank."

Mrs. Cluff hurried past the kitchen window with Mr. Cluff following behind. Both did a double take when they saw Eddie standing at the table. Eva met them at the back door and spoke in a low voice. They came into the large kitchen. Mr. Cluff had on a suit and tie, and Mrs. Cluff wore a lime-green dress.

"Hello." Mrs. Cluff walked to the stove and lifted the lid on the pot of soup.

Mr. Cluff went into the bedroom. A few minutes later he reappeared, tieless, with his sleeves rolled up to his elbows. He sat at the table.

"We're all really sorry about your grandmother, Eddie," Mr. Cluff said. "She was a good woman. I don't think in all the time I knew her that she ever asked for anything. If she didn't have it, she just went without. I wish more people thought that way. Anyhow, it's a real shame when somebody dies that didn't have the Lord in their heart. A crying shame."

Eddie didn't answer. He fixed a hard stare at Mr. Cluff. His face felt hot, and he wanted to tell him to shut up. How could a person say something nice and then give an insult in the same breath?

"Uncle Jack and your cousin Rennie are joining us for lunch today, Eva," Mrs. Cluff said. "They're on their way to the coast so Rennie can catch a plane to a military school back east somewhere. Put two more settings on the table and make sure there's enough food. Let's get a move on. They'll be here any minute. You know, you could have picked a better time to invite company to lunch."

Eddie felt like walking out the door.

"I already ate, Mom. I'm going riding," Albert said.

"You can go riding after your cousin leaves. This was the second Sunday in a row you missed church with another stomachache," she replied.

"And I think after we're alone we'll just have to have a little talk about what's been going on around here. I can't figure out why a son should be so rebellious when he has so much to be thankful for," Mr. Cluff said.

There was a loud knock on the front door. Mrs. Cluff leaned over the kitchen sink, straining her neck to see. "Well, they're here. I suppose there's nothing we can do now. You really shouldn't have brought him here, Eva. You weren't thinking."

"Mother, for heaven's sake, why are you being like this? Eddie is a friend of mine, and I wanted him to have lunch with us."

"It's him I'm worried about. You know your uncle isn't the most open-minded person in the world."

The friendly knock turned into loud pounding. Mrs. Cluff banged the ladle on the stove. She looked frustrated. "Will someone let him in? And why is he knocking anyway?"

Mr. Cluff stood and walked toward the front door. "Get ready for your brother's big joke. You watch. He'll do his travelling salesman act or something."

The door opened.

"Good afternoon, kind sir. We're Jehovah Witnesses and we're here to leave you some of this fine reading material. I must tell you that if you feel like getting mad, you go right ahead. We get more points that way." The man laughed with an exaggerated loudness.

Eddie sat next to Mrs. Cluff, and Eva sat between her uncle and Eddie. Albert sat on the opposite side with his cousin. Eddie was about to pick up his spoon when Mr. Cluff cleared his throat.

Eddie looked around the table. Everyone had their heads bowed and their eyes closed. After Mr. Cluff said grace, he waited for the others to begin eating. The soup was the best Eddie had ever had.

"Eva is a good cook, isn't she, Eddie?" Mrs. Cluff said.

Eddie had just filled his mouth with another large spoonful. "Hmm-hmm," he mumbled.

"I'll miss having the extra set of hands around here when she leaves tomorrow."

Eva's uncle spoke up. "You're going back tomorrow? Well, why don't you save your money and come with us? It'll be better than sitting on the Greyhound for twelve hours with nobody to talk to. The way I drive, we can have you sitting in your dorm in half the time. It's hard to believe you're going to a brand new university. At your age. See, that's the big difference between you and me. You skipped a grade. Me, I skipped a grade back. I guess I'm just a dumb farmer. Heavy on the dumb." He banged his palm on the table and laughed noisily.

"I can't, Uncle Jack. I have a round-trip ticket. But thanks for offering. So Rennie, where is this school I've been hearing about?"

Rennie sat up, anxious to speak about himself. "It's actually a military base. I'll be finishing my training there. I figure I'll be away for at least—two years."

He drew out the words "two years" with a smile. Albert looked over at his cousin. "What's the place called? Where is it?"

"It's called Camp Petawawa. It's in Ontario."

"Petawawa. What kind of name is that?" Mrs. Cluff asked.

Eva's uncle cleared his throat. "It's Algonquin. I told Rennie if he gets lonely and he gets a weekend pass, he can go get himself a squaw on the reservation."

There was a mild chuckling around the table. Even Mrs. Cluff thought it was funny. Eva quickly changed the subject. "Let me make you a sandwich, Eddie. What do you like? Pickles, mustard?"

Eddie shook his head. "No. This is all I need."

As soon as he finished his soup, Eddie was going to leave. He didn't care what anybody at the table thought of him. It was a big mistake thinking he could join a white family to eat in their home, and he promised himself to never make that mistake again.

"Now who is that wounded young soldier there sitting beside you, Eva?" her uncle asked.

"It's Eddie. He's a friend."

"Is he now? I thought maybe my good Samaritan sister pulled in another stray off the highway or something."

Albert stood. "Can I be excused, please?"

"Don't you want a bowl of cherries and a cookie?" Mrs. Cluff asked.

"No. Can I . . . you know . . . please be excused?"

"Certainly you can, my dear. But like your father said, don't ride off anywhere before we have that little chat."

"Good luck, Rennie," Albert said as he pushed his chair up to the table.

Eddie dropped his spoon into the bowl. "Can I be excused?"

All eyes at the table turned toward him. Without waiting for an answer, he went around the table toward the front door.

"Eddie! Wait a minute," Eva said.

Eddie grabbed his shoes. He pushed the door open and it slammed hard behind him. He ran shoeless up the steep bank to the highway. At the bridge he saw the road had been opened, and trucks and cars whizzed by almost bumper to bumper. He was forced to wait for the traffic to ease, and when Eva called out to him again, he ignored her. Whenever it looked like there might be a break in the line of vehicles, he saw more cars speeding around the corner. It was time for him to go because if he wanted to get away without talking to Eva, he couldn't wait any longer. He slipped on his shoes. Without tying his laces, he climbed onto the top of the bridge railing. It took him a few seconds to get his balance before he began making his way across the narrow railing.

The bridge shook under his feet but Eddie kept his eyes locked onto the plank while he slid his feet ahead of him. A driver honked his horn. Eddie lost his concentration for a moment and his arms went out to catch his balance. In the middle of the bridge he paused to look down at the rushing water. He'd always tried to get across the bridge as fast as he could, so it was his first chance to see the riverbed from this angle. Beneath the water he could make out different shapes and colours of stones and trash gathered around a log close to shore. He hoped the water was cleaner by the time it got down to where he filled the buckets.

He heard Eva's voice again and looked back to see her on Albert's horse. She kicked and urged the horse up the steep path.

The traffic had died out except for a lone semi-trailer a mile up the highway. When she reached flat ground, Eva whipped the horse's flanks with the reins until they were going at full gallop. The sound of its own hooves echoing off the bridge spooked the horse, and Eva had to stand in the stirrups as she see-sawed back and forth on the reins. The horse lifted its head and slid to a stop on its hindquarters in front of Eddie. The semi-trailer rounded the corner.

"Eddie, get on behind. Please. We'll go up to the range and talk. I'm really sorry about my dad and my uncle. They didn't mean it the way it sounded. They just don't know any better. But I told them both—"

The horse rose up on its rear legs. Eva patted the horse on top of the head. It brought its feet back down to the ground. "I told them they should have never spoken to you like that and that you were a friend of mine."

There was a loud shout.

"Eva. You get off my horse right now."

It was Albert, running toward them with a look of panic on his face.

"Come on, Eddie. Let's get out of here. Hey, I'm in trouble already, so we might as well go for a little fun ride, okay? I'm really sorry about everything I said to you. And I'm sorry about my family. But please. Come on. What do you say?"

Albert came onto the bridge just as the truck driver gave a blast of his horn. The nervous horse skittered out into the middle of the road.

"Damn you, Eva," Albert yelled.

Eva managed to maneuver the horse closer to Eddie. "Hurry. Please. We don't have much time," she said.

Just as the driver of the semi let go another blast of his horn, the horse banged into the railing, and Eddie fell more than jumped onto the saddle behind Eva. He clamped his arms around her waist as the horse lunged forward. Eva kicked the horse with both feet and slashed its flanks with the reins. Eddie felt the leather go across his legs. Pressing the side of his face against her back, he closed his eyes. The ringing clatter of driving hooves, the growling motor, and blaring horn began to slip away until he was only aware of a rocking motion, the warmth of Eva's body, the smell of her hair and the warmth of her skin.

28

Eddie wondered how he came to be lying on his back. Something bad had happened, but his jumbled thoughts didn't make sense. There was screaming next to him, but he couldn't move to see what was happening. It went quiet, and then the screaming started again. His hearing was coming to him in waves as if someone were covering and uncovering his ears with their hands. Salty liquid streamed into his eyes and down his throat, choking him. When he couldn't move or feel anything except cold gravel digging into his back, he wondered if this was how it felt to die. He had a faint memory that he'd liked to do this when he was little, lie on his back and watch the sky.

The blurred figure of a man with a rifle appeared. He raised the gun, and there was a loud bang. Eddie twitched. He could feel himself slipping away into unconsciousness when the clouds parted and the sun shone in his eyes. The brightness lingered until reduced to a pinpoint, and then the light was gone.

Eddie heard noises echoing all around him. He thought they were crows or seagulls, but they turned out to be voices calling to him from far away. Persistent hands prodded and poked him constantly. It was like being dragged out of a delicious sleep in a night that seemed to go on and on. Why wouldn't people stop bothering him? Slowly the sounds formed into words he could recognize. And when a voice let out an unusually loud shout, he forced his eyes open. The light was so bright that his eyes hurt. He tried to move his head, but a shot of pain in his temple made him cry out. A figure in white appeared beside him.

"Well, well. Look who it is, back from the dead," a woman's voice said.

Eddie felt an eyelid lifted by cold fingers that smelled of bleach. A sudden weariness came over him and he tried to pull his head away so he could sleep again.

"You're going to have to stay awake for a bit longer. After I finish, you can sleep all you want."

He wanted a drink of water but couldn't put the words together. He could only make smacking noises with his lips. When the woman placed a straw in his mouth, the cool water washed away the soreness in his throat. Soon he was able to see her more clearly. She was a nurse in a starched white dress that rustled and hissed as she moved, and her cap looked like a white butterfly had landed on her head. She unravelled the bandage from around his head. When she peeled off a large square of gauze, Eddie saw a touch of pink in the centre.

"You took a good bump on the noggin there, young man. Do you have any idea where you are?"

"Huh?"

"You're in the hospital. For the past couple days or so you've been going in and out of consciousness. You're one lucky boy. For a while we didn't think you were going to make it. Your mother has been here every day, pacing up and down the halls, driving us all crazy."

A loud voice shouted from the other side of the curtain. "Somebody help me. This is too much. I can't take this anymore."

The nurse shoved a thermometer under Eddie's tongue before she stepped around the curtain. "Oh, for heaven's sakes, Mr. Anderson. Stop acting like such a big baby. What's the matter now?"

"You've got to stop."

"It's almost over. Goodness sakes. The way you're going on, you'd think you were the first person in the world to ever have an enema."

"It's not supposed to hurt this much, is it?"

"It's just a little bit of pressure you're feeling, that's all."

"I'm going to pop."

"You're not going to pop. It's practically empty anyway. Here, I'll pull the tube out, and you can get yourself into the bathroom. I never heard such a ruckus from a grown man."

By the time she returned to take the thermometer out of Eddie's mouth, he was asleep.

Eddie wondered if the nurse enjoyed waking him up just to poke another needle into him and then leave without saying a word. He vaguely recalled his mother and Lewis at the side of the bed speaking to him, but he couldn't answer because of a nagging pain in his throat.

Each time he awoke, he saw his mother sitting beside his bed. He couldn't have any conversation with her; he could only nod his head before drifting off to sleep. Each time he was surprised to see her still there.

Then one morning, before Eddie was completely awake, he smelled food. He couldn't tell what was making the tempting aroma, but it made him think of a hamburger steak with brown gravy on mashed potatoes and peas and carrots. Opening his eyes, he sat up slowly and looked for the nurse so he could tell her that he was starving. But as he reached for the buzzer pinned to his pillow, a shooting pain in his head forced him back down. It felt like hours before his throbbing temples calmed down enough so that he could open his eyes again.

The afternoon sun reflecting off the white walls and ceiling was blinding. Out in the hallway nurses and orderlies hurried past. The curtains of his bed had been drawn back against the wall, and he saw the bed next to him was empty. His neck didn't feel as stiff as it had been, and if he moved his head slowly, the pain was bearable.

As he looked around the room trying to recall the events that brought him to the hospital, he saw the back of a man standing at the window waving to someone outside. He was tall and slim with shoulders that stooped forward, giving him the appearance of being in a hurry even while standing still. His flat-top crew cut was speckled with grey, and when he pulled a hand out of his pocket to cover up a wide yawn, Eddie saw the tattoo of a cross. The man turned around. It was Ray.

Eddie wanted to hide under the sheets. Ray stared across the room at him for a long time until a metal tray or bedpan clattering to the floor somewhere jarred him out of his thoughts, and he walked toward Eddie. As he pulled up a chair, Eddie recognized the frown that had always made those around Ray a little fearful. Except for a few new lines on his forehead, he looked the same as the last time Eddie had seen him years earlier. There was a movement at the door. It was an old man walking with a cane.

"Oh, look," the old man said. "Well, you're finally awake. Now I got somebody to talk to. How you—"

"Hey. We're talking," Ray said.

The old man looked surprised. "I just wanted—"

"I said we're talking."

The old man shuffled to his bed. When he turned around to lower himself, his gown opened, exposing his bare behind.

"Jesus Christ, look at this," Ray muttered as he reached over to draw the curtain. He spoke to the old man in a clear voice. "You mind your own business. And keep your bony ass on that side of the curtain."

Eddie felt the room become charged with an old familiar tension. Ray sat down on a chair beside the bed, wary of the intravenous bottle hanging from the steel pole and the gadgets and instruments with wires and tubes that all seemed to be attached to Eddie. A door slamming shut made him jump, and his eyes darted everywhere. Beads of sweat popped out on Ray's forehead. Ray was about to say something when a woman on the other side of the curtain spoke to the old man.

"How are you doing today, Mr. Anderson?"

"Fine," he answered in a hushed voice.

"Why are you whispering?"

"I don't want to bother the boy."

"Oh, he's much better now. He'll probably enjoy the company. Okay now, let's take the blue pills and make sure you drink all the water."

The metal rings on the chrome bar screeched as the curtain was pulled swiftly back. Ray leaned back in his chair and crossed his arms. The nurse looked surprised to see him.

"I didn't know you had a visitor, Eddie. Who is this? Your father?"

Ray glared at the nurse.

"Well, don't mind me. I'll just get your temperature and I'll be out of your way," she said.

After scribbling on the chart at the foot of the bed, the nurse left the room. The old man seemed to cower when Ray rose from his chair to draw the curtain shut. He pulled his chair closer to the bed.

"Did you know your mom's been writing letters to Isabel ever since Gregory died?"

"No."

"Well, she did. I think she's going crazy thinking about you and worrying. Back then she said sometimes she could hear you crying and how you were even pissing the bed for a while. You still do that?"

"No."

"You sure?"

Eddie was too angry to answer. The old man's bed squeaked as he stood and hobbled out of the room.

"Well, if you're gonna lay there like a sulky old woman, I'm gonna go. Isabel's waitin' for me down in the car anyway. She don't like hospitals. She's scared a mean nurse will grab her and give her a needle in the ass. Looks like we're gonna be staying with you guys for a little bit. Look, Eddie, I got lots I want to say to you, but not in here. And nobody knows how long it's gonna be until you can go home. Boy, you were lucky. Looks like you finally found a use for that knot head of yours.

"I told your mom to go home. I found her sleeping in the chair when I came in. Anyway, I'll see you when you get out. I won't be coming in here again. This place gives me the willies."

"Do you know what happened, Ray? Do you know how Eva is?"

"You talk to your mom. We just got here."

"Don't you know?"

"I said, ask your mom. We came up because we heard about your grandma. Sure wished I could have made it to the funeral. That's not going to happen again. I'm here to stay now. It's too hard trying to make a living picking beans and pulling weeds. It's time me and the old girl stopped running around."

"Is Eva still in the hospital? Do you know what room she's in?"

Ray let out a weary sigh.

"I told you. Ask your mom. I don't know everything. Christ, you know how lucky you are? You don't have any broken bones, just a little knock on the head and a couple scratches. Don't worry about it. You'll be kissing your sweetheart soon enough."

Ray pulled something out of his shirt pocket and placed it on the table beside the bed. It was a pack of Juicy Fruit gum.

29

A week after being admitted to the emergency ward, Eddie pushed open the glass doors and stepped outside the hospital. Birds dashed from tree to leafless tree, and the fresh air smelled sweet. It was a cool autumn day, but the sun still had power to warm his body and enough glare to make his head hurt.

Eddie had mixed feelings about leaving the hospital. He would miss the bed that he didn't have to share with his brother and also all the attention the nurses gave him. And even if most of the other patients complained, he thought the food was good, much better than what he ate at home. But he longed to be on his own, outside, far away from the ringing bells, the flushing toilet that woke him from a good sleep, and someone down the hallway coughing until they choked. As soon he had the chance, he would go down to the river to hunt for grouse. If he didn't see any game, it wouldn't matter. He would just sit on the bank and listen to the sound of the water.

He limped carefully down the steps to the parking lot. Ray waited in a car, and Isabel stood next to it. There was no sign of his mother or Lewis.

Isabel hurried toward him. She held his face in her hands and hugged him, looking into his eyes. "Let's go home."

Ray and Isabel sat on opposite sides of the car, and Eddie wondered if something was wrong. He'd expected to see Isabel sitting right beside Ray and running her fingers through his hair as always. Their silence made him wonder if it was him they were mad at and not each other. When Ray turned the car down the driveway, Eddie let out a long breath, glad he'd be out of the car soon.

Eddie opened the car door and saw Lewis pat a barking dog tied to the clothesline tree.

"That's my dog, Rip," Ray said. "He's an Australian blue heeler. You know, he can round up a herd of cattle all by himself. Only thing is, he won't stop barking. I figure you and me and Lewis can work the hell out of him. Maybe that'll shut him up."

"I think we should just get used to the barking," Isabel said dryly.

That night in bed Lewis was full of questions about life in the hospital. Eddie told him how some of the old men had a tube shoved up their behinds, then were filled with water, and the funny way they hobbled to the bathroom as fast as they could. When one of the old men didn't quite make it to the toilet and leaked water on the floor, a man with a mop had to clean it up. Lewis laughed so loud that Grace pounded on the wall. In a low voice he told Lewis about a pretty nurse who leaned over him when she changed the dressing on his head and how he could see down the front of her dress to the cups of her brassiere.

Eddie had a few questions he hadn't dared to ask Grace. "Did you hear anything about Eva or Albert? Did Mom say anything?"

"Nobody tells me nothing, but I listen when I hear them talking. After I went to bed once, I knew they were talking about you, so I got up and stood behind the bedroom door. Mom said when Alphonse went for the mail, he saw Albert Cluff behind the barn crying. Ray said crying won't bring back his horse and Albert should just go out and get himself a new one. Isabel said how did he know that was what he was crying about and it could have been his sister that was making him cry. Mom told them how pretty Eva was, and if Ray could have seen her for himself, he would have thought so too. Ray caught me and told me to get to bed. I didn't hear any more. Now, whenever they see me listening, they tell me to go away."

Eddie couldn't sleep. He could only think of Eva. He wanted to find out if she was angry with him for leaving her house that way. As he stared up at the ceiling, he felt calmed as he thought of her. He pictured the two of them walking by the river holding hands, her pretty face smiling at him, the sound of her voice when she laughed, and the way her hair lit up when the sun was behind her. They would stop, and she would take his face in her hands and kiss him again. He closed his eyes to linger on the dream. Suddenly the dog began barking. Eddie opened his eyes, and Eva was gone.

The dog wouldn't let up. When it was obvious he wasn't about to stop anytime soon, Eddie heard Ray get up off the couch. The door squeaked open. A few seconds later the dog let out a yelp and was quiet. An hour later the barking started again.

Electricity gave a whole new feeling to the house. Ray and Isabel had gone back to the States for their furniture. Now they slept in the living room on a fold-down couch. They had a record player with speakers that Ray placed in opposite corners of the room. When Eddie sat in a certain spot between them, the music sounded so much better than the scratchy tunes played on the old phonograph Jimmy had left. With so many electrical appliances plugged into the outlets, the fuses kept blowing.

Ray even bought a used television set in town and spent most of the afternoon walking around the yard holding up the antenna while Alphonse shouted to him if the picture got better or worse. All Eddie could see on the screen was a rolling black bar that looked like a windshield wiper in a snowstorm. But Ray wouldn't give up. He tried every trick he knew to fix the TV picture.

"I have to go to the hardware store in town for a bigger antenna. Whoever wants to come with me, I'll buy them a hamburger. Huh? Who's all coming?"

Eddie put on a clean shirt, combed his hair, and was outside standing on the top step before anyone else. A hamburger in town was something he couldn't pass up. But when he came home, he was going to walk over to see Eva. Nobody could stop him.

Ray leaned under the open hood of the car working on the engine. He stayed outdoors a lot, mostly because he and Isabel couldn't seem to say anything to each other without an argument breaking out. The only time they were together was at the supper table or when they drove into town.

Ray pulled out the dipstick, checked the oil, and slid the dipstick back into place. He rubbed a smudge off the oil cap with his thumb, closed the hood, and wiped his hands with a rag. Eddie looked down toward the river. A gentle wind wobbled a treetop, and pine siskins rose up and circled the tree before flying away. Eddie walked up to Ray.

"See them birds there stopping and starting?" Ray said. "Know what it reminds me of? You and Gregory playing that game. What was it called? The one where you had your back turned and you would call out something while Gregory tried to sneak up on you before you turned around. Remember? What was it called?"

"Go Go Stop."

"Yeah, that's right. The first time you guys played it, Gregory laughed so hard he pissed his pants. I remember giving him hell for it."

Ray watched the birds darting about below the house. Even though the sun was blocked out by high clouds, he shielded his eyes and squinted as he watched the way they streamed up and touched down, then lifted off again like a trembling shadow.

"I always used to like watching you two. It reminded me of my brother and how he couldn't beat me at anything. I was always the one that come out on top in the little games we used to play, the foot races and rock throwing. And he could never find me when we played hide and seek."

"Gregory was a better swimmer than me," Eddie said.

"Yeah, well, my brother was better with horses than me. I didn't care for them at all. Just when you think you can relax and take it easy, boom, you're on the ground with the wind knocked outta you and a sore ass."

Eddie felt a calmness coming from Ray that seemed to encourage conversation.

"Gregory could go out into the middle of the river where the current was so strong that I could hardly stand up. He was so good at swimming. I wonder why he drowned like that," Eddie said.

Ray cocked his head to the side and looked down at Eddie. "Swimming? You think that's what he was doing? Swimming? Jesus Christ.

"He wasn't in the river. That was the first damn place we looked for him. They found him in a swamp out in the middle of that field behind the cabin. They said he had a goddamn fishin' line and it looked like he went out on a plank, and it give way, and he fell in. His legs were tangled in wire, or cables, and he couldn't get out. I don't know why in hell nobody thought of looking in there. Did you and him go into that swamp? Did you know about it?"

"Yeah," Eddie said.

"Well, why the hell didn't you say somethin'? We would have found him in time if we looked there right away. I can't believe it. I told the both a you to stay away from there. You always were a dumb, useless little bastard back then."

Eddie's head throbbed with a pain worse than when he was in the hospital. He placed a hand on the side of his head and winced.

"What, you gonna start cryin' now?" Ray asked angrily. He stepped in front of Eddie so close that his breath moved Eddie's hair.

Eddie looked up, surprised at the sudden rage in Ray. It made him wonder what would happen if they were all alone. Ray looked like he wanted to kill him. In the corner of his eye Eddie saw Grace standing on the path from Grandma's house, arms folded, watching, listening.

"You should be a shamed a yourself." Ray turned away.

"It's one word, not two," Eddie said defiantly. His own anger made him reckless.

Ray looked over his shoulder, confused.

"What did you say?"

"Ashamed is only one word," Eddie said. "Not two."

Ray stared at Eddie, his eyes black and fierce.

"Just like your goddamned mom. Both a you with a big mouth and no sense. You don't know how lucky you are right now," Ray growled as he walked toward the house.

Eddie looked over at his mother. She unfolded her arms and surged ahead so fast that a dry leaf lifted and curled behind her. She looked at Eddie as she went past him.

"Ray," she screamed. "You get the hell outta here. You think you can talk to him like that in my house and get away with it? You sonofabitch."

"Did you hear what he said about—" Ray said loudly.

"I don't care. Just get out. Get out while you can. If you're not gone in ten minutes, I'll put a bullet in you," Grace said.

"Don't you threaten me," Ray warned.

Grace bolted into the house. Then Eddie heard loud scuffling of feet on the floor.

"Grace. Stop it," Isabel said.

Lewis ran outside and jumped off the steps, looking terrified. He stood behind Eddie and peered around at his mother.

Isabel looked surprisingly agile holding back Grace from getting to Ray. She said quickly, "Ray, look what you done. You can't stay here no more. Leave your stuff and go. I don't want no part of you. I had it. Grab your jacket and go. Now."

Ray pulled his coat off the nail by the door and walked slowly down the steps toward his car, stopping by the two boys. He put his hand on Eddie's forehead and shoved him hard. Eddie fell to the ground and groaned at the pain.

Grace screamed and broke away from Isabel. "You bastard, Ray. You chicken shit bastard."

She grabbed her rifle off the wall. Isabel stepped in front of her and took hold of the gun. "Don't, Grace. Please stop." The gun dropped to the floor.

Lewis started to cry. Eddie had never seen him so frightened. Ray started the car and spun the tires. They never seemed to stop churning up dust until he turned onto Range Road toward the highway.

An hour later Grace and Isabel sat at the table, drinking tea. Lewis sat between them. Eddie sat on the steps sipping cold water as the aspirin finally began to work.

"I been waiting a long time to get away from him," Isabel said to Grace. "He really changed after Gregory died. He was mean and miserable all the time and never thought about anybody else. It's like I took a sack of rocks off my back. The hell with him. Good riddance."

Grace nodded. "You know what? I'm not going to sit around and talk about another man that can't grow up. Been around too many of those. Why don't we all go to town and have us a hamburger steak at the Silver Grill? What do you think, Eddie? And no half orders either."

Eddie shook his head. "I don't wanna go to town. That dog kept me up all night."

After Grace changed and finished her hair and lipstick, she came and sat on the doorsill beside Eddie. Her perfume and hairspray made him queasy.

"I don't want to leave you here all alone, Eddie. Why don't I stay with you? We can listen to music, or I could cook something up for you."

"Mom, I'll probably just lie down and have a good sleep," he said. "And I really just want to go down to the river."

"Okay." Grace sighed. "What is it about the river? You know, one time when you were barely old enough to walk, you wandered away from the house, and we found you sitting on a log by the river with a smile on your face, like you found a big stash of candy. Huh? Why do you go there by yourself?"

Eddie shrugged. "I dunno."

"Okay. I'll bring you back something from town. I think Alphonse is home if you need a visitor."

She squeezed Eddie's knee and tousled his hair.

As soon as the car was out of sight, the dog began barking. A sharp pain like a finger touching a sore tooth began throbbing in Eddie's temples. He looked at his reflection in the mirror, at his face that had been swollen and bruised for a long time but was finally beginning to mend. The bruises on his forehead were now a faint yellow on the outside edges. The gash on his cheek was now broken up into a smaller series of scabs, and his red eye looked almost normal.

He took his old .22 down from the wall and opened the box of shells. A walk along the river was all he'd been able to think about lying in his hospital bed. And he might even get lucky and see a grouse. There were only two shells left. One of them dropped to the floor just as Alphonse appeared in the doorway.

"Going hunting?"

Eddie loaded the gun and put on the safety. "Yeah."

"See if you can get a blue grouse. I can never get close enough to them anymore. They hear me every time."

Eddie hoped Alphonse would see that he was in a hurry and didn't have time to visit.

"Did your mom tell you? Henry Tuttle had a stroke a while back."

"Huh-uh."

"A month ago his old lady found him on the floor in the bathroom with his pants down to his ankles. Now he can't say a word. May said he just lays in bed drooling all over himself. She even has to wipe his ass for him now. You know, I think she was giving me the eye when she told me. Hah. Maybe sometime when you walk in the store and you don't see anybody behind the counter, I'll be in the back putting some colour into old May."

Eddie didn't respond to Alphonse's joke.

"Hey. Pay attention when I'm talking to you."

Eddie felt annoyed with his uncle. He didn't want to waste time talking or visiting. All he wanted was to walk up to the bridge and maybe catch a glimpse of Eva out in her yard, though she might have gone back to university by now. It didn't matter. He just wanted to be on his way.

"I said, I'm talking to you."

Eddie looked up at Alphonse. "What?"

"I seen that Cluff kid the other day behind the hay barn. His saddle was setting on the top rail of the corral and he was humped over it bawling his eyes out. Boy, I don't know how that kid could care about that damn shitter more than his sister."

Something in what Alphonse said didn't sound right.

"What? What do you mean? What are you talking about?"

"What do you think I'm talkin' about? You telling me you don't know?"

"Know what?"

"Your mom didn't tell you?"

"Tell me what?"

"Jesus Christ, Eddie. I was up at the road and I seen everything. You were hanging on to that girl for dear life on the back of that horse. There was a tanker truck coming right up on you two, and when the driver honked his horn, that horse spooked and shifted into high gear. When you guys come around that corner to go onto Range Road and I saw the gate was closed, I knew there was gonna be a bad wreck. That little girl was standing in her stirrups and pulling on the reins to get that shitter to stop, but that horse tried to jump over the cattle guard. He didn't make it. He landed a foot away from the other side. His front legs went down between the rails and flipped him ass over tea kettle, snapping his front legs.

"You were both thrown over that horse's head, and that girl landed on the hardpan road with you right on top. I thought you was both goners, but she broke your fall. Christ, that horse was screaming and kicking and waving his broken legs in the air. That girl's brother came around the corner just when I put a bullet behind that horse's ear.

"Ambulance showed up and took both of you to the hospital. Sorry to say, Eddie, but that poor little girl died right there on that road with you beside her. I seen her. I had to shoot that shitter, or he would have kicked your head off.

"You didn't know? Why the hell didn't anybody tell you? I should have just shut up, dammit. I shouldn't have said nothin.'"

Alphonse hurried out the door. He tossed a rock at the barking dog. The barking stopped until he went over the hill out of sight.

Eddie picked up the gun and went into the bedroom to grab what he had kept hidden under the mattress. His leg felt stiff as he hurried outside. He needed to get as far away from the house as fast he could. The dog jumped at the end of its chain whining and spinning in circles. When Eddie's foot turned on a rock, he called out in pain, surprising the dog and sending it into a new frenzy of yelping.

Eddie pulled off the safety, brought up the barrel, and placed the front sight in the vee of the rear sight, right in the middle of the dog's forehead. The dog's head kept changing positions but Eddie was surprised at his steady hand. For a split second he considered letting the dog off the chain to see if he could bring it down on the run. He took a breath and pulled the trigger. The stock gave a slight bump against his shoulder. The report was soft like a struck match. The dog fell to the ground as if its legs had suddenly turned to jelly while the crack of the gun washed over the nearby bushes and trees.

Eddie walked over to the dog. If it needed another bullet in the head to finish it off, then the dog would have to suffer. There was only one shell left. A scarlet puddle formed on the ground below the dog's open mouth, and the long tongue began folding itself into bubblegum-pink layers.

Eddie unhooked the chain and shoved the dog inside a potato sack Ray had put under the tree for a blanket. He swung the sack over his shoulder and kicked dirt over the patch of blood. Stumbling with the weight of the dog and the pain in his leg, he hurried down the bank straight through the Oregon grape.

The smell of the bush was thick in his nose. Sharp leaves scratched his neck. Hawthorn spikes grabbed at his shirt. A squirrel squatting on a high tree branch observed him with a sideways stare as Eddie slipped quietly into the bush. Where the undergrowth thickened, he recognized landmarks and soon picked up his old trail. It swerved back and forth, the way he had designed it, to throw off trackers.

Stepping out onto the shore of the river, he dropped the sack to the ground. He kneeled on the gravel and scooped handfuls of water onto his face to wash away the sweat stinging his old cuts and stitches. He swallowed noisily until his scratchy throat felt soothed and his stomach felt heavy. Then he slumped down on the ground near the end of the log where he had spent the day, weeks earlier, worrying about his fight with Rodney Bell, thinking it was the worst thing that could ever happen to him. This had once been a place of comfort where he felt safe and out of the way, but now it was just an old log in a place no one cared about.

Ragged clouds floated at the edges of the hills like puffs of smoke. Turkey vultures circled beneath the colourless sky, still looking to feast on the salmon run that Eddie knew was over weeks ago. But there was an unmistakable aroma of dead fish in the air, and it always carried with it a dim memory of the ocean.

To Eddie's surprise he saw a lone spawner close to shore barely moving, just enough to keep it from being carried away. By the number of scales spread around the gravel Eddie could tell that it had struggled for a long time trying to stay alive. The gashes and open wounds on the silver body showed the wear and tear of the journey upstream over beaver dams and through open rapids where bears and gaff-pole fishermen tried to pick off the salmon one by one. Jostled up and down against the rocks by the rolling water, the fish jerked three times, took a gulp of air, and was still.

A gust of wind felt cold on Eddie's face, and he opened his eyes. He sat up shivering and realized he had fallen asleep. He'd used the dead dog as a pillow; there was a wet spot where his head had been. He picked up the sack and tossed it out into the deep water. The rolling action of the river bobbed the sack up and down for a time before it slipped under. As he watched small bubbles float to the surface, he knew exactly what he wanted to do. He loaded the gun with the last shell, pulled on the safety, and turned back up the trail.

Pulling back the branches of a low poplar, Eddie found what he was looking for: the hollow tree he'd often crawled inside when he was little. It had made him feel safe. Looking at the tree now, he thought how silly he had been then. He found the entrance behind bushes and dug out the dead leaves and sticks with the butt of the gun, stopping now and then to catch his breath and let the pain in his head pass. Then he went down to his hands and knees, shoved the gun inside, and squeezed through the hole. Using the side of his foot, he cleared more debris back out through the entrance. When he sat down in the tight space, his good knee touched his chest while the now-throbbing sore one poked out the opening. He released the safety on the gun.

The air was so cold his breath rose up and out the top of the tree like smoke up a chimney. He closed his eyes and shook his head. During his stay at the hospital he had foolishly believed that when he came home, everything that was wrong would somehow have fixed itself and his troubles would be over. But nothing had changed since he crawled inside the tree as a little boy and imagined himself flying above everybody among the white puffy clouds. It had all been in his imagination. They were just dreams.

He leaned back and bumped the tree with the back of his head. Bits of spongy rotten wood landed on his shoulders. After a few moments he was able to calm himself and breathe slower. His headache went away, and his thoughts cleared.

Eddie pictured the store where he and Gregory stood outside on the porch looking in at the shelves of everything a boy could want, imagining what it would be like if they were allowed to pick out anything. If Ray hadn't said Gregory would be alive today if anyone had looked for him in the swamp, Eddie might never have remembered it. But there were so many other places that he and Gregory had found by braving spiders and snakes. Once they came across an old outhouse with a rotting floor and dared each other to jump up and down in it. And when they stood on a high hill overlooking the highway below and threw rocks down at the cars, Gregory had nailed the windshield of a pickup truck. The driver had slammed on his brakes, got out, and looked all around. They'd laughed.

The eye that had been scratched in the fight with Rodney began to water, which set off the other eye. Soon his old cuts and stitches were stinging again from the tears rolling down his face. It was a long time before he could take deep breaths without his body shaking and trembling. He wiped the tears from his face with his shirt sleeve and put Gregory out of his mind. Then his thoughts turned to Eva.

Maybe he should do what he'd seen in the movies, leave a letter. But the only two people in the world who'd ever seemed to care about him, Eva and Grandma, were gone now. Nobody would even bother to read it. Isabel would take over his bed, and Lewis would sleep on the couch. His brother would like that. He could go outside for a pee or walk around the sleeping house to look in on everybody and see what they were doing. He could come and go as he pleased. Everybody would be better off.

Eddie took a last look around. When he looked up through the open top of the tree to the sky that was now the clearest blue, he saw the sun reflecting off the wing of a jet that glided across. Its vapour trail floated behind as if it were unzipping the sky. It wasn't until the aircraft had gone out of sight that he heard the growl of its engines.

Most of the leaves from the poplars were gone. He stared through a crack in the wood through bare branches down toward the river and all the way up to the dark faraway hills against the northern sky. Many times he'd stopped to admire the sight and wonder what was on the other side.

Eddie pulled Eva's yellow kerchief out of his pocket, buried his face in it, and took a deep breath. He held the faint, soapy, lemony scent of her inside of him for as long as he could. When he let his breath go, he knew he was ready.

His shaking finger curled around the cold curve of the trigger. As he closed his eyes, a woodpecker began hammering away on a rock-hard fir. He paused. In that brief moment of hesitation, he heard the fluttering of little birds' wings, fir cones swishing down through the boughs of trees as they fell but never seemed to land, the faraway cooing of an inconsolable mourning dove, and the nearby river washing over rocks and logs.

Author's note

Throughout this novel characters use the Syilx word sámaʔ, meaning non-Indigenous Caucasian person. For ease of pronunciation I've spelled this *summa*. For consulting with me on this I'd like to thank SʔímlaʔxʷMichele Johnson, PhD, of the Syilx Language House (thelanguagehouse.ca).

Acknowledgements

I want to thank the Canada Council for the Arts for the grant I received when I needed it most.

Thanks also to my patient, encouraging wife, Marlene—although at times she was frustrated by my progress—since this book would not have been possible without her; and to the beautiful, always fashion-conscious and fun-loving Kate Gilchrist for being a great friend in the short time we had her—she loved the book as much as we did and would have been so proud to see it published; and to Susan Mayse, my editor, for being the best teacher in the world except for Mrs. Fraser in grade one.

This story is for my son Brodie and daughter-in-law Karen, and for my grandchildren, Sienna, Huxley, and Rebel. On the day you sit in front of a fire and read it to *your* grandkids—of course you will skip over the swear words and sex parts—when one of them asks you, "Who wrote this?" you will say, "My Papa."